"With a sexy train ride, a cocky hero, and a big heart to match, *Witcha Gonna Do?* blends romance, heat, and wickedly modern magic." —#1 *New York Times* bestselling author Lauren Blakely

"*Witcha Gonna Do?* will make your heart bubble, swoon, and giggle with its fantastic mix of hilarity and heat. Appealing characters and a delightfully unique setting make this vibrant, witchy rom-com really shine!"

—India Holton, national bestselling author of
The League of Gentlewomen Witches

"Adorable, hilarious, and positively sizzling with charm, this is a delightfully magical read I'm going to come back to again and again!"

—Sangu Mandanna, author of
The Very Secret Society of Irregular Witches

"Flynn wants you to feel like you're hearing about your best friend's latest romantic adventures—it's meant to be a fun read that keeps you entertained and giggling. There's a heavy amount of lust and biting dialogue early on between archnemeses-to-lovers Tilda Sherwood and the handsome Gil Connolly. . . . *Witcha Gonna Do?* is silly and hot—with both characters competently secure in how to give and receive pleasure." —BuzzFeed

"Sexy and hilarious, *Witcha Gonna Do?* is an ideal mash-up of contemporary romance and magic." —Book Riot

"There's plenty of charm in the wisecracking characters, hot-as-hell chemistry, and pun-filled world-building. This sexy romp of a romance is sure to win fans." —*Publishers Weekly*

"Flynn's enemies-to-lovers romp is replete with the titillating details of Tilda and Gil's escalating relationship. Fans of fast-paced, sexy romances in magically transformed contemporary settings will enjoy this clever, breezy rom-com." —*Booklist*

Berkley Romance titles by Avery Flynn

Witcha Gonna Do?
Head Witch in Charge

Head Witch in Charge

AVERY FLYNN

BERKLEY ROMANCE ✦ NEW YORK

BERKLEY ROMANCE
Published by Berkley
An imprint of Penguin Random House LLC
penguinrandomhouse.com

Copyright © 2025 by Avery Flynn
Excerpt from *Hexy Beast* copyright © 2025 by Avery Flynn

Book design by Elke Sigal

Library of Congress Cataloging-in-Publication Data

Names: Flynn, Avery, author.
Title: Head witch in charge / Avery Flynn.
Description: First edition. | New York: Berkley Romance, 2025. |
Series: The Sherwood witches
Identifiers: LCCN 2024052715 (print) | LCCN 2024052716 (ebook) |
ISBN 9780593335239 (trade paperback) | ISBN 9780593335246 (ebook)
Subjects: LCGFT: Paranormal romance fiction. | Witch fiction. | Novels.
Classification: LCC PS3606.L93 H43 2025 (print) | LCC PS3606.L93 (ebook) |
DDC 813/.6—dc23/eng/20250211
LC record available at https://lccn.loc.gov/2024052715
LC ebook record available at https://lccn.loc.gov/2024052716

First Edition: September 2025

Printed in the United States of America
1st Printing

To all the responsible-for-everything eldest daughters
(and those who act as the responsible-for-everything
eldest daughters even if they aren't technically the oldest)
out there. We appreciate your service,
even us youngest spoiled daughters. ☺
Xoxo, Avery

Head Witch in Charge

Chapter One

Leona Sherwood . . .

A year ago . . .

$\mathcal{E}$ver wake up and realize from the moment you open your eyes that *this* is the day when everything is going to go wrong?

You know what I'm talking about, right?

It's the kind of day when you get shampoo in your eye, nick your shin with the razor, and trip over your sister's rooster (literally) when you're walking out of the shower.

The next thing you know, you are buck naked on your belly and all but kissing the hardwood floorboards because you went ass over teakettle. Sure, a quickly whispered gentle-fall spell saves you from face-planting completely and breaking your nose in the process, but your triumph only lasts a moment because that's when the stupid rooster decides to stand right on your big, round, naked ass.

Just let that sit with you for a minute.

Four toes that each go in a different direction—three of which are tipped with little claws and one with a gnarly and sharp upturned spur—on your bare flesh. Creepy, gross, weirdly human-skin-feeling rooster feet on your butt.

I'm telling you, some days are just like this. The thing is, for me, I can't ever let anyone know I have those days because everyone—including my family, who I love dearly—has to believe that I'm calm, cool, and collected at all times.

Why? Because I'm Leona Sherwood, the witch who will someday lead the most powerful magical family in all of Witchingdom, the Sherwoods. Yep. That's right. I'll be the head witch in charge—whether I want to be or not.

As such, there are certain expectations about how I should act, how I must speak, and how I have to breathe—at least that's how it feels sometimes.

Also, being the Sherwood heir means I have responsibilities and expectations. I have to get it right the first time, and I have to set the example for all my sisters—which is why I can't give in to the urge right now to let my forehead thump against the floor repeatedly because of this cursed day.

As Mother always says, a Sherwood never admits defeat. A Sherwood keeps their chin pointing upward, their icy gaze unflinching, and their intimidation factor setting on one billion—all while making it look easy, because we never let them see us sweat.

It's not exactly a family mantra, but it has been drilled into my head since I was three and cast my first spell. So there is no way my sister Bea's rooster familiar and his nasty feet are going to beat me.

"Barkley," I say, making my voice as intimidating as possible, which I admit is about a tenth as scary as my mom's. "Get off my ass or I'm going to magic you into fried chicken."

The miserable rooster crows a complaining cock-a-doodle-doo but hops off my butt.

"I'd ask," my mom says from the direction of my door, which I swear I'd closed, "but I'm afraid the explanation is more than I would want to process."

I look up, and there's my mom in all her regal perfection without a single thread of her reddish-tinged blond hair out of place. She narrows her blue eyes. They're the same Caribbean Sea shade as my right eye, while my left is the same mossy green color as my dad's. She is—as always—assessing the situation and sussing out the advantages.

Her shoulders are back, her spine unbending, and her serene smile unbothered.

As the head of the Sherwood family, she is one of the most powerful witches in all of Witchingdom. She unnerves everyone—including (to a lesser extent) me and my four sisters. And it's her size six-and-a-half shoes I will be filling when I take over as the family matriarch.

Mom whispers a few words in Latin and waves her fingers. The peanut butter scent of her magic fills the room a half second before her spell lifts me and twirls me around. A robe appears out of nowhere and wraps itself around me. Then I'm carried through the air and deposited on the overstuffed chair by my bedroom's bay window.

"Now, that's much better," Mom says as she gracefully walks into my room. "We need to discuss your options."

"For lunch?" I ask hopefully, knowing full well that is very much not what she meant.

She frowns and sits down on the chair across from me, doing a little hand wave and making a small table appear that is covered in all the fixings for a high tea. There are scones and clotted cream, little crustless sandwiches, square bite-sized cakes, and my favorite strawberry preserves. I like strawberries because I love tart and sweet tastes together at the same time— it's my jam.

Ha! You get it?

Okay, fine, I'm not the funny Sherwood sister. That's my older sister, Effie. She has the snark on lockdown and has all the benefits of being the eldest Sherwood daughter without the responsibilities of being the heir. The woman lucked out when the magic didn't choose her to be the next Sherwood matriarch. Nope. I had to be the one who came out of the womb sparkling like I'd been glitter bombed in utero. Why did the magic choose me instead of the firstborn, per usual? If anyone knows the answer to that, they aren't sharing it with me.

It's not like it matters anyway. I am what I am: the Sherwood sister most likely to end up with a rooster on her ass, regardless of whether anyone ever gets to see the bad luck chaos queen under the mostly uncrackable veneer of the Sherwood heir.

Under my mom's watchful eye, I slather my scone with clotted cream and strawberry preserves. She gets that ah-exactly-what-I-wanted look of superiority when I do it. I know what she's about, but I keep it to myself. I'd rather eat than argue again. You see, most of the really powerful magic in Witchingdom takes place in the kitchen. The whole family forms a circle around the cauldron, we chant the spell, and voilà: magic. The preserves I'm eating came out of one of these kitchen witchery spells. Strawberries aid in love, fertility, romance, luck, and success—all things the Sherwood heir must have in abundance—hence why my matchmaking-minded momma is thrilled I'm eating it.

I'm still in tastebud heaven when my mom clears her throat, drawing my attention. The look on her face can succinctly be described as "on a mission."

"Leona, darling, we have important things to discuss," Mom says as she pours us each a cup of elderberry tea. "As the heir, you have very specific responsibilities. Our entire family from your great-grandmother to your second cousin's newborn baby is depending on you."

"I know, Mom," I say before stuffing the last bite of scone into my mouth.

The expression on her face softens and she covers my hand with hers and squeezes. "I know it's hard, but I know you can do it." She sits back and puts her business face back on as she does a little finger wave and the images of three men appear in midair. "You need to pick one of these eligible bachelors. Each will help the family grow stronger so we can better fight the

Council's efforts to turn Witchingdom into an authoritarian state."

What's the Council? Well, it's pretty much the witches' version of the boogeyman, only worse. Just what the world needs, right?

Made up of an unknown number of witches from other families who feel they've lost their hold on the power they used to wield, they want to use their political influence to remake Witchingdom into a rigid world where everyone fits into their designated boxes (as determined by them), adheres to the status quo (as determined by them), and gives them one hundred percent support (as determined by them). Basically, these people are the absolute worst kind of assholes you can imagine times eleven billion.

If they are able to make that happen, there sure wouldn't be any witches like my sister Tilda, whose power doesn't work like anyone else's. Nope. Those witches who don't weave spells the same way everyone else does would be banished, or worse.

And for as much as Barkley is the bane of my existence, there's no way those assholes in the Council would ever allow my sister Bea's witch's familiar to be anything but a green-eyed black cat. The rooster would literally be dinner. (And he'd taste horrible. There's no way that much unhinged animal energy would make for a decent Sunday roast.)

As for me? Well, if the Council had their way, I *would* be the oldest Sherwood sister, because the firstborn always had to be the heir, the one through whom the family magic flowed. Effie would have had to be hidden away from birth, never to be pub-licly acknowledged, or abandoned in the woods like the non-heir firstborns from centuries ago.

Those are the stakes if the Council wins, and that awful future wouldn't be just for my family. The shifters would be considered second-class citizens, the magical misfits would be banished from society, and the other creatures of the realm would be locked into subservient castes.

For too long, the most powerful families in Witchingdom laughed the Council off as some kind of wannabe boogeyman organization not to be taken seriously—after all, there couldn't possibly be that many people who agreed with their bullshit ideas.

That was a mistake, to put it mildly, but Juniper is always saying that deep down, witches are better than I give them credit for. All I can say to that is that witches are usually worse. (Cynical witch? Me? Abso-fucking-lutely yes.)

Don't bother telling me I'm just too jaded. My sister Bea already has, and it hasn't worked because I'm a realist. That's why I know that what's coming next will be beyond bad if the Council finds its members elected to Witchingdom's High Coven.

Still, I really wish there was a way I could help other than be part of a politically expedient wedding. Witchingdom as we know it could end, and my part in stopping that from hap-pening is to get married? What is this, the Middle Ages?

Yeah, yeah, I get that our family has to consolidate power

and build alliances with the other families in Witchingdom to fight the Council. I understand that each of us has sacrifices to make. I know it's my place as the heir to do what's best for the family no matter what. Still, you have to admit this is shitty.

And less importantly, but still a factor, is that it sure doesn't help that my choices for a husband are as dull as they are logical. Quinton Quince, Wilmont Lumin, and Ommin Zedler are all heirs to families with connections in every part of Witchingdom. Sure, they don't have as many ins with powerful people as we do, but the only family that rivals the Sherwoods in that aspect is the Svensens, and marrying someone from that family is *never* going to happen.

It would be like making a peanut butter and tuna fish sandwich. Objectively awful all around.

The Sherwoods and the Svensens have been archenemies since time immemorial, so there's no way their heir would make my mom's list of eligible bachelors. Plus the Svensen heir, Erik, is a real dick. He's the kind of cocky, hot rich guy who always gets exactly what he wants without ever having to work for it. There quite literally couldn't be a worse husband choice than him. I mean, sure, I could be faced with marrying a cursed rock, but at least the rock wouldn't run off with the family silver like a Svensen definitely would.

So Mom's choices, dull as they may be, make sense. However, there's a part of me that can't help but think there has to be another way to defeat the Council that doesn't involve me marrying for political power. And as long as I can avoid picking a fiancé, I have time to come up with that better solution. I can do it. I know I can. I just need more time. Too bad Mom is getting more than a little tired of my deflections whenever she brings up the subject.

"I know an arranged marriage for power reasons doesn't sound romantic," Mom says as she snags a miniature chocolate raspberry cake, "but it worked out well for your father and me."

I sink back in my seat. "But you *love* each other."

She chuckles. "We didn't at first."

I can't even imagine that. The two of them are so lovey-dovey. Mom is always sneaking kisses whenever Dad sits down, since at seven feet tall, he towers over her. Then Dad lets out his bear-shifter side just enough to say her name with a rough growl, which always makes her giggle. You can then smell the peanut butter scent of her magic and the grape jelly smell of his for a few seconds before poof! They've magicked to their bedroom. You won't see them again for at least a few hours.

My parents are not just in love—they are *in love*.

"I know you're not very interested in marriage," Mom says, "but it has to happen eventually, and with all that the Council is up to, it needs to be with someone who will help our alliance. The stakes are too great not to."

And that was the rub of it.

Unable to deny it, I glance over at the floating photos of my husband choices and sigh. It's not like I'm going to walk away from my responsibilities to my family or my obligations to

AVERY FLYNN

Witchingdom. The reality is, Mom and I both know I'm going to marry one of those three men because the heir does whatever is necessary to take care of everyone else.

But that doesn't mean not having a choice doesn't suck.

Mom lets out a little sigh that doesn't scream "disappointed," but definitely whispers it loudly. "You don't have to pick today, but please promise me you'll at least think about which bachelor it will be while you're on your girls' trip to Las Vegas."

Yeah, figuring out who to hitch myself to forever is the last thing I want to think about during my girls' trip. I love my family, but if I don't get away and have the opportunity to let my hair down and just be Leona instead of the Sherwood heir for five blissful days and four wine-filled nights, I am going to lose it.

"I'll try, but we're going to be busy seeing shows and shopping," I say, leaving out our plans for day-drinking by the pool, strip-club shenanigans, and playing high-stakes poker. "Kacee made reservations at her favorite restaurants every night."

"It sounds like fun," Mom says as she gets up and walks toward my bedroom door. "Just make sure you don't have *too* much fun. You're a Sherwood; people will be watching."

It's true. Love the Sherwoods or hate them, everyone in Witchingdom always wants to know the latest family gossip.

I pick up the last scone. "You worry too much."

Mom raises a brow in an imperious gesture. "I worry just the right amount."

"Well, you never have to lose sleep over me," I tell her. "I'm the responsible daughter, remember?"

She smiles, and then poof, she's gone, leaving the peanut butter scent of her magic lingering in the air. She's probably off to her office, where she'll work on plans to thwart the Council via official government channels. In a few years, that will be me. But not yet. In a few hours, I'm going to Vegas, where even a Sherwood gets to relax and just have fun without repercussions.

Really, what's the worst that could happen? I wake up married? Please. As if.

Chapter Two

Erik Svensen . . .

*Y*ou and I need to get one thing straight right off the bat: I am *not* the good guy.

I'm exactly who you think the heir to the Svensen magic would be.

I cheat.

I lie.

I steal.

I excel in double-dealing.

I'll use every advantage, every loophole, every witch's awww-he's-not-that-bad-you-just-have-to-get-to-know-him good intention without hesitation.

And I do it all while looking like a WitchyGram model who does thirst traps in well-worn sweaters that scream "old money." Using pretty privilege and charm for my benefit? Every damn time and twice on Sunday. Only an idiot wouldn't use every single tool at their disposal to do what needs to be done.

I am a lot of things, but a fool isn't one of them.

Of course, some plots call for a little more finesse and subterfuge than slick charisma or a strong-arm push. That's why I'm sitting here at the Lunar Resort and Casino's rooftop pool bar reading a book I'd never take off the shelf, nursing a too-fruity mai tai complete with a stupid yellow umbrella, and using a camouflage spell to look like every other basic, dorky white guy who is only in Vegas to have a little fun.

It wouldn't do for my target to know who I am. If she did, she'd probably turn me into a toadstool on sight. I'd magic my way out of that, but it would take some time, and that's the one thing I don't have.

Next year, I take over as head of the Svensen family, which means I'll control the family magic after the traditional power transfer ceremony.

The Witchingdom tradition is for the next generation's heir to take over as head after thirty or so years to ensure magical continuity in a power sharing ceremony. This also helps stop the heirs from offing the current heads to gain that power—or the other way around. That used to be a real problem a few centuries ago. However, we're supposedly more civilized now, which really just means we do our bad shit in the dark rather than at high noon in front of the entirety of Witchingdom.

Of course, my father made other plans.

The kind of plans you'd expect from a Svensen—the deceptive kind.

His big idea, as I recently discovered, is to pull a swap spell during the ceremony, which will strip me of all my powers.

Yes.

All of them.

Then he's going to tell the other families that the family magic rejected me. Therefore, he has no other choice but to continue being the family's magic source—so much sacrifice, he'll tell them, but that's just what the head of a family does.

As far as plans to rid oneself of an heir go, it's not a bad one. I might have never realized the extent of his plans, but his ego got the best of him and he ignored the number one rule of screwing people over: Keep your big mouth shut about it until the deed is done.

But the only thing my narcissistic father loves more than fucking people over for his own benefit is to brag to his sycophants about just how damn clever he is. If he were half as smart as he was an evil bastard, he just might have gotten away with it. But he isn't, and now he's not gonna.

I spot Leona Sherwood the second she walks out of the elevator surrounded by a group of friends.

Because this is the most popular you-don't-ask-about-me-I-won't-ask-about-you witches' resort in Vegas, she doesn't *look* like herself—or more correctly, she's using magic to make other people think she doesn't look like herself. It's part of the allure of the place (and why they can charge a premium) that you come as you are or as you want to be, and no one asks any questions. For most folks it's because they're married or attached or hiding their real identity for Svensen-like reasons. None of those apply to Miss Too Sweet Sherwood. So it doesn't take a genius to realize she's using a camouflage spell to hide from the WitchyGram users with weirdo levels of parasocial relationship entitlement who follow every member of their family around, trying to be the first to post a new sighting.

And if that's what she gets for being one of the good witches, I'll pick being bad any day of the week.

However, to be honest, I choose that anyway—which is why I'm using the revelare spell to see past the brown hair, dark eyes, and tanned skin to get a look at the real Leona Sherwood, with her signature red hair, big round eyes (one blue eye and one green), and the kind of pale skin that only looks a little bit tan if you squint so all her freckles seem to meld together.

Is me doing that playing by the resort's rules? No.

Is it legal according to Magic Regulations and the analretentive witches who police them? It is if you don't get caught.

And I never do.

That doesn't mean the revelare spell doesn't come with drawbacks. In this case, it's the ground primrose in my mai tai, making it taste like shit. As far as sacrifices went, it wasn't cutting off a limb, but I was having to remind myself what was at stake if this plan works—which it will—to stop myself from gagging with every sip.

I made a few plans of my own that include bringing a

surprise to the power transfer ceremony: the worst possible thing for my dad, the thing that will make it impossible for him to double-cross me—a Sherwood wife.

That's right, my father's downfall will come because of the sugar-and-spice-and-only-things-that-are-nice family who've been the Svensens' enemies for generations. Even better, my bride will bring with her so much influence, power, and magic to back my claim as heir that my father won't have any choice but to relinquish his position as head of the family. At that point, I'll do to him what he's planning for me and cut off his access to our family magic. Impotent in all the ways that matter in Witchingdom, he'll have to make a choice: either face the public shame and shunning or run away and die in some miserable corner of Witchingdom. It'll be societal death or actual death—I'm good with either.

My second act will be to banish my brother and sister from the family so they can live their lives with as little taint from our ancestors' dirty legacy as possible. Then, finally, after forty or fifty years, I'll die without an heir and the Svensen magic will cease to exist. Our family Mississippi will dry up and die, like it should have long ago.

And *that* will be the best fucking day of my whole entire life.

But that day is not today. Unfortunately. Today I have to balance being the unscrupulous Svensen heir on assignment for my dad to get some intel about the location of an ancient spell book and my own mission to bag a Sherwood bride by hook or by crook.

So I sit at the bar and watch my mark as she laughs with her friends like a woman who has had the world offered up to her on a silver platter and has never had to make a hard decision in her life. The thick rope of her braided hair points straight down to her black bikini–clad ass—and her ass, her real ass? It's epic. Big. Round. Definitely hold-on-able. It's the kind of ass a man doesn't forget—even if they've only seen it once at a distance during some mind-numbingly boring society event when she was wearing an emerald-green dress that clung to it.

Seriously.

That happened five years ago and I'm still jerking off to the memory on the regular. You would too if you'd seen it.

Trust me, the woman has a juicy fucking ass that has been living rent-free in my head for years. It's inspired a lot more than just this plan to depose my dad.

Does it make me an asshole to tell you all that? If it does, I can live with that. I've definitely been called worse.

By my own dad.

About five seconds ago.

And he's still going on and on during the phone call that will not end.

Don't bother with the pity. I'm used to it. If I couldn't put up with the old man's diatribes, I would've crumbled into dust years ago. But until it's time to go public with my wife in a year at the power transfer ceremony, I have to play dutiful son—even when I don't want to.

Especially when I don't want to.

"You need to get home now before you fuck up this deal any more," Dad says, his bitter voice coming in through my earbuds and jabbing me right in the brain. "It's not every day a line on where to find The Liber Umbrarum comes in. You do what it takes to get that information from the Kiehls by any means necessary."

"I thought they were our partners in this little endeavor to recover the spell book," I say, just to wind him up.

"Partners," my dad scoffs. "Don't be simple, boy."

I can't see him over the phone, but I can picture his scowl—it's his usual expression whenever he paces his dark office at the family home and lists out the many errors committed by his disappointments, which is what other fathers would call their children.

"This deal with the Kiehls to use The Liber Umbrarum's ancient alchemy spells to pay off your debts was your baby, not mine," I say as I watch Leona lounging in the cabana with her friends.

"Family debts. Not mine! Family debts. And I'm making it your baby." Translation, dear old dad is in over his head with the Boston werewolf pack and needs me to get the job done that he couldn't. "The meeting has already been set. You go. You talk. You get the information we need."

The Sherwood heir picks that moment to take off the fabric tied around her waist over her bikini and walk from her cabana to the pool. My dad's voice fades into the distance, because I never thought she'd look any better than she had in that emerald dress. Fucking A was I ever wrong. Curvy with the kind of tits that overflow a man's hands and an ass that could not be contained, she has long legs, thick thighs, and a wide, honest smile that almost makes me feel bad about what I'm going to do.

At least it would if I actually gave two shits about anyone other than myself, my brother Cy, and our sister Sigrid. Lucky for me, I don't, so don't get your hopes up about a redemption arc. I know *exactly* who I am, and a secret nice guy is not it—and everyone knows it. According to Witchingdom gossip, all of us Svensens are gorgeous, greedy assholes always looking for a way to one-up the other witch.

They aren't wrong.

"Erik Aldus Svensen, are you listening to me?" Dad asks, his annoyance palpable in the zip of electric magic that comes through the earbud and sends a small shock down my spine.

I shake off the pain, used to what he calls an "attention-getter." "Yes, Dad."

"You better be, because if you fuck this up, I'll have to resort to other measures to raise some capital. Cy's lab equipment would get some fast cash on the black market. Then I could marry your sister off. Fitzwilliam came by the other day. His third wife died a few months ago just as mysteriously as the previous two. He's on the market for wife number four, and everyone in Witchingdom knows he only loans money to family."

Fury blasts through me at the idea and the truth escapes before I remember who I'm supposed to be around my dad. "And you think selling your daughter off to the highest—probably murderous—bidder is the best option, do you?"

"I don't need you to tell me my business, boy," he snaps back. "I can't keep up the pretense of our wealth much longer. We need a cash infusion and we need it now. I've sacrificed all I can for this family. It's up to you to make it happen by doing whatever it takes to get The Liber Umbrarum, keep the best money-making spells for ourselves, and auction off the love potions and other idiot candy magic to the highest bidder, or your siblings will have to pick up the slack for your failing. What. Ever. It. Takes."

Oh yes. "Whatever it takes" should be the family motto—especially if it involves blackmail, deception, and outright thievery.

However, before I can tell him exactly that, Leona Sherwood gets out of the pool and my brain goes blank for a second. There's just something about seeing her wet, happy, and smiling up at the sun while wearing a pair of ridiculously huge sunglasses that hits me like a right hook from a pissed-off construction gnome.

I watch as Leona saunters over to her cabana, grabs a tropical-themed sarong that she ties around her waist, and starts toward the pool bar. The same bar where I'm sitting. The same bar where I've been sitting for hours with my book, nursing the same mai tai, waiting for Leona and her friends to come out to the pool.

The universe, however, decides to blow a little good luck my way and she is finally heading straight for me.

"I gotta go, Dad."

"It better be so you can get your ass to that meetup and get the location of that damn book," he says. "The clock is ticking on the rest of Witchingdom finding out how flat broke we are. I will not be publicly humiliated like that. I will not lose my power and my place in society because you can't do a simple thing like get a tiny bit of information from those stupid fucking werewolves who have absolutely no idea what's in the spell book. I'd like to think that my heir couldn't fuck up something that's practically idiotproof, but you've disappointed me before."

My anger that's always simmering under the surface threatens to boil over, making my skin burn with a heat that the desert sun couldn't even dream of producing. It's enough that the edges of my spell altering how I look start to shimmer and weaken.

Of course that's what the old man is most concerned with. Not my brother's and sister's lives, not the rest of the Svensen relations, and not the general caring for and well-being of those under the family's protection, but being revealed as cash-poor gentry and, thereby, losing any social power he has among Witchingdom's elite.

I hang up while he's still talking.

It doesn't matter. I know what he's going to say anyway: "It's only the head of the family that matters. Everyone else can fend for themselves."

If you're thinking there's a reason why I'm such an asshole, you'd be right, and it doesn't change a damn thing. I am who I was born to be.

Keeping Leona in my peripheral vision, I let out a calming breath and lock my false appearance spell back in place. Then I turn back to my book. It's a rare first edition of Elini Horsnäs's biography, one of many that my dad had ordered me to put up for anonymous auction so he could get a new wardrobe for the social season. I'd pocketed it instead.

You never know when an oddity will come in handy— like now.

Leona stops a stool down from me and orders drinks for her and her friends before glancing over at me and doing a double take. "Oh, I *love* that book."

Bingo. I just love it when a plan comes together.

Everyone in Witchingdom knows the Sherwood heir is a voracious reader. With only the minimum amount of research, I locked in on her genre (biographies) and niche (badass women). And now my dad's throwaway for quick cash is going to gain me a lot more than a new tuxedo.

"It's great." I close the book and hand it over to her so she can look at it. "I came across this first edition in a secondhand shop and it just grabbed me."

"You found a first edition Elini Horsnäs biography in a used bookstore?" she asks as she turns the pages with reverence and care, a soft smile curling her lips. "You might be the luckiest person I've ever met."

"Well," I say, laying the awkward charm on thick, "since it led me to getting to meet you, I'm going to agree."

She lets out an amused snort and hands me the book. "That was a horrible pickup line."

I take the book back, making sure not to touch her fingers with mine. The key when reeling in a mark is to always make sure they think they're the one making the decisions.

Dialing my smile to bashful, I ask, "Too much?"

"Definitely too much, but I appreciate the laugh," she says with a chuckle as the bartender places a tray with four fruity drinks topped with little umbrellas on the bar. "I'm LeLe Collins."

"Nice to meet you, LeLe." I offer my hand. "Erik Phillips."

She shakes it, her grip firm and confident. There's a zing of something that makes my balls tight. Yeah, she's hot and I'm horny, so what? It's not like I haven't played with my prey before—nothing like a handful of orgasms to make getting screwed over go down a little easier. They have fun. I get what I want.

I'm not Mr. Nice Witch, remember?

So yeah, the idea of finding out how tight her thighs would grip my head while I'm tongue-deep crosses my mind. Sue me.

I don't want to let go of the Sherwood heir's hand, but there's too much on the line for me to give in to what I want. Instead, I do a silent spell that sets off a text notification on my phone.

I glance down at the screen as if I don't know what it's

going to say. "Sorry, it's my friend. We're here so he can forget his now ex-girlfriend."

Her face scrunches up into a sympathetic grimace. "Bad breakup?"

"Let's just say finding out she cheated on him with his dad is doing a number on him." Which was the plot of the latest romance book Sigrid insisted I read.

"Oh." The heir—LeLe—puts her hand to her heart. "Ouch."

"Yeah." I stand up and scoot my barstool back into place. Time to drop the next little crumb. "It was nice to meet you, LeLe, but I gotta go. I have a poker game tonight in the Reservoir Room, but maybe I'll see you after?"

A smile lights up her face as she does a finger wave and her tray of drinks floats up in the air and over to her side. "Oh, you'll see me there. I'll be the one taking all your chips."

Her skill at the table is legendary according to all the digging I've done on her, but I needed the confirmation she just provided that she'd be at the high-stakes table tonight.

"I don't know." I tuck the book under my arm. "I'm pretty good for a book nerd."

Her grin turns flirty as she looks me up and down. "Well, I look forward to seeing if you're the player you think you are."

Then she walks away, the tray of drinks keeping pace next to her. I don't need to watch her stroll all the way to her cabana, but I can't look away. She glances over her shoulder at me and smiles.

Yep. Lady Luck is definitely with me in Vegas.

I may not have much, considering Dad has decimated our

family fortune, but I'm as lucky as a leprechaun on a hot streak. Things just work out for me. That's how I know my plans for getting rid of dear old Dad are going to work out perfectly.

And if LeLe and her family pay the price? That's just the cost of getting what I want.

Chapter Three

Leona . . .

One look at the players standing around the dark green felt table in the Reservoir Room told me everything I needed to know about the level of play there will be tonight. In about five minutes, every chair will be occupied by a heavy hitter—with two notable exceptions, the first of which is me. I'm good, but I'm not at their level of good.

Who's *not* the exception? The three titans of Witchingdom's poker world.

Razor McGee is pacing in front of the large window overlooking the neon strip. A tall slip of a witch, she's known for her sterling-silver fingernails, which are down to sharp points, and has a whole WitchyGram following for her ASMR account, where all she does is shuffle decks of cards.

Over at the bar sucking on a plastic drink sword lined with five green olives is Hal Onions. As short and square as Razor is tall and slim, the gnome is known for his quick quips on fan-paid-for Fairy Twinkle personal video messages. The man also has more wins under his pink elephant belt than any other poker player on the circuit this year.

Huddling in the corner, looking as guilty as three finance bros who'd just scored some fairy dust, are the Quarter triplets. No casino will let all three of the groundhog shifters play in the same game. They swore they don't have telepathy, but the way they bet, called, and folded said differently to the odds-makers. If I had to guess, I figure it's the youngest, Alfonse, playing tonight, since he's wearing the family signet ring.

Besides me, there's only one other exception to the murders' row of poker players.

That one?

Erik from the pool bar. He's sitting with the Elini Horsnäs biography in front of him at the poker table. The book is opened to at least a hundred pages farther than it was this afternoon. His long finger skims down the middle of the page in an old speed-reading technique I tried one summer but stopped when my recollection of a spell to summon a kangaroo resulted in a French bulldog in a kangaroo costume poofing out of thin air.

He doesn't look up from his reading despite the loud laughter coming from the Quarter triplets or the loud clink of ice in Hal Onion's glass as he takes the seat next to Erik. The man is sucked into his book. I can appreciate it. But that's not what has my magic swirling in my belly without me even calling it.

That happens sometimes when you run a long-term camouflage spell, but it hasn't even been a full day for me. Add to that the fact that I keep smelling fresh-brewed coffee when my magic smells like warm donuts, and the hairs on the back of my neck stand up. Someone must be working an intimidation hex in the room.

Razor and Hal both look completely at ease, so it can't be them. My gaze lingers on Erik, and there's something on the edge of my brain, an itch or a tick or a whisper of something that I just can't place, but it's not a working intimidation hex. That leaves one of the Quarter triplets, which really is something they would try to pull off. Assholes.

Ignoring their curious gazes as I cross the room, I take the seat across from Erik. He looks up, his focus fuzzy behind the round glasses he's wearing. As soon as he zones in on me, though, he whips the glasses off and stuffs them in the inside pocket of his navy blue sports coat before shooting me an awkward, shy smile.

"It's a good read?" I ask, nodding toward the biography.

Before he can answer, though, the dealer calls the other players to the table and the game begins.

An hour later, I can definitively say that Erik couldn't bluff his way out of a toddler's birthday party.

So why aren't you calling him out and taking all his chips, then, LeLe?

Yeah, the inner bitch in my head added some snide emphasis on my fake name along with the question I have no answer for. The fact is that I'm having a blast watching Erik flail at poker. I can't keep the smile off my face—not because he's fumbling so badly, but because he's having so much fun playing anyway.

That is something I am definitely *not* familiar with. Losing is not an option when you're a Sherwood, let alone when you're the Sherwood heir.

For the past three rounds, I've been three cards away from an even straight. Usually I'd be hunched down in my seat, running the numbers (yes, counting cards is technically illegal, but that doesn't mean no one does it), and chomping a stick of gum to give the competitive anxiety a release. Not tonight though. Instead, I'm loose limbed, clearheaded, and enjoying the butterflies-in-my-stomach feeling every time Erik looks my way with a self-deprecating oops-I-did-it-again grin when he misplays a card.

The fact that there is a huge mountain of plastic betting chips in the middle of the table (some of which are worth as much as five hundred dollars) doesn't seem to factor into his enjoyment level at all. He's not playing the odds or stressing over the amount of money on the line. He's just having fun being absolutely awful at something. Seriously, the man cannot play. It's kind of like watching a troll use its huge hands trying to unwind a knot tied by tiny little fairy fingers. The will is there. The actual ability? Not so much.

"You're full of shit, Phillips," Hal says as he tosses a handful of red plastic chips on the table. "I call."

"You think so?" Erik asks before his gaze cuts over to me. "What do you think?"

I shake my head. "There's no way you've got it."

He doesn't say anything; he just shoots me a sly smile that makes my breath catch and lays down his cards.

Everyone freezes in surprise. It is so silent, you could have heard the paper wrapper of an eye of newt muffin being pulled off, and everyone is so entranced a leprechaun could have come through and picked every pocket in the place (including the sixteen running up the goblin's sleeve).

There, lying on the dark green felt-covered table, is a straight flush.

The first to recover is Razor.

She tosses her cards on the table face down and says with a chuckle, "You lucky bastard."

"Every witch has their day, I guess," Erik says as he scoops up all the chips and puts them into a velvet bag with the resort's logo embroidered on it.

Alfonse's pointy nose twitches and his teeth get a little pointier as he glares at Erik. "Yeah, let's see if it's still your day after the next hand."

"No can do," Erik says as he pushes his chair back and locks his eyes with mine.

The shy bookish guy vibe from earlier is gone, replaced by a confident bordering on cocky one that I really shouldn't find attractive, but I do. There's something about Erik that makes my magic take notice, a subtle edge of something I can't help but want to run my fingertip across.

He rounds the poker table, stopping next to where I sit

with my winnings, which rival his. "I have a date with the lovely lady."

"You do?" I ask, even as I start to tidy my pile into even stacks of chips I can magic over to the cash-in booth.

"If my luck holds." Hand resting on the back of my chair, he leans down and whispers into my ear, "Wanna help me spend these chips on a ridiculously overpriced gourmet picnic?"

A delicious shiver of attraction works its way across my skin. "Will there be cherry bark pie?"

"Whatever you want," he says, "I'll make it happen."

All of a sudden, I want a lot of things, absolutely none of which are cherry bark pie.

Chapter Four

Erik . . .

$\mathcal{I}$ have no idea how I managed to last as long as I did at the poker table. I folded on a full house because LeLe was toying with the thin strap of her low-cut green dress. Then there was the time I called on nothing but a pair of twos because she was reapplying lipstick. If she had touched her hair at all during the poker game, I would have magicked the rest of the room into oblivion just to have her to myself.

Now I did.

Sort of.

We're in the elevator, and it's taking its sweet time going down to the lobby. Despite the others crowded in with us, everywhere I look in the mirrored walls, all I can see is LeLe. I don't even have to work to see through her camouflage spell at this point. To me, she's exactly as she is—full curves, red hair, one blue eye, one green eye, and an attitude that says *dare you*.

Fuck do I want to dare.

She turns toward me and tucks a strand of hair behind her ear as she looks me over. I've been looked over a lot in my life. Women and men both love a taste of bad boy now and then. It's not about me—it never is—and I'm okay with that. Everyone walks away satisfied, they have a fun story to tell their friends, and I have a new piece of insider information or bit of gossip that can be used for my benefit later.

It's never about feelings or love or anything as unnecessary as all that. Sex, like life, is transactional. The sooner you understand that, the better off you'll be.

So what does LeLe want from me? She doesn't know I'm a Svensen—unless, of course, she came to Vegas prepared to violate the resort's rules about seeing through camouflage spells. I don't buy it though. A con always knows a con. She's too soft and hopeful for that. All that do-good optimism comes off of her in waves. Yeah, it's tinged with a ribbon of frustration and a tempting thread of badness just begging to be pulled to see her come undone, but it's right there in her aura: my girl LeLe is one of the good ones, more's the pity. It's gotta suck to go through life as a sucker.

"So tell me, Erik Phillips," she says as she winds one thick strand of wavy hair behind her ear, "why do I get the feeling that you aren't exactly as you present yourself to be?"

Huh. Maybe there's more to LeLe than a gorgeous face and an ass worth going to war for.

"It is Vegas," I tell her, not meaning for my gaze to drop to those cherry lips of hers, but they're like a tractor beam. "Isn't that part of the fun?"

She smiles, revealing the dimple in her left cheek. It's off-center and a little crooked in a way that shouldn't be sexy but is.

"I suppose that depends," she says, moving a step closer so we're both tucked into the back corner of the elevator.

Yes, there are other people in here with us as we inch our way down, but it doesn't feel like it. My magic keeps waking up inside me without me calling it, peeking out at LeLe and basking in the warm donut smell of her magic, which seems to be doing the same thing. I've heard about this kind of connection before—usually it's just in my sister Sigrid's romance books, but there are old stories handed down from one generation of witches to another. It's all bullshit, of course. What we have here is a mix of pheromones, the hedonism that Vegas brings out in people, and the excitement of something new.

"Are you," she goes on, her dimple getting deeper as her teasing grin gets bigger, "a serial killer planning to wear me as a skin suit?"

"I'm more of a jeans and T-shirt guy." I dip my head down so my lips are temptingly close to the curve of her ear. "You're not planning on wearing me as a skin suit, are you?"

She gives her head the slightest shake. "I can't sew."

"That's a relief." I pull back before I do something stupid like kiss her in a crowded elevator or smell her hair. "I'm just taking you out to dinner."

She purses her lips in a mocking frown. "Just?"

"That depends on you." I shove my hands in the pockets of my jeans to keep from reaching out and touching her because I'm not sure I'll be able to stop once I start, strangers surrounding us or not. "I did say you could have whatever you want."

"Good," she says. "I'm really in the mood for a cheeseburger."

The L lights up above the elevator doors as a bell dings, announcing our arrival. Thank the fucking fates. "The resort has a great burger joint on level three."

"I don't know," she says when the doors open and the people in front of us walk off the elevator, squeezing through the crowd waiting outside the now-open doors to get on and go up to the higher floors. "I'm in the mood for room service."

I don't need to think, my magic just responds. Before the last person steps into the lobby, the scent of fresh-brewed coffee spills out from the elevator. Everyone waiting to get on gets a momentary confused look on their face before they wander off, talking to one another about how they suddenly changed their minds about going up.

LeLe and I stay in our spots in opposite corners of the elevator as the doors close, anticipation and awareness making the air electric.

"I like how you think," LeLe says, and then waves her fingers and sends a shot of warm donut scent into the air before the elevator's already unhurried pace grows slower as it climbs back up toward the top floor.

"The feeling's mutual." My gaze goes to the thin strip of fabric curving over her shoulder and holding her dress up. "You were very distracting during the poker game. Teasing me with your strap wasn't nice."

"Oh, you noticed that?" She brushes her fingers over the bit of fabric in question, pushing it off her shoulder. "Oops."

My mouth goes dry and I can't look away. The top of her dress on that side clings like a rock climber to the tip of her nipple. A deep breath, a small movement, a barely-there sigh would send it sliding down, revealing the rest of her. I can't look away, which is very much not part of my plan.

My plan is simple:

One—Arouse her curiosity.

Two—Draw her in.

Three—Walk away but linger in her mind so that when
    we continue to accidentally-on-purpose cross
    paths, it's almost as if she willed me to be there.

That's how it's supposed to go.

I'm not supposed to be the one being seduced.

And yet, here I am, ready to drop to my knees if she only asks.

Now *that* sounds like a good idea, the perfect idea, the best idea I've ever had.

Before I can even think twice, I'm across the elevator in front of her, my fingers hovering in the air above her shoulder, almost touching her skin where her strap was.

"Can I touch you?" I ask, unable to stop the request from coming out of my mouth.

"Yes," she says with a sigh.

"Where?" Ground rules, I need ground rules or I'm going to get lost in this woman.

Her eyes darken with lust. "Everywhere."

I'm not normally one to deny myself when tempted, but I can't stop myself from talking even though I know it will fuck up my plan. "You were right before, I'm not who you think I am."

She chuckles as if to say, *no shit*. "Who out there is exactly as they present?"

"LeLe—"

She cuts off my last desperate attempt not to be as much of an asshole as I know I am with a touch, pressing her palm against my chest as she leans forward and lifts herself up onto her tiptoes, not stopping until she's millimeters away from my mouth.

"I don't care who you are outside of here," she says. "For once in my life, I just want to forget about everything out there and just be right here in the moment. Can you help me do that?"

Forget talking.

Forget breathing.

Forget the plan.

I can deal with all that later; what I need now is her. "I'm going to kiss you."

She takes my hand and brings it up to her full breast,

stopping just short of pressing my palm to her nearly bare skin. "I hope you'll do much more than that."

The last string holding me in check snaps, and I whisper a quick secretum spell to ensure the elevator's security cameras glitch and that the elevator ignores all calls to stop its upward climb to board new passengers. Yeah, it would be better for my plan if we're caught, if whatever happens next lands at the top of WitchyGram's trending topics, but my scheme is currently in shreds. I can't think about plots and cons when LeLe is looking at me like this, as if I'm the only one who can fix that delicious ache inside her.

Instead of tugging her dress the rest of the way down or sinking to my knees and pushing her skirt up so I can feast on her until she comes in my mouth, I snake an arm around her waist and turn her around so she's facing the elevator's mirrored walls. There's not an inch of space between us. My hard cock is pressed against the upper swell of her ass and her back is plastered to my chest.

"I'll close my eyes if you want so I don't see, but look at yourself—your real self—like this." My voice is so low, so tight with lust, I barely recognize it. "You're fucking fantastic."

Her eyes go wide with surprise. "But you'll know who—"

"I already do." I'm not supposed to be telling her this. She isn't supposed to know I know who she really is. But what's happening right now isn't a part of any scheme. This is outside of it, uncontrolled by it, and free of everything else there is in this world. We're just LeLe and Erik, nothing more, nothing less. "I can see you, the *actual* you, the one who wants to let go

of the responsibility and the expectations and the requirements." I hook my finger around the strap of her dress hanging
loosely against her upper arm, ready to tug it down and break
whatever spell is keeping her dress up over her glorious tits,
but not yet. "It's Vegas; if you can't let yourself be a little bad
here, what's the point?"

The urge to yank on the strap has me by the balls, but I
can't give in. This has to be all LeLe—the actual LeLe—calling
the shots.

The air shimmers around us, and the scent of warm donuts
fills the space before her reflection in the mirror changes to
reveal Leona Sherwood with her signature red hair, freckles,
and mind-blowing curves.

"Fuck, you are gorgeous."

Or at least that's what I mean to say, but all that comes out
is a desperate groan, because her reveal spell also sends the
one side of her dress that had been improbably clinging to her
down, revealing her full, luscious tit topped with a pale pink
nipple that's hard and begging for attention. There's no way I
can resist her, plan be fucking damned.

Chapter Five

Leona . . .

*S*pread your legs for me."

Anticipation zings across my skin as I do what he demands. I don't have to think about it first. I don't have to wonder if it's the right thing. It just is. Nothing that feels this fucking good could be wrong.

"That's it," he says, his voice practically a hot groan against the sensitive skin of my neck. "Keep your eyes open and watch. I want you to see yourself come all over my fingers."

He slips his hand beneath the high slit of my dress.

"Open. Your. Eyes." He nips the spot where my neck meets my shoulder. "Now, LeLe, or I'll stop."

At that moment, with my thighs already tingling and my core aching with unfulfilled need, I'd do just about anything for him to keep going. I open my eyes and gasp at what I see in the reflective walls of the elevator. It's all me, no camouflage spell. My wavy hair is a mess, half down from the partial ponytail I'd pulled it into during the poker game. My bottom lip is swollen from me biting down on it to keep from moaning loud enough that the entire hotel will hear. One boob is hanging out as that side of my deep-V dress pools around my waist. I'm leaning back against Erik, letting him hold me up as I just revel in pleasure. I look vulgar and wanton and as hot as I have ever looked in my entire life.

"That's my LeLe." He reaches up and cups my exposed breast and then pinches my nipple, rolling it between his fingers while tugging it with just the right amount of pressure to make me forget to bite down on my lip before my moan escapes. "Now look down at what I'm doing to that sweet pussy of yours."

My gaze falls as if I'm in a trance. Under the long skirt of my green dress, I can see the movement of Erik's hand as he alternates between teasing my clit and sinking his long, thick fingers inside me. A tease of almost seeing without actually seeing, along with the feel of my orgasm building with each stroke and push.

"Look at the color build in your face as you get closer," he says as he increases the speed of his thumb as he circles it around my clit. "And the way you squeeze my fingers, getting tighter and tighter. The smell of your magic is fucking delicious. I can't wait to put my mouth, my hard cock, where my fingers are. I'm going to make you come so many times this weekend, you'll never be the same again."

The images his words build in my head, along with the way he touches me and the feel of his dick against the small of my back, letting me know exactly how big it is and how completely it would fill me up, is more than I can take. My climax comes without warning, a sudden hard wave of pleasure that doesn't seem to end, just continuing to roll over me for minutes, hours, days, I have no fucking clue.

When it's over and I come floating back into reality, it's in time to see Erik sucking my pleasure off his fingers. Then, instead of pulling me close or stripping me completely, he lifts the spaghetti strap of my dress back into place, covering me up just as the elevator doors open.

"This is your floor," he says, stepping back into the opposite corner.

My brain is still too blissed out to process what's happening. "Are you coming?"

"I'm on a different floor. You need time to think about if you want what I promised without being on the edge of coming." His gaze drops to my mouth, my breasts, lower. Then he shoves his hands into his pockets. "I'll be at the fountain tomorrow night. Eight o'clock. I promise to bring cheeseburgers."

I'm weak-kneed and discombobulated when I step out into the hallway, which is why it takes me until the elevator doors close for me to wonder how he knows which floor my room is on.

Chapter Six

Erik . . .

$\mathcal{I}$ haven't been this nervous in, well, basically ever. But here I am, fucking pacing in front of the resort's huge fountain with a picnic basket of cheeseburgers, fries, two malted elderberry shakes, and a cherry bark pie, staring at the sliding glass doors, hoping that every time they open, LeLe will walk out.

What. The. Fuck.

I never second-guess myself. If I did, my dad would pounce on that weakness and exploit it for his own gain. As a Svensen, you learn that lesson young and you never, ever forget it.

I'm about to chuck the damn basket into the fountain when the resort's doors open up and LeLe walks out in a sundress that should be illegal. It's not that it's all that low-cut or tight, but it's because I know exactly what's underneath the pink fabric that sways with each step.

"Sorry I'm late," she says, stopping in front of me and holding out a small jar. "I stopped for some strawberry jam."

My stomach rebels at the offering. "For the cheeseburgers?"

"Ewww, no!" she says while making a gagging face. "You haven't experienced life until you've dunked your fries in strawberry jam."

"That is disgusting." Not even Cy would try that during one of his experiments about taste buds.

LeLe shrugs and makes what sounds like a chicken bwaking.

Did she just squawk at me? At *me*? Oh no, that is not how this is going to go.

Without giving myself time for second thoughts, I open up the basket and swipe a few fries. She has the jar opened before I'm even done with that, a knowing grin on her face.

"Fine, I'll try it." I dip the fries into the red goo and then take a bite. It is, without question, even better than dunking my fries in a chocolate shake. "Fuck me."

She doesn't say *I told you so*, at least not with words, and we go find a spot on the grass to watch the fountain show and enjoy our burgers and strawberry jam fries.

An hour later we're out of food, but not of stories about our siblings and all the trouble they get into. I shouldn't be having fun telling her about Cy and Sigrid—without using their names, of course—but I am. There's something about watching her nose scrunch up when she laughs that makes me want to tell her more and more just to make her laugh again.

"So, after my sister hexed my brother so every goat on the farm followed him around all summer like he was some kind of Bovidae Pied Piper," I say, "that's how he ended up with a goat familiar, which you have to admit is weird."

LeLe rolls her eyes. "My family has no room to talk on weird familiars. My sister has a rooster. It lives in a coop in the yard, but always seems to be shadowing me inside the house anyway. The number of times the big jerk has cock-a-doodle-dooed at me before I've had my first elderberry tea in the morning and scared the crap out of me." She presses her hand over her heart and shakes her head. "That rooster is mostly evil, I swear."

"You think you know evil familiars?" I counter. "My brother's goat ate my sister's favorite book. She'd waited hours in line to get it signed by the author, and he just snagged it off her nightstand and gobbled it up."

"Oh," LeLe gasps, "that's bad."

"Very." Cy has no idea how close that goat came to being dinner that night. "My brother had to go deep into his savings to buy another copy off of HexBay."

"Your sister's and my brother's familiars can never meet," she says, and begins to put our now-empty dishes back in the picnic basket.

I whisper a quick clean-up spell that sends everything but the picnic blanket we're on back to the resort's kitchen and pull her down so she's lying with me on it, tucking her close against my side as we look up at the night sky. "So you've told me about the wild things your sisters have done; what about you?"

"Me?" She snorts dismissively. "I am the boring sister. I just do what I'm supposed to do."

"I don't believe that. I know how you are in elevators." An image of her face as she watched me sink my fingers inside her flashes in my mind, and my dick hardens at the memory. The temptation to roll onto my side and kiss her until we have to go back to one of our rooms or get charged with public indecency is turning my whole body into one tensed muscle. "I think we just need to prove it."

Her cheeks are pink because she must be remembering the same thing. "You want me to be followed around by all of the goats in Vegas?"

That reminder of Cy couldn't come at a better time. Another thirty seconds and I would forget about my carefully laid plans to save him and Sigrid from my father. I can't do that. They are all that matter.

"Already been done." I jump up and stand at the far corner of the blanket, needing to put space between LeLe and myself before I forget again. "Nope, we have to go big. If this is your one go-out-and-be-outrageous moment in time before you go home and back to your regular life, we need to really do it up."

She sits up and pulls her knees close to her chest. "Just coming to Vegas is adventurous enough for me."

I could leave it here. Walk away. Nothing has been done yet that can't be undone.

Who are you, Svensen? Don't go soft now. She's a spoiled, beloved Sherwood and the only answer to the problem of how to get rid of your despot of a dad. Pull your shit together.

Listening to that inner voice I know is right, I square my shoulders and force my mouth to shape itself into the teasing, conspiratorial smile that has almost always gotten me exactly what I want.

"You're selling yourself short," I say, keeping my tone light and fun. "You've got it in you, you just need to let it out like you did in the elevator. It felt good, didn't it? Don't you want to do that again? Come on, we're going to walk until we find some good, dumb fun."

LeLe purses her full lips together and lets out a little breath. "I don't know."

"Let me be your bad influence, just for tonight." I hold out my hand to her. "Let's both be the people we wish we could be at home."

She hesitates for a second and then takes my hand. We start walking down the strip, past the casinos, restaurants, and tourist shops. I keep the pace casual, stopping here and there as if we're just aimlessly wandering even though our destination is the little white chapel underneath a giant neon Elvis.

Chapter Seven

Leona . . .

*M*aybe it's because it's Vegas, or maybe it's because I know what I have to do as soon as I get home, but the second we stop in front of the Hunka Hunka Burning Love Wedding Chapel, I know exactly what outrageous thing I want to do.

I jerk to a stop in front of the huge window with its neon sign advertising old-magic temporary handfast marriages. "You up for something completely unexpected?"

Erik looks at me with a skeptical expression. "I'm not sure either of us is ready to get married."

"It's only temporary," I reassure him. "You know how weak old magic is; it'll probably only last until sunrise."

He looks down at me, some emotion lurking in his eyes that I can't read. "Are you sure you want to do this?"

Was I sure?

Yes.

No.

Mostly?

What I know deep down all the way to my bone marrow, though, is that this will be the last chance I'll have to do something that isn't all about making the best choice for the Sherwood family. I love my family. I want the best for them. But I also just want to be me every once in a while. Next year I'll become the family matriarch, get married to one of the politically smart matches my mom picked out, and never have a chance like this again.

It's now or never.

"Come on." I open the doors and tug him inside what looks like a shrine to Elvis and old magic. "We'll be laughing about this for years."

He gives me a quick kiss that only makes me want more. "How can I say no to you?"

I'm high on the rush of doing something unexpected and amusing just because I can.

There's no family obligations or expectations, no spying eyes taking pics for gossipy WitchyGram accounts, and no logical reason to do this at all.

I'm here because it's fun. It's Vegas. It's a tiny, temporary rebellion from being Leona Sherwood, heir, with all the weight that carries.

Even head witches in charge just want to have fun. It's not like anything could go wrong.

Chapter Eight

Erik . . .

*T*can't do this.

I *should* do this.

I *need* to do this.

But I *can't* do this.

It's taking everything I have not to snatch the pen out of LeLe's hand before she signs the Hunka Hunka Burning Love Wedding Chapel's liability waiver stating that while the handfast marriage ceremony is only a temporary bond, participants won't hold the chapel responsible if the handfast becomes permanent or never works at all.

The waiver doesn't list why that could happen, but I know.

1. Getting married under false identities won't impact the handfast spell. It's not two witches' names getting married, after all.

2. If the spell is taken under duress of any kind or while someone is unable to consent, the handfast won't take, not even for a few minutes.

3. A handfast spell made during the full moon at the exact moment of its fullest presentation (which happens in exactly seven minutes) can't be broken without a special, almost-impossible-to-complete spell and the participation of both parties (which I'll never do).

My mouth is opening to say something—tell her it was a joke, say I feel sick all of a sudden, anything else, but LeLe signs the waiver before I can make a sound, and it's done. The only thing left is to say a few words under the arbor. Then we'll be married. And my plan to depose my dad will move on to the next stage. By this time next year, the old man will be out of the picture one way or another, Cy and Sigrid will be safe, and I'll sit back and watch the poisoned line I come from die out.

That's good.

It's perfect.

It's exactly what needs to happen.

This is what I keep reminding myself as LeLe hooks her arm through mine and we walk out back to the moonlit garden. There's an arbor at the back with a sparkly white cauldron that's already smoking with the ingredients of the handfast spell.

"Go ahead and pick out your handfast wedding bouquet," the Elvis impersonator who is going to perform the ceremony says. "I'll meet you two under the arbor in two hip swivels."

She starts forward but I can't move. LeLe turns and looks at me with a million questions in her eyes but before she can ask a single one, my phone buzzes with an incoming text.

Sigrid's face flashes on the screen and worry snaps my spine straight. "It's my sister. I'm sorry, I have to take this."

"We're just being dorks with this goofed-up ceremony anyway," LeLe says with a wink. "Take your time."

That's one thing I can't do. The moon is at its fullest percentage in five minutes. After that it won't matter. She walks toward the flowers and I stay behind, clenching my jaw tight as all the warning bells go off with Sigrid's text.

> **SIGRID:** Where are you?

> **ERIK:** Vegas.

> **SIGRID:** Get home. Now.

The warning bells turn into alarm bells.

> **ERIK:** I can't.

> **SIGRID:** Please, E. Dad's up to something.

That's pretty much a given if he's breathing.

ERIK: He's always up to something.

SIGRID: This is different. He's making me dress up for dinner.

I force my face to stay neutral. Thanks to years of practice when faced with some horrible scam that the old man is working pays off in numerous ways, it's not a problem. If my sister even gets a hint about just how worried I am, though, she's going to go straight to full-on panic mode. And even though she can't see me, it always seems like she can *see* me.

ERIK: So.

SIGRID: Fitzpatrick is here. He's coming to dinner. Dad wants me to play piano for him later like I'm at some kind of weird audition. E, please!

ERIK: Dinner's nothing. You'll be fine.

And if she's not, forget my power sharing ceremony plan, I'll kill the rat bastard with my bare hands even if it means I'll go down with him.

SIGRID: I need you, E.

And that's why I can't change course. I have to stick to the plan. Every other option is temporary. Marrying LeLe and taking out my dad during the power sharing ceremony is the only way to stop him for good.

ERIK: I can't.

The three dots showing she's typing appear and disappear several times before she sends her response.

SIGRID: Fine.

A second later the in-Do-Not-Disturb-mode alert appears next to my sister's name.

If I had any doubts about Sigrid's ability to hold her own, even against our shitty dad, I'd be on the first magic carpet out of here, but she's smart, strong, and savvy. She can avoid his trap for the next few days, which will give me enough time to marry LeLe and explain how our marriage is going to work.

My chest burns.

My head throbs.

I can't get enough oxygen in my lungs.

I try to inhale, but it's like trying to suck a boulder through a straw. My father is sending a message: Fuck with me and your sister pays the price. Will he follow through with marrying her off to the in-all-probability murderous old man for enough cash to keep the loan sharks off his ass for a year? Without a second thought.

"Let's rock 'n' roll, you hunka hunka hot couple," the witch dressed up as young Elvis in tight black leather says as he struts through the twenty-four-hour wedding chapel's back garden.

LeLe is already standing beneath the rose-covered arbor with a bouquet of peonies, the huge full moon bathing her in a soft glow. "It's time to get temporarily married."

It's times like these when I'm glad I'm under no illusions about who I am. Another guy—a good guy—wouldn't do this to LeLe. That guy would find another way to save his family.

As we both know, though, I'm not a good guy. Not even a little. Not even when being around LeLe has me pretending more than I need to that I could be.

As everyone in Witchingdom loves to say (but usually only behind my back), I am my father's son. I do what's efficient. What's easy. What will get me to where I want to be no matter who gets hurt in the process.

And tonight that means stuffing any hesitation I may have about my plan in a deep, dark hole and walking over to the woman whose life I'm about to ruin.

My steps barely even falter.

"Everything okay?" LeLe asks, concern crinkling the corners of her eyes.

"How could anything possibly be wrong?" I hedge, bricking up even the hint of hesitation or pity for this woman who simply had the same misfortune I did to be born an heir. "You ready to be spontaneous and wild?"

"Born ready," she says with a giggle, obviously riding the

rush of being impulsive for probably the first time in her entire life.

"If you'll hold hands," fake Elvis says, "we'll get this show started."

I take LeLe's hand, ignoring the guilt so foreign to me that I can barely identify it twisting my insides and the sizzle of something lighter and brighter that hits me in the chest, and face the Elvis impersonator. "Let's get married."

And we do.

Chapter Nine

Leona . . .

The next morning my body is still loose and lazy from the night before, wrung out from orgasms and the killer massage Erik gave me that led to more orgasms. The sex has been so mind-meltingly fantastic that its made the handfast mark linger on my wrist, a golden glow that brightens each time he touches me. I'll kinda miss that when all of this is over. But that moment isn't quite yet. Thank the fates. Reaching out for him so we can start the day off right with more orgasms, my palm slides across cool sheets instead. I crack my eyes open and confirm what I already know—I'm in bed alone.

On his pillow, however, there's a white notecard embossed with the resort's logo.

Off to find more strawberry jam. Can you believe we emptied out the resort's supply?

> *Xo,*
>
> *E*

Jam. Yeah, we went through a lot of that over the past few days, and that was before that silly handfast ceremony last night and all the naked fun we had after. Running my fingertips over my wrist, I gasp as a golden tattoo of a bracelet appears on what had been my unmarked skin only heartbeats before. It almost looks real, as if last night's spell is more than just impotent old magic that will last about as long as this temporary tattoo will—until my next shower.

Thinking of which, I smell like well-satisfied funk, and a shower isn't a luxury at this point, it's a necessity.

Getting out of bed with an audible groan—there are sore spots, and then there are the good kind of sore spots—I can't flatten my lips from the permagrin I woke up with as I walk toward the bathroom. I have a deep conditioning treatment on my mind and my hand on the bathroom door, but the sound of Erik's voice outside the closed hotel room door freezes me to the spot.

"We'll talk about The Liber Umbrarum's location later, Kiehl," Erik says, his voice sounding harder than it had to me before.

"That's not gonna happen," the other man shoots back. "We talk now."

"Fuck off. I don't have time for you right now."

My hand's on the doorknob, ready to whip the door open and back up Erik with this guy who sounds like a real charmer, but some whisper of warning holds me back.

"Then you better make time," the other man says. "I don't give a shit if you are the heir or whatever it is you witch ass-holes call it, you're just a shitbird to me, and we have a deal, Svensen."

Svensen?

Why would he call Erik that? He's a Phillips.

"Shut the fuck up," Erik says, sounding nothing like the man who sang in my ear last night as we danced under the full moon. "I told you not to call me that here."

Unless he is, because this is Vegas, after all, and nothing is exactly as it appears.

My hand goes to my stomach, pressing hard against it. If I could feel anything at this moment, I'm sure the heel of my palm jammed up against my diaphragm would hurt, but right now, I'm not sure even having a troll step on my foot would make me blink twice. I'm frozen. I'm in shock. I'm halfway to cracking in half.

Svensen?

Erik Svensen?

Not him. It couldn't be him. It has to be anyone *but* him. That family is horrible. They're dishonest. They're the worst people in Witchingdom. But why do this? Because he's an asshole? Because he's bored?

Because . . .

The whole world fades away as realization hits.

Because he wanted to marry the Sherwood heir for all the monetary and power benefits it would give him. Family means everything in Witchingdom, and even if the circumstances aren't ideal, to say the least, my family will have no choice but to accept him (and his family by proxy). Money would be given. Support would be shown. Power would be shared.

Forget letting the wolf into the henhouse. That is nothing. I've let the Svensens into the heart of our family.

My stomach twists and flips like a fish tossed from the sea onto the shore. I'm going to throw up.

A million recriminations rush through my head as I run into the bathroom.

Foolish.

Too horny to be trusted.

Ruined things for your family.

Failure.

Bad heir.

A fucking loser.

As soon as I reach for the door, I notice the handfast mark and my lungs seize. It's old magic. That kind never lasts because nature is always evolving, so all the ingredients we use in spells act differently. I mean, the newts' eyes we use today are three times stronger than in the past, so everyone knows to cut the amount that goes into the cauldron or else it will throw the magic ratios off. If you don't, the spells you work will only be for temporary use. The other night's handfast ceremony won't stick.

It can't.

No matter what, it can't.

But I can't stop the panic washing over me in giant waves. I need to call my sister to figure out my next steps. Not Effie, she'll get the truth out of me in about thirty seconds, and no one can know what I've done. It can't be Tilda because she's busy with her magical misfits group. Juniper is out; she sees through bullshit like other witches see through a window. That leaves my sweetest, most trusting sister. I'm too freaked out to feel like throwing up anymore, so I hustle out of the bathroom—pausing in front of the door to make sure Erik the Evil and the other guy aren't out there anymore—and then go grab my cell phone off the bedside table.

Bea answers on the second ring.

"Do you need bail money?" she asks, unable to keep the giggle out of her voice. "Oh my . . . could . . . you . . . even . . . imagine?" Now she's laughing so hard she's having trouble getting the words out. "You? Bail?" She lets out a loud bark of laughter. "As if."

"No, I don't need bail money." Sounding almost exactly like my mother at her most imperious, because if I sounded like me, it would just be sobbing.

"Shocker," my sister says with a snort-laugh. "You never need anything. You're a one-witch power machine."

I wish. It's more like I'm a one-witch mistake machine. And a liar, considering what's about to come out of my mouth next.

"The girls and I have a disagreement we need you to decide,"

I tell her, looking around the empty room as if my friends who I came to Vegas with are in here.

"About roosters or old spells?"

It's a logical question; those are her two areas of expertise.

My bottom lip trembles, and it takes me a second to get myself under control. "Old spells."

Bea claps with excitement. "Hit me."

"How difficult is it to reverse a handfast marriage?"

"Oh, a handfast is weak magic," Bea says with a disappointed sigh at what I'm assuming is a simple question for her. "Barkley could probably break it."

My shoulders inch down from my ears and some of the panic ebbs from my veins. If something is so easy a rooster could fix it, I have nothing to worry about.

"Unless the handfast was done last night."

My heart comes to a dead stop in my chest and all my blood drains to my toes. "Why's that?" I ask, trying my best not to sound like someone on the edge of disaster.

"Well, last night was a full moon, and old magic, even the weak stuff, when done on a full moon, is super strong," she says, excitement building in her tone. "There's all sorts of old-timey ingredients that no one uses anymore that have to go into the cauldron, extra steps that have to go into spell weaving, and usually the cooperation of all of the involved parties."

Fuck, fuck, fuck.

Every part of me that was ice-cold gets eaten up by a blast of terror-fueled heat. I have beyond screwed everything up for my family and for Witchingdom. This is so bad, there isn't even a name for it.

"In short, breaking a handfast made under a full moon is a pain in the ass." She lets out another big chuckle. "Aren't you glad you don't have to deal with that?"

"Yeah," I manage to get out, "really glad."

Bea keeps talking about how lucky I am not to have to work out an old magic spell, but her words fade into the background and all I can hear is the blood rushing through my ears. If my family finds out the truth—if my mother finds out the truth—they are going to know how big of a fuckup I really am.

That can't happen.

Whatever it takes, I'm going to fix this, and then Erik Phillips—correction, Erik Svensen—is going to rue the day he thought it was a good idea to fuck with me.

Chapter Ten

Leona . . .

One year later . . .

*E*rik motherfucking Svensen.

Of all the lying, good-for-nothing, still-maddeningly-hot assholes in all of Witchingdom to walk off of a train in the middle of nowhere Virginia, it has to be my secret husband who keeps avoiding our divorce spell.

I really do have the absolute worst fucking luck. And to make everything even more shitty, he's wearing a tux.

An ordinary man looks hot in formal wear, and Erik is already a million on the ten-point hotness scale without the outfit help (yes, he's well aware of that fact and, like the shithead he is, uses it to his advantage). It's not fair—especially since I'm wearing the leggings and oversized hoodie with a strawberry jam stain over my left boob that I had on when a spell gone wrong left me frozen in a block of ice for a week.

Lets out a deep breath.

Sorry. I got on a bit of a rant there. Let me catch you up on what's happened since I walked down the aisle at the outdoor Hunka Hunka Burning Love Wedding Chapel and handfast married the absolute worst man in Witchingdom.

First, I found out that divorcing Erik isn't as easy as a quick trip to the lawyer. Nope. It turns out that a handfast marriage begun under the full moon needs a very particular and difficult dimitto spell to break the marital ties—and it gets worse from there. Not only does the spell have to be completed within a year of the handfast marriage, the dimitto spell requires that both parties agree to take part in it. If either of those requirements are not met, then the dimitto spell is useless.

No good.

A waste of air.

Pointless pontificating.

In other words, I'll be married to Erik for the rest of my life.

It won't take you three guesses to figure out which one of the two of us doesn't want to get divorced—not that he'll tell me why. The guy's a Svensen; he's probably just doing it because torture is one of his hobbies.

Second, the Council's power has grown, and it's starting to break free from the shadows and make its move to take over Witchingdom.

Third, my sister Tilda accidentally froze everyone in the

family—literally—during a spell gone wrong. Then she, this guy named Gil, who she's totally in love with, and her friends stole The Liber Umbrarum, an ancient spell book that gives whoever possesses it massive power because of all the ancient knowledge contained in it. Tilda, good witch that she is, used The Liber Umbrarum to defrost all the Sherwoods.

That—not surprisingly—got the Council's attention. They tried to execute a whole smash and grab of The Liber Umbrarum themselves, but Tilda and her friends saved Witchingdom by foiling the attempt. Yeah, they crashed a train in this meadow in the process, and it looked like things were not going to end happily, but every newly unfrozen Sherwood magicked their way to Tilda's side to help her face down the goons sent by the Council to take the spell book from her. Not that she needed much help from us, because it turns out she has more power than just about any other witch alive.

The good news is the Council's enforcers have scattered to lick their wounds in private.

The bad news? There's no way the Council is going to give up after one little skirmish, not when the spells in The Liber Umbrarum are the key to them gaining total control over Witchingdom.

Really, you need to hear the whole story about the heist from her if you haven't already. I can't believe I missed being a part of it all because of being a temporary witch popsicle.

That's a lot, right? Well, deep breaths, because we're not done yet.

Who do you think Tilda and her friends stole The Liber

Umbrarum from? If you said the Svensens—as in Erik Svensen—then you are right.

Yeah, don't say I didn't warn you that it is an interconnected dramafest over here.

And that's why I'm standing in the middle of a field, surrounded by my entire family, staring at the biggest mistake of my life and trying to figure out if he's going to spill the truth to my family. And then they'll know that I, the Sherwood heir, the one who has to do everything right the first time because that's what is expected and demanded of me, fucked up.

Big-time.

Add to that the fact that I've been hiding the whole handfast marriage thing from my family for the past year and you get why I'm white-knuckling life right now. Not only am I an idiot, I'm an idiot who's been living in fear for the past year that her family would find out the truth.

Oh yeah, and I've been doing whatever it takes to keep my mother from making me pick a husband. You do not even want to know what I've done. Let's just say a week of Barkley talking like a witch to distract the whole family was pretty dire. The things a rooster familiar thinks about on a daily basis are both bizarre and boring in the same breath. But it's not like I had a choice. My only other option was either telling my mom everything or bigamy.

I hope you understand by now that neither of those are an option and why I wake up with the two a.m. panics every night. It really has been the shittiest year of my life, and it's all my fault.

"I hate to be the bearer of bad news, but we have a problem," Erik says after walking near to where I'm standing with my sister Tilda and our parents. "My dad is absolutely livid about your family stealing The Liber Umbrarum. However, if we get it back to our secured facility right away, there's a chance I can talk him out of involving the cops or worse."

There is no way he's telling the truth—at least not all of it. More than likely, this is an excuse for him to take The Liber Umbrarum for his own selfish purposes because that's what the Svensens do. They lie. They steal. They cheat. They fake their way into marrying you.

Well, not this time.

He's not getting any alone time with that spell book, not with all the power that's between its pages. The Council getting their hands on The Liber Umbrarum would be the worst, but Erik Svensen using it for his own purposes runs a close second in my book.

I crunch a pile of fallen orange leaves under my tennis shoes as I march up to him. (Am I picturing each dead leaf as Erik's coal-black heart? Abso-fucking-lutely.) "So *we* take it back."

"*We?*" he asks, one of his dark eyebrows shooting up.

I give him a dirty look that would send most witches for cover. Erik doesn't even flinch. Overconfident bastard.

"After what happened in Vegas," I say, keeping my voice low so only he can hear, "there's no way I'd trust you with The Liber Umbrarum on your own."

I could say more, but I don't have to. Of course, that doesn't stop my heart from beating against my ribs like it's about to make a break for it. All my years of training as the Sherwood heir come in handy though. My palms might be clammy, and I've got a whole squadron of butterflies having the zoomies in my stomach, but I keep that shit locked up tight—at least as far as anyone can tell from the outside.

Getting the spell book to safety will take a few hours. Tops. I can put up with him even for twelve hours. Plus it will give me the perfect opportunity to finally persuade him (or force, or threaten, whatever it takes) to participate in the spell to break the handfast.

"Whatever you want, LeLe," he says with a wink that people who don't know him probably think is charming and flirty.

His grin matches mine just for showiness as he all but beams at my family, but there's more to it, an intensity in his blue eyes that sends a shiver down my spine. Damn it. He shouldn't be able to still do that to me, not after what he's done.

He drops his hand the size of a dinner plate to the small of my back, his palm and long fingers spanning the space and making my whole body get all melty and wanty. The smug look on his handsome face shows that he knows exactly what he's doing.

It takes everything I have not to let my annoyance show to the rest of my family, who are all sneaking looks at us, no doubt trying to figure out when we got so chummy and what is going on between us. I've got to get out of here before any of them start to ask questions.

"Shall we, LeLe?" he asks, his tone deferential as we walk past my mom and dad.

"You know I hate it when you call me LeLe." He is the only one who does, because he obviously doesn't value his kneecaps.

"Fine." His hand drops a few millimeters, his fingertips almost but not quite brushing my ass. Typical Erik, tiptoeing along that line of acceptable and what will get him kneed in the balls. "I'll just call you 'wife' instead. Is that better?"

My lungs seize as I whip my head around to make sure no one overheard.

"Not in the least." Side-eyeing him, I take a small step forward and find myself missing the sizzle from his touch as soon as I break contact.

He grins at me. "But it's what you are."

"Only because you won't participate in the dimitto spell." The spell I've sent to him multiple times with little yellow Post-it Notes marking every line he'd need to chant.

"I have no plans to do that," he says, not even bothering to pretend to be ashamed.

Yeah, no shock there. The first time I sent the spell, he opened the package and returned it with only the word *nope* scrawled across the top of the parchment. The second time, the envelope with the spell came back unopened and stamped "return to sender." The third time, I sent the spell via flying monkey couriers. All I got back were pics of Erik and the monkey living their best life in a beach resort somewhere tropical.

Knocking my glare up a few notches, I keep my volume low as I tell him, "We are doing that divorce spell."

"Oh, wife." He steps closer so he's just outside my personal bubble. "You're breaking my heart. You are my one and only."

I roll my eyes.

His reputation is well-known. He's a natural-born flirt with women, men, and everyone else. There are at least five hundred fan accounts on social media that document his every rumored romance. Not that I follow them. Okay. Fine. I do, but only so I can keep tabs on him to know where to send the dimitto spell.

"Erik Svensen, you can't sweet-talk your way into my pants again."

And maybe if you say it enough, Leona Amber Sherwood, it'll actually be true.

Yeah, my inner horny self can just shut it about now.

"Now, LeLe." Erik reaches out and brushes his thumb across my wrist, his touch sending a jolt of desire straight to my core and exposing the otherwise invisible golden glow of the handfast chain magically tattooed on my skin. "We both know that's not true."

"You're the worst." But in the absolute best way if you're naked and in the mood to get your back blown out.

No!

I will not think about that now. I will not think about how we spent our time in Vegas naked and utilizing every horizontal surface and quite a few vertical ones to fuck each other boneless. I will not think about how my panties are already damp, my nipples hard, and every horny hormone in my body is shouting, "Just fuck him already." Instead, I'm focusing on how satisfying it will be to never have to think about this awful man ever again.

"I may be the worst, but you bring out the best in me," Erik says, letting go of my wrist and flexing his fingers as if he felt the same electric spark when he touched me, just like I had. Then he takes a few steps toward Tilda and Gil standing across the meadow. They are holding the ancient spell book, so of course they have his attention. "Come on, LeLe, let's get out of here before the Council gets it in their heads that this is the perfect time to send in reinforcements and steal The Liber Umbrarum back."

My eyes go wide as the last word registers.

"Back?" I sputter as I turn up the speed to catch up with Erik's long strides. "They want it *back*? You stole The Liber Umbrarum from the Council?"

Of all the stupid, foolhardy, impulsive things to do, stealing from the Council is number one through ten on the list.

"It has spent the last hundred years mislabeled as a cookbook in one of their own archives. They didn't know what they had, and so I liberated it from them. It takes a Svensen to really appreciate something as amazing as The Liber Umbrarum . . ." He stops next to me and smirks down at me. "Or a wife."

My pulse skyrockets, and I look around to make sure no one overheard before I turn back to him and hiss, "I'm *not* your wife."

Erik dips his head down, his lips brushing the curve of my ear in a way guaranteed to drive me to distraction and turn me on at the same time.

"LeLe, my bride, you most definitely are and always will be," he says, his voice velvet sandpaper on every one of my most sensitive spots. Then, he brushes a fingertip across my wrist, making my skin sizzle with awareness and setting off the warm glow of the handfast mark. "I excel at many things, one of which is finding loopholes in any and all verbal and written agreements. I can guarantee you there isn't one when it comes to our vows." He gives me that sexy smirk of his again. "You're stuck with me, wife. Forever."

A blast of heat steams through me so fast I'm surprised there aren't tendrils of smoke coming out of my nose. And it's because I'm that mad and frustrated and—fine—so turned on that kissing him and killing him both seem like reasonable reactions to his smug announcement.

I'm hot.

I'm bothered.

I'm very fucking confused right now. Not about our marriage—that has to go, no ifs, ands, or buts about it, and I know that. It's just more of trying to figure out how in the world I can want to tell him to fuck off and fuck me in equal parts.

It must be the aftereffects of spending seven days frozen. It has to be.

I glare at him as he stands there with his loose body language and easy grin as if nothing in the world—not even the Council—can touch him.

Can he not take anything seriously? This is the Council we're talking about, the big baddie of the Witchingdom that's doing everything it can to take over and enact a dictatorship. It's my duty as the Sherwood heir to make sure that no matter what it takes, the Council will not get possession of The Liber Umbrarum.

A few hours alone with Erik to ensure the spell book is locked up away from the Council, and then I'll strong-arm him into completing the divorce spell so my family never finds out how badly I failed them. Then I marry whoever my mom decides is the best political move. Love? Who needs it. Lust? Look where that got me in Vegas.

I can do this.

I will do this.

Today will be the best day of my life—the last one I ever have to see Erik motherfucking Svensen ever again.

Chapter Eleven

Leona . . .

$\mathcal{I}$ am trying my best to appear like I'm not freaking the fuck out when my older sister Effie sweeps in and strong-arms me away from Erik.

Oh, it doesn't look like I am being moved by force from the outside, my sister is too good at making everyone think she's just the sweetest thing since pink Pixy Stix for that. My sisters and I, however, know better.

Effie is a terror.

I might be the heir to our family magic, but as the oldest, Effie is the bossy brains and badassery of the family. Am I afraid of her? No. Am I knee-jerk gonna go to her for advice, and has she wheedled every secret I've ever had out of me for my entire existence? Oh yeah.

She's my older sister. I'd step in front of a herd of stampeding water buffalo for her, right after I hexed the book she's reading so the last chapter disappears. If you have sisters, you totally understand. If you don't, you have way less mutual trauma and fewer closets to steal clothes from.

"Are you sure you want to do this?" Effie asks as she looks over her shoulder at Erik. "With him?"

Yeah, she knows the whole story about what went down in Vegas (she got me to fess up within hours of me returning home). From the staged meet-cute to the fake names, to the elevator sex to the handfast marriage under the full moonlight. Like I said, if Effie wants to know something, she's going to find it out.

"Don't I look sure?" I straighten myself and tilt my chin up a few degrees, taking it from witch next door to untouchable bitch.

I can make that transformation in my sleep—no spell necessary. My mom makes things happen by the sheer force of her personality. She's intimidated presidents, queens, and even a pair of trolls who quickly changed their minds about making her answer a riddle to pass over their bridge. I'm nowhere near that good, but I'm working on it—as the heir, I don't have a choice.

My sister looks me up and down before her lips curl into a self-satisfied smile, as if my resting witch face was all her doing. "You look exactly like you normally do—completely and utterly impenetrable."

"So, like the Sherwood heir." Which should make me happy, but instead just makes my shoulders slump a little lower.

She nods, trouble glimmering in her dark eyes. "The Sherwood heir married to the Svensen heir."

"Shhhhh." Panic rockets through me and I grab her arm, yanking her farther away from all the Sherwoods crowding the meadow and into the shadows, my heart pounding against my ribs the whole time. "Someone could hear you! *Mom* could hear you!"

I can already hear Mom's I'm-not-mad-I'm-disappointed voice as she tells me that everyone had been depending on me to stick to the plan of marrying the right man from the right family for the right reason. Shit. Could I have fucked anything up more?

"What?" Effie shrugs. "Everyone is too busy getting all of the meet-cute-and-fell-in-love information from Tilda and Gil to pay attention to us."

She glances over at our little sister and her obviously adoring brand-new boyfriend and gets the same sappy, happy grin on her face that's on mine. We might give Tilda a hard time— she is the youngest, after all—but we love her more than words can say.

"They do look cute together," I say, the truth tumbling out of my mouth before things click into place and I realize what my conniving sister is doing. "That is the worst attempt at changing the subject I've ever heard."

Effie opens her eyes wide and presses her palm to her heart as if she's been wrongly accused. "It's true!"

"Of course it's true." That is like saying water is wet, newt muffins are delicious, Barkley is mostly evil, or my sister Juniper loves studying underutilized spells. "Hot professor type and our adorable little sister is a good pairing."

"And the fact that they are obviously head over heels for each other helps," Effie says with a happy sigh. "She does have that glow about her. Kinda like the hot pink aura you're sporting right now. The one that says you're in love."

Heat blooms in my cheeks—the annoyed kind, not the oh-you-figured-out-my-secret kind. "You need to get your psychic vision checked."

"Hmmm." She cocks her head to the side and squints at me as she draws out the syllable.

Unease dances the conga up my spine like a parade of electric ants. "What?"

"What makes you think I have anything to say?" she asks, all sunshine and innocence.

Yeah, that bird is not flying. "You always have something to say. About everything. To everyone."

It's true. Maybe it's because she's the oldest, maybe it's because she's never been worried about rocking the boat, maybe it's just because she's Effie. Whatever the reason, the woman has never hesitated to tell anyone what she was thinking. Sometimes I'm jealous of that and other times I'm glad there's a strong, working filter between my brain and my mouth.

"Is it my fault I see the solutions when other people only see problems?" she says, her tone making it plain that she doesn't think it is her fault at all. "And just so you know, your aura is more red than pink."

Before I can stop, I'm looking down at myself. I don't see red. I don't see pink or blue or gray or anything other than my favorite pair of supersoft leggings and Fizzy Clementine band hoodie that I was wearing when the oops-you're-frozen spell happened. Unlike Effie, aura colors are not my area of magical expertise. I deal with strategic magic, spells about logistics and organization.

I know.

It's too sexy for words.

I'm gonna regret this, but I gotta ask, "So what does red mean? Anger?"

That would totally track. No one makes me as angry as Erik I'm-a-smug-asshole Svensen.

Effie all but vibrates with excitement; the woman loves nothing more than to stir the pot. "It means passion. Lust. Desire. Especially when you're looking at your husband."

Memories flash through my mind. The desperate need rolling through me as Erik stood behind me, his dick pressed against the small of my back as he cupped a breast with one hand and slid the other between my legs. The thrum of our magic swirling together as I sank to my knees in front of him. The feel of him inside me and that look he got in his blue eyes in the seconds before I came. It wasn't cocky satisfaction. It wasn't a smug I-told-you-so. It wasn't a finally-now-I-can-get-mine. It was different than all of that, and part of me—a small, tiny part that barely made itself known—wants more than anything to see it again, something that definitely cannot happen.

So I stuff that idea down into a deep, dark well and fall into the part I play best—imperial Sherwood heir.

"I think being frozen really did mess with your magical abilities if you think my passion is leaning toward the sexy side instead of the murdering side when it comes to Erik Svensen."

Effie rolls her eyes. "Would being married to him really be so bad? I mean, you saw something in him, or you wouldn't have said your I dos under the full moon."

Yeah. I saw a hot funny guy named Erik Phillips, not Svensen, who made smart jokes and treated me like I was Leona and not the Sherwood heir with a duty to my family that superseded anything I actually wanted.

Too bad what I saw was a lie.

"He *is* a Svensen," I say between gritted teeth.

Effie shrugs. "So?"

"You know what they're like." Really, the stories are legendary. Blackmail. Thefts. Espionage. Vile threats. The Svensens are implicated in it all. "They can't be trusted. They're villains. I mean, come on, he used a spell to hide his identity in Las Vegas."

For most witches, that would be enough to banish someone from their life for good. Effie, however, isn't put off.

"Weren't you using a camouflage spell too?" she asks. "Doesn't everyone there?"

I let out an offended gasp. Of all the people to say that, it comes out of my sister's mouth?! Where is the loyalty?

I sputter, but manage to get out the words to defend myself. "But the rest of the world does it for regular reasons, not so they could trap someone into marriage."

A fact that she well knows because I tell her everything and she is supposed to be my ride or die.

Effie rolls her eyes. "Everyone makes mistakes."

If my sister had just said that the sky is green, it couldn't have been weirder. Look, we all have those people in our lives who are the ones who when you say someone did you wrong, they remind you they have a shovel and land. That's my sister Effie, which makes her whole "everyone makes mistakes" comment about the guy who tricked me into marriage not just weird but totally bizarre.

Crossing my arms, I shoot her a don't-fuck-with-me look. "What are you up to?"

She giggles at my pose, totally unfazed. "Nothing, but you should still listen to me and your raspberry-colored aura."

None of that seems like a good idea—especially not with Erik Svensen. I'll be spending the next few hours with him, taking the ancient spell book to a secured location so the Council can't use it to take over Witchingdom. And because I'm the Sherwood heir and thus always figuring out how to use a situation to my advantage, I'll also use the alone time with Erik to get him to agree to perform the spell that will dissolve our marriage. Then I can go on with my life according to the plans laid out for me. Never mind they aren't exactly what I want. No one gets everything they want in this world. Life doesn't work that way, so I'll just suck it up and do what needs to be done per usual.

And maybe if I say that enough, it will start to feel less depressing.

"You wanna come with?" I ask my sister with a little more pleading than I meant to have leak out.

"Not a chance," she says as she hugs me goodbye, "but if you need anything, just holler. I'll be there. Flying monkeys couldn't keep me away."

And speaking of flying monkeys, the man who had a great time at the beach with the Hamadryas baboon instead of agreeing to do the dimitto spell is standing a few feet away next to a shiny canary-yellow Cadillac convertible that wasn't there five minutes ago.

Going over there is both the last thing and the only thing I want to do. Why can't anything be simple when it comes to Erik?

I should hate him.

I do hate him.

Sorta.

Can I hate him if I keep dreaming about him? Yes. I can find a way to make that work. It's just my subconscious working out all the hate, along with a few orgasms, I'll admit.

Ugh. Why does he make me like this?

Thoroughly annoyed with myself, Erik, and (let's face it) the whole world, I leave my sister behind and march my way over, keeping my attention focused on the classic Cadillac instead of the broad-shouldered slice of hotness standing next to it.

I succeed.

Mostly.

The convertible has fins in the back, cream-colored leather seats, and instead of a touch-screen entertainment system, there's an old-fashioned radio with knobs you have to turn to tune in to a local radio station. Stepping closer, I can't help but admire how the polished wood dashboard gleams in the light of the moon, and the pair of black fuzzy dice hanging from the rearview mirror has me smiling before I stop myself and pull my bitch face back into place.

The car is absolutely ridiculously gorgeous, over-the-top, and the one thing we don't need, since a simple spell will take us anywhere in Witchingdom that we need to go.

Still, I can't help trailing my fingertips across the back of the passenger seat's soft leather headrest, which is surprisingly warm and welcoming. I can already picture how nice it will be to sink back into the seat, let my eyes close, and feel the wind rushing through my hair as we speed down the highway. The car feels like freedom—something I'm not allowed as the Sherwood heir.

And that bummer of a thought is enough to remind me of the where, why, and who of the situation.

"You magicked a car here?" I ask, even though it's not a question, because who else would have done it?

"Oh, this isn't just any car," Erik says, skimming his palm

across the hood as he walks around the vehicle. "This is Bessie, and she's going to take us to the secured facility."

That is not going to happen. A transport spell is nearly instantaneous. Even a magic carpet could get anywhere in Witchingdom within an hour. But a car? That would make the trip take hours, or even days, depending on where the Svensens' secret hiding spot is.

"And don't worry about clothes," Erik goes on, impervious to the death glare I am shooting at him as he stops at the back of the car. "I already summoned up a suitcase full of them for you."

He pops open the trunk, and there in the middle of the ginormous empty space are two blue suitcases, each of which is monogrammed—"Mr." on one and "Mrs." on the other, both in gold script. Turning to face me, he smiles. My gut drops and nervous energy starts pinballing through me, because it's not his usual cocky smirk. Instead, it's a sweet, innocent curve of his lips that makes his whole face light up. My internal oh-shit meter was already going off, but that guileless grin sent it into full-on panic mode even though I know it's about as real as a unicorn shifter who hates Lucky Charms.

"Why are the suitcases so big?" I ask, already knowing I'm not going to like the answer.

He closes the trunk with a thunk. "It'll take us a few days to get to the secured facility."

"A few days?" The words come out louder than I meant, and I can feel the eyes of all the Sherwoods turning toward us. Forcing a calm, nonchalant expression even though I'm about to commit murder, I wave off their concern, waiting until their attention is focused anywhere but on me before continuing in a tight, quiet voice that should scare the shit out of my soon-to-be ex. "No. Forget it. You give me the location and I'll cast the spell to get us there tonight."

He makes a regretful tutting sound and gives me an aw-shucks shrug. "No can do."

The man must have absolutely zero sense of self-preservation, because instead of walking back around the car so that there are nearly five thousand pounds of metal, leather, and machinery between us, he curves around the tail fin and walks right up to me. I'm in the process of deciding exactly which spell I'm going to use to make him poof out of my sight when he takes my hand.

Instead of the most annoying man in all of Witchingdom magicking into thin air, it's all of my thoughts that do the disappearing act. My breath catches. My heart speeds up. My mouth goes dry. Without meaning to, I wet my lips with the tip of my tongue and bite down on my bottom lip. Erik's blue eyes darken with desire as he stares at my mouth.

His jaw tenses.

He steps forward.

And for a single, solitary moment, it's not a fanciful thought that he's going to kiss me—it's a fact.

But he doesn't.

And I'm fucking thrilled about that.

Really.

One hundred million percent thrilled.

Kissing Erik is not a thing I want. Not at all. Not even a little teeny-tiny bit.

You can keep all of your *uh-huh, sure*s to yourself right about now. I know I'm lying, but let me hold on to what little bit of dignity I still have at this moment when all I can think about is dragging the man I hate into the nearest dark corner and fucking him senseless.

He blinks a few times and moves his gaze so he's looking just to the side of my face instead of directly at me. However, he doesn't let go of my hand.

"My great-great-great-grandfather cursed the secured facility so that it can't be reached by magic. So that's why Bessie isn't only beautiful, she's necessary. Oh, and one more thing." He lifts my hand and runs his thumb across my wrist, sending a shiver of anticipation through me as the otherwise invisible gold bracelet tattooed on my skin as a result of the handfast ceremony glitters in the night. "No one can enter who isn't a Svensen by birth or"—he pauses and looks right at me—"by marriage."

"There has to be another way," I say, the words coming out all breathy.

"Generations of Svensens have tried and failed to get to it by magic, and we don't exactly have the time to research a different solution if we're going to get The Liber Umbrarum safe in the secured facility before the Council comes after it."

Why does he have to be right?

I suck in a deep, cleansing breath as I beg the universe for another option.

If there is one, the fates aren't sharing it with me.

"Of course," he says, letting go of my hand, "I could go by myself if you trust me not to use the spell book for my own benefit."

As if. "I wouldn't trust you with a half-eaten newt muffin I was planning to toss in the trash."

Grinning, Erik opens the passenger door for me. "Then your chariot awaits, wife."

If there was any other way—seriously, *any other way*, I'd do it. But there's not.

Fuck me.

I really am the unluckiest witch alive.

Chapter Twelve

Erik . . .

$\mathcal{A}$ll the shit they say about my family and me? The blackmail? The extortion? The double-dealing? The underhanded plots? All of it's true.

Yes, I dognapped our neighbor's pug (he's living a much better life with a family in Toledo who doesn't lock him up in a closet or forget to feed him, but best of all, I don't have to hear his high-pitched yips anymore while I'm trying to sleep).

The stories about sneaking into the city council's office and replacing the official cauldron with a rotten pumpkin spelled to look like the real thing? That was me. (It's hard to take votes on eliminating city services when your cauldron is a fast-deteriorating squash. I only did it so my sister, who is always at the local library, would stop ranting about the cuts. It was ruining my dinner every night because it's all she would talk about.)

Did I take compromising photos of the CEO of Hex House Inc. and blackmail him into not buying the historical home of my brother's favorite alchemist just to bulldoze it down and put up a parking lot? Yes. And it saved me hours of my brother reciting all of the witch's accomplishments every morning before I'd even finished my first cup of elderberry tea. (Fine, I also posted the pics on my WitchyGram alt profile because the guy was a dick and it made me happy to do it. So I'm petty. Big whoop.)

Then there's the stories about my family. Selling state secrets for cash. Ransoming people to get the deed of what is now our family seat. Being double agents who are actually triple agents who are actually quadruple agents in tense state-level negotiations with the real beneficiary being ourselves? Without a doubt, that's us. We've been like this since the first Svensen witch set foot in the United States and reneged on a peaceful deal with the local tribe already here for a thousand acres of prime coastline. Why pay for something when you could just steal it? That is the Svensen way.

Well, mostly.

Unlike me, my siblings, Cy and Sigrid, don't fit the Svensen mold. I've always wondered what it's like to be them and have people look at you and say all the shit they do about your family and know they are wrong when it comes to you.

That question was purely academic for me until Vegas—until LeLe. With her, I was just Erik who made a mean martini, was shit at cards, and knew exactly where to kiss to make her whole body tighten with anticipation.

But now?

Even going seventy miles per hour down the highway, there's no mistaking that all she sees when she glances in my direction is one of those dirty, rotten, no-good Svensens—not that I care. That's who I am, and I don't make any apologies for it.

So there really is no point in breaking LeLe's impressive two-hour silent marathon as we speed down the two-lane road. She wants a divorce. That's not going to happen. Marrying her is a vital part of my plan to get rid of dear old Dad.

I relax my hold on the steering wheel because I am not going to let her silence get to me. I don't give a shit what she thinks. The time in Vegas with her had me second-guessing my plan, thinking that maybe there was another way when I know damn well there isn't. It is what it is, and there's not one chance in a billion that I'll change my mind.

Still, I can't stop sneaking glances at her. LeLe doesn't rant and rave like my dad. She doesn't promise retribution. She doesn't swear to take it out on anyone I care about so I'd suffer by knowing that their pain was my fault.

Instead, she's back to being the ice princess I've met over the years at various Witchingdom events. The LeLe from Vegas— the one who danced in the hotel lobby, who ate whipped cream straight from the spray can, and who bluffed her way into winning a pot of chips with a pair of fours—doesn't exist any more than the good guy Erik does.

If she were anything to me beyond a means to an end, that would sting. It might even have haunted me every time I walked by a bakery with a "Hot Donuts" sign or looked in a mirror or even fucking inhaled.

I can assure you it didn't.

I've barely thought about that moment at all.

And the fact that I avoid any dessert with whipped topping is for my own reasons that have nothing to do with LeLe.

All of that is exactly why I keep my mouth shut and drive, why I keep my breathing steady despite the pressure in my chest (to be expected after a long fucking day), and why I'm ignoring the woman in the passenger seat just as hard as she's ignoring me.

When Bessie drops to a quarter of a tank, I start scanning the side of the highway for gas station signs. However, it's not a gas station that has me flicking on my blinker a few miles later. It's a sign for the Strawbery Banke Inn.

LeLe whips around in her seat to face me, annoyance as clear as the line of freckles across her nose. "Why are we turning off?"

"We need to stop for the night." A good night's sleep will work out the chest tightness that has crawled up to my shoulders and settled in for what feels like an eternity.

"I can drive," she says.

I don't take my eyes off the narrow country road that looks like it was designed by someone who'd had twelve too many pints of mugwort ale. LeLe, though, is not about to take my silence as an answer, judging by the way she's glaring at me with her arms crossed and her chin tilted up in the universal position of try-me-asshole.

It's cute.

Now don't start chewing my ass, I don't mean that in a patronizing way. It actually is cute.

Hot.

Sexy.

Fuck. I tighten my grip on the steering wheel and concentrate on keeping my foot on the gas pedal instead of moving it over to the brake so I can pull off to the side of the road and—What? Kiss her? *Oh yeah, she definitely wants to make out with you, Svensen. It's written all over her face. Oh wait. Her expression says* fuck you, *not* fuck me.

I swear to the fates I'm going to get a twitch in my left eye if I can't get my shit together around her. This is exactly what happened in Vegas. Every time I was with her for longer than a few minutes, I forgot the mission, the plan, the whole point of being with her. That can't happen again, not with only a few weeks until the power transfer ceremony.

"One, you haven't slept either," I say as I keep my eyes peeled for anything that goes bump in the night and is hiding in the woods crowding the road, half hoping to see something so I can use it as an outlet for all the annoyance at myself running through my veins. "Two, no one drives Bessie but me. Three, you don't know where you're going."

She snorts. "You could tell me."

"I can't. In addition to cursing the secret facility so it couldn't be reached by magic, my ever-trusting great-great-

great-grandfather laid a hex down on all future generations that we could never give anyone directions to it." The Svensens don't just distrust anyone outside of the family. In fact, I'd say we're most suspicious of those who share our DNA.

She lets out an unhappy harrumph and turns her attention back to the road. "Your family has issues."

I laugh, but it sounds hollow even to me. "Finally, something we can agree on."

"Is that your plan this time?" she asks, her tone sharp. "Make me feel bad for you because your entire family is awful so that I get all ooey-gooey and forget about the divorce?"

Yeah, that divorce spell is never going to happen, but I keep my mouth shut about that. No reason to piss off the woman even more than she already is.

"Not everyone in my family is bad," I say, imagining Cy in his lab, his hair going every which way, and Sigrid curled up with a book, the pages of which are all waved because she'd dropped it reading in the pool. "Just the vast majority of us."

She rolls her eyes and gives a little snort that doesn't take a genius to translate as "uh-huh, sure."

Then she turns her body away from me and stares out at the woods on either side of the road, returning to the silent treatment.

My shoulders cinch up a little more until I swear it feels like they're about to brush my earlobes. I have got to work her out of my system.

No. Not like that.

At least not this time.

It takes a few more minutes of driving slow down a twisting gravel drive that has me wincing every time a pebble shoots up from the road and pings Bessie's undercarriage to get to the inn. I pull into a spot in the small parking lot next to an ancient pickup truck that might be more rust than metal at this point. I double-check the wards over Bessie's glove box, where The Liber Umbrarum is stored away, and the Cadillac itself. Then I'm out and around the front of the car to open her door vampire-quick. I'm a dick, but I do have manners.

LeLe, however, opens her door before I get the chance. She raises an eyebrow as if to ask what I am going to do about it. There are a lot of things I'd like to do right now, but absolutely none of them involve fighting about the car door, so I swerve around her and pop the trunk and pull out both of our suitcases.

She struts over and holds out her hand. "I can carry mine."

I shoot her a wink and a sly smile. "I know."

"So give it to me," she says through clenched teeth, obviously annoyed.

Her cheeks are flushed the same shade as when she's coming down from an orgasm, and there's a snap, crackle, pop in her one-blue-and-one-green eyes that promises all sorts of trouble.

And that's the thing.

I like trouble.

"You're such a jerk," she says, her gaze dropping to my mouth before jerking back up.

A nice guy would pretend not to have noticed, however,

we've already established I'm not that guy. "That may be true, but you still want to kiss me."

Her breath catches and her eyes darken with desire as she starts to take a step toward me before she catches herself. It's impressive seeing how she reels herself back, squaring her jaw, straightening her shoulders, and narrowing her eyes. She's good, but even she can't hide the want when she looks at me and lets out a shaky breath.

"Been there, did that, got the—"

"Sixty-three orgasms to show for it," I finish for her.

"I was going to say 'T-shirt,'" she says half a second before her cheeks go three shades brighter.

I know exactly what she's remembering. Our shopping trip in Vegas. I'd sat outside the changing space in the private dressing room reserved for VIPs. The sales assistant had dropped off several outfits before closing the door and leaving us alone.

"Erik," LeLe says, her voice low and breathy. "Stop it."

"What?" I ask as if I don't know. "I'm just standing here, not doing a damn thing. I'm not touching you. Or kissing you. Or asking you to try on another outfit."

In Vegas, LeLe had tried on one dress after the other, each one getting smaller and smaller. She'd strut close to the chair where I sat and do a three-sixty just out of my reach, teasing me with what I could almost see and touch. I played along until she came out of the changing space in a distressed, threadbare designer T-shirt masquerading as a dress that gave me a new appreciation for the bottom curve of a woman's ass. When she came in close that time, there was no teasing turn or walking back.

"Stop thinking about it," she says as she fans herself with her hand as if it's suddenly gone from almost winter to the dog days of August and lets out a sound that is a lot of want and a little can't have. "I cannot wait to divorce you when this is over."

"Oh, LeLe." I take a step closer, still white-knuckling the suitcases because they are the last thing I want to touch when I'm this close to her. "You couldn't wait when we were in that elevator or the shower or when you were wearing that T-shirt. Always so impatient and demanding—especially when you know what you want."

For once, LeLe is without words, and for my part I'm about half a second away from dropping these stupid suitcases, tossing her over my shoulder, and going to find the closest at least semiprivate spot where I can fuck her happy like we did in Las Vegas.

One: Hold on for dear life to the luggage handles.

and

Two: Get as far away from my wife for the night so I can remember which head is in charge of things.

Too much is riding on my plan to mess things up now.

"Come on, wife," I say as I start down the path toward the inn. "Your room awaits."

"Don't call me that," she grumbles.

But she says it to my back, because I'm already walking down the winding stone path leading to our home for the night.

The Strawbery Banke Inn is a narrow three-story house painted pink and set aglow by the massive amount of fireflies hovering around it. Oversized strawberry bushes line the stone walkway to the front porch, where a wizened old man with a pipe sits carving swans out of white cedar with lightning speed.

As soon as we get to the base of the five steps leading up to the porch, he pauses and gives us a slow up and down before folding the knife closed and dropping it into the front pocket of his worn denim overalls.

"Took you long enough." He holds up his hand, the knuckles twisted and swollen with arthritis. "There's only so many swans I can make before my joints start screaming. I strongly recommend you never piss off a pixie to the point where they curse you."

LeLe and I look at each other and then back at the old man, who maybe shouldn't be out this late on his own.

"I don't think we're the people you were expecting," LeLe says, her tone soft as if she's trying to coax a lost kitten into trusting her. "We just pulled over when we saw the sign."

The old man gives us a slow look over. "Erik and LeLe?"

We nod, and I take a step closer to LeLe, angling myself so I'm between the old man and her. Yeah, he might look like a harmless old guy out way past his bedtime, but in Witchingdom, things are often not exactly as they appear. And before you get all sentimental, I didn't move in front of her because I care. It's because I need her, or my plan falls apart. That's it. Nothing else.

The old man tugs on his long wiry white beard and makes a few uh-huh noises. "Then you're the ones."

He stands up, and I swear I can hear all his joints cracking at once. Whatever he did to the pixie who cursed him, it must have been bad. He might be ancient, but he moves quickly. He is across the porch and at the front door in a blink. Yeah, my magic detector is buzzing like crazy. Something is totally off about this place.

I glance over at LeLe and raise an eyebrow in question, but she just shrugs and climbs the stairs.

"How did you know we were coming?" she asks.

"Didn't. The house did." He holds the screen door open for us. "I'm Eustis Neale, the caretaker. Let's get you squared away."

LeLe walks in first, shooting me a what-the-fuck-is-going-on look over her shoulder. If I had an answer, I'd give it, but I am clueless.

She narrows her eyes at me and whispers, "Did you set this up like you did the heist at the unicorn shifter convention?"

"No one can prove that," I tell her, adding in a wink just to make her blood boil.

That's true. No one could prove it no matter how they tried. But let's just say I did come into a good amount of cash when there was a sudden and unexpected Lucky Charms shortage and I was the only supplier in Witchingdom with (purloined) boxes on hand.

She grumbles something I don't quite catch and turns away from me.

"Hold on, gotta turn out the lights outside." Eustis leans half out the door while still holding the screen. "Averte lumina."

In the next breath, all the fireflies lingering around the inn scatter in all different directions, disappearing into the woods. Before the screen door bangs shut behind Eustis, it's so dark I can barely spot Bessie's chrome gleaming in the moonlight coming through the canopy of trees.

"Come on," Eustis says as he heads down a hallway. "I got a room set aside for ya."

LeLe speeds up, trying and failing to match the old man's surprisingly swift pace. "I was hoping you had two rooms?"

He shakes his head. "Nope."

"Does it have two beds?" she asks, sounding way more hopeful than she should.

"Just the one." He stops in front of the last door on the left.

She closes her eyes and I swear I can hear her muttered prayer to the fates for patience.

Throwing her a bone, I say, "A comfortable chair?"

Eustis opens the door. "Not enough space."

He isn't lying. There's a gigantic heart-shaped bed in the middle of the room that leaves only enough space around it to walk on either side if a person turns sideways and shuffles.

"That's okay, I got this," LeLe says before waving her fingers. "Fac unum duo."

Even though the doubling spell is a basic one, it should work. And it does. The scent of warm cake donuts fills the room right as a jagged crack starts at the top of the crushed-velvet comforter and doesn't stop until it splits the heart right down the middle. Then an invisible force pushes the beds apart so there's enough space to walk between them.

LeLe lets out a satisfied sigh and brushes her palms together like a blackjack dealer after they've dealt all the cards. "All better."

Eustis snorts. "Give it a sec."

A vibration rushes through the room fast enough that LeLe's hair whooshes to the side. There's a loud boing and the beds smash back together and the tear dividing them into two zips closed.

LeLe lets out a little squeak of surprise and takes a step back.

Look, there's magic and then there's *magic*. This is the second kind. Whatever is going on, it isn't witch-related.

Both of us turn and look at Eustis. Not surprisingly, there isn't a hint of the smell of magic in the air, which is always left behind after a witch's spell. Instead, the room smells of old books, worn leather, and the sweet vanilla tobacco scent of the old man's pipe.

He shrugs his bony shoulders. "The house doesn't like anyone messing with its decor or room assignments."

And that explains it. The adrenaline pumping through my veins slows down, and LeLe lets out a surprised breath. The Strawbery Banke Inn is a sentient house.

They aren't common, but there are at least a hundred or so in Witchingdom. The good news is they're friendly. The bad news is they're stubborn, which means whenever a sentient house takes a curiosity about you, your life is about to get more interesting. And, as the whole bed thing just demonstrated, there isn't any point in working my magic while we're on the property, because just like in Vegas, the house always wins.

Something that LeLe isn't ready to accept, going by the determined tilt of her chin.

"Can I talk to the house?" she asks, as if the answer of *yes* is a foregone conclusion.

Eustis hooks his thumbs into the straps of his denim overalls and rocks back and forth on his heels. "It's asleep."

She scoffs. "But it still makes the bed go back together?"

Yeah, even for a sentient house that seems like a reach.

Eustis grins, totally unfazed by being caught in what has to be a bald-faced lie. "It's a funny house."

LeLe takes in a deep breath like she's gearing up to go to battle, one she won't win. As a Sherwood, she probably doesn't see it. Really, when has someone like her ever not gotten her way? The family and everyone in it are almost universally adored. Being a Svensen, however, means that I know firsthand what it's like to be looked down upon and to lose. I know when to fight dirty and when to back off and find another way to win. This is one of those times.

"We have a long day tomorrow. The bed is huge. I'll stay on my side. We can put pillows down the middle. I promise no funny business." I hold out my last finger to LeLe. "Pinkie promise."

She glares at me but curls her finger around mine. A shot of awareness blasts its way straight to my dick. Her eyes darken and her lips part. Every single nerve in my body is tuned in on her, *only* her. The air thickens around us and I swear it's like the rest of the world disappears. It's just LeLe, me, and that undeniable attraction that is so strong it's palpable. She must feel it too, because her eyes go wide a half a second before she pulls her hand away.

She narrows her eyes, but her cheeks are still flush with desire. "You don't even want to imagine the hex I'd put on you if you do anything to even remotely piss me off any more than you already have."

Eustis lets out a croak of a laugh, the sound dry and rusty, before turning his back on us and walking out of the room.

"Young love," he says as he ambles down the hall, gliding his fingers along the chair rail. "Yes, Amarilla, they sound just like we used to."

I'm way too fucking tired to think about that old man dating a sentient house, so I close the door. Really, some things a person doesn't need to know a damn thing about.

By the time I turn around, LeLe has a line of pillows going down the middle of the heart bed and is already under the covers with her eyes closed and her arms crossed over her chest like a vampire.

"Good night to you too, wife," I say as I reach behind my neck, pull my shirt over my head, and make my way to the bed.

Her eyes snap open.

"You know I'm not—" Whatever she is about to say next fizzles out when she looks at me.

Her gaze travels over me, slow and hungry. I know that

look. That's how we ended up naked in one of the curtained-off poolside bungalows while the rest of Vegas played in the sun.

When she looks at me like this, it's easy to believe I could be that man she saw then instead of who I really am even though I know there's not a chance of it actually being true.

My jaw hurts from clenching it tight as I get under the covers, sticking as close to the edge of my side of the bed as I can before turning out the light.

I lie there staring at the ceiling, knowing there's no way I'm going to sleep tonight, not with LeLe this close.

The mattress jiggles with movement half a second before LeLe says, "You said not all of your family are awful. Who did you mean?"

The tightness in my chest is back and a prickly sensation inches up my spine.

"My sister, Sigrid, just wants to stay tucked into the library reading books, while my brother, Cy, spends almost every day in his laboratory trying to brew up new spells. Neither of them asked to be a Svensen. They just got stuck with it. Still, they don't act like Svensens, and yeah, I know how we act. But Cy and Sigrid? They're better. They're different." Like a chump, my voice gets all thin and tight at the end, and it's all I can do to keep my shit together. What is it about this woman that fucks with me so hard? "They're both good despite all of our family's shit surrounding them."

"But not you?" she asks, her voice so quiet I almost don't hear.

"No, not me," I say, forcing myself to sound as if I don't give a shit—a skill I learned by my tenth birthday once Dad realized he could use what I cared about to get me to do what he wanted. "And you know that for yourself already, don't you?"

The reality of it is my birthright as the Svensen heir. It's who I have to be.

All the things Witchingdom attributes to me? It's mostly true. The thefts, the backroom dealing, the schemes petty and large—they can't pin them on me, but they know I'm responsible. Maybe some of them hold it against me, but the majority just see it as the universe evening itself out as nature tends to do. For every Sherwood family with pure intentions, there has to be a Svensen family that's always on the take.

Next to me, LeLe lets out a determined breath. I can't see her, but I know what face she's making. No doubt, she has that stubborn tilt to her jaw and her lips are pressed together in a straight line, and if she's annoyed, she's probably squinting with her right eye.

I'm holding my breath in anticipation of whatever withering put-down she's about to deliver when she moves her hand under the covers, finding an opening in the pillow wall, and her pinkie finger hooks around mine like a promise to believe I'm more than my last name. It only lasts for a few seconds, and I can't breathe or think. Then she lets go and turns over without a good-night.

It all happens so fast that I'm not even sure it happened at all.

What in the hell was that?

The back of my hand is tingling with awareness, my dick has woken up, and I am one hundred percent awake to the point that I'm not sure I'm ever going to need sleep again.

Was she trying to comfort me or torture me with that touch? Honestly, I'm not sure which option would be worse.

Chapter Thirteen

Leona . . .

The world is still mostly dark when I crack my eyes open a smidge the next morning. Hate to disappoint you and all your romantic notions, but the pillow wall is still up, I'm fully dressed, and I am not the little spoon with Erik's arms wrapped around me and holding me close while his hard cock is nestled up against my ass.

I'm not bitter about it though. Quite the opposite. I'm glad. Happy. Thrilled. Joyful. I am abso-fucking-lutely euphoric—so much so that my jaw is sore from clenching my teeth with glee.

Letting out the quietest of slow and steady calming breaths, I squint at the wall across from the bed. It takes my vision a minute to adjust. I can just pick out the hands on the clock shaped like a toadstool. Five thirty. It'll be dawn soon. Then I can stop pretending to be asleep.

I've been lying in bed for what feels like all night trying to coax, bully, and bribe my brain into shutting off. It would not do so. Instead, it kept giving me information I most definitely did not need and most assuredly did not want.

Oh, did you hear that? Erik mumbles in his sleep. That's cute.

No. It's not. It's annoying.

Take a deep inhale. Go on. You know you want to. See? He has a nice woodsy, warm scent mixed in with a hint of fresh-brewed coffee.

My nose is stuffed so I can't smell a thing.

Wonder if he is going to wake up too? A little full arm stretch placed just right and that pillow wall would go tumbling down.

I'm not moving a muscle. I'm going to lie here in absolute perfect stillness until it's late enough that I can get up without it being weird.

A tired sigh comes from the other side of the pillow wall, followed by a sleep-roughed, "Good morning, wife."

That sandpaper timbre in his voice makes my breath catch and my eyes snap all the way open. "How did you know I was awake?"

Erik mumbles a quick spell before he snaps his fingers and the lights turn on. "A husband knows."

I blink about a million times at the sudden brightness filling the room, and my heart's racing. There's something about how he sounds in the morning that just gets to me. Every time we woke up together in Vegas, he pulled me in close until he was spooning every inch of me and told me stories in this voice. Some of the stories were obviously made up (really, how much trouble could one goat familiar cause) and others brushed the edges of a jagged sadness, but they were all completely engrossing. I could have spent a good portion of my life listening to him tell me stories. Erik really does have a gift.

If only I'd realized in the beginning that he was using that gift to spin tales for evil; if only I'd realized he was a Svensen, then I wouldn't have been such an idiot and believed.

Ouch. That little reminder makes my heart pinch.

"I think you do that just to get under my skin," I grumble as I yank up the covers to my neck like a shield even though he can't see me.

"What?" he asks, his amusement clear. "Breathe?"

I fight it, but a goofy grin pulls up the corners of my mouth anyway. A guy who can make me laugh is always my downfall.

"Aha!" Erik lets out a maniacal laugh. "I knew you were a softie."

How did he know? My gaze bounces from the pillow wall (still intact) to the ceiling (no mirrors, thank you, house) and lands on the window, where I can see our reflection because it's still dark outside.

The man has no right to look that good at this time in the morning. His dark hair is longer than it was in Vegas and it's going every which way, including hanging in his eyes, giving him a sexy disheveled look and making him seem more imp than nemesis. He must have kicked off the velvet comforter during the night, because the only thing covering him is the sheet resting on his hips. I get an eyeful of broad shoulders, sinewy arms, and washboard abs. Fuck. I don't have to close my eyes to remember what it felt like to glide my fingers over that stomach or kiss my way across his chest. It's all right there, a nearly tangible, hot desire that leaves me keyed up and needy for the last man I should ever lust after. It's hard, and honestly, I don't want to, but I yank my gaze back up to Erik's face.

The bastard grins and winks at me.

Asshole.

You mean hot, sexy asshole.

Shut up, brain.

"If you don't mind," I say, glaring at his reflection. "I need to get up and go shower."

He doesn't hesitate. "I'd never stop you."

Then he just stares at me. I swear he doesn't even blink. I can practically feel his gaze traveling over me, stopping at all the places he'd spent so much time kissing in Vegas.

There is *a lot* of stopping.

The room is getting warmer (especially under the comforter), my skin is becoming more sensitive, and the act of putting thoughts together is harder because my body is screaming at me to knock down that stupid pillow wall I'd insisted on last night.

I try to take in a calming breath, but all that does is inflate my chest so my hard nipples rub against the sheets, a teasing reminder of what it is like when Erik delivers those feather-light touches that drive me to the edge. I bite down on my lip to keep myself from saying anything I'd regret later—like "fuck me right this second"—but all that little bit of pain does is make me want some pleasure even more.

It's almost more than I can take (celibacy has never been my brand), but someone must be looking out for me, because the sun rises just enough that the light glints off the Sherwood signet ring on my thumb. The reminder of what's expected of me and what my duty to my family is hits at exactly the right moment, and I'm relieved. Yeah, that's right. Relieved.

Gathering myself up, I stare at the spot on the window just above Erik's reflection. "Close your eyes."

Petty? Whiny? Ridiculous? Yes to all of the above, but I just can't seem to help myself around him. He drives me to it.

One of his eyebrows shoots up. "Really, wife?"

I don't have to look at him to know he's doing that signature smirk of his—the one I hate and love in the same breath.

"I need to get up and go take a shower," I say with as much dignity as I can muster considering I have a blanket pulled up to my neck like a Victorian-era virgin. "We have a long day ahead."

Bracing myself for battle (yes, even a small one like this), my mind is already spinning coming up with what I'll say next when his smile softens around the edges. Then he grabs his pillow from behind his head and places it over his face and throws both arms crisscross over top of it.

"So you know I'm not peeking," he says, his voice muffled by the heavy down feathers.

It's over-the-top, way too dramatic, and—I hate to admit it—kinda sweet. I bite back my groan of disgust. What is wrong with me when it comes to this man?

I know he's only doing this to make me forget about the divorce, and yet it still makes me smile. Thank the fates he can't see it.

Doing my best to ignore all that, I quickstep it around the bed and into the tiny en suite bathroom.

There's enough room in here to turn around, but not much else. I twist on the water in the shower and crank it to blistering—or at least that's the way Erik described the temperature I like my water when we showered together in Vegas. It was supposed to be a sexy shower, the kind you see in the movies. Instead it was a negotiation in water temperature, with him swearing his skin was melting at my preferred heat level and me turning blue when he adjusted the water to frigid. By the time we found an acceptable medium, we were both laughing so hard that we almost slipped and fell on our asses multiple times. One giggle led to another, which led to me clinging to him for support and then him pulling me close and then we were kissing and the next thing I knew he had scooped me up and carried me soaking wet to the hotel bed.

The inn's bathroom is full of steam when I strip off my clothes and step into the shower. Like the rest of the bathroom, it's tiny, but the water pressure is hard enough to massage the knots out of my shoulders. Normally I don't carry my tension in my shoulders, but then again, normally I don't have to spend every waking—and sleeping—moment with the guy who duped me into marrying him.

The shower is good, but as I flip open the mini bottle of pomegranate-scented bodywash, I can't get the Vegas memories out of my thoughts. Even worse, I'm not sure I want to. I tip my head back so the water can soak my hair and glide the soap over my body, lingering on my breasts the way Erik always would. Cupping them gently at first, a mere tease of what was coming. Then he'd push them together before he'd suck one hard nipple into his warm mouth. His teeth would graze the sensitive peak, teasing and tempting me until I was ready to beg for more. All the annoyingly self-satisfied man would do, though, would be to move to the other nipple and start the whole process over again. By the time he was done with that one, I wasn't a woman so much as I was the personification of jelly-kneed lust.

The warm water beats against my shoulders as I rub the bodywash over my skin, slowing and taking my time covering my breasts, cupping them, brushing my nipples to taut peaks, and then pinching them. Closing my eyes, I give in to the fantasy that it's Erik doing this. It's Erik kissing his way down my stomach to the apex of my thighs. As I slip my fingers between my legs, it's his face I'm picturing looking up at me from a kneeling position, that damn smirk of his on full display. His shoulders are slick with the water from the shower and I have to brace my hands against the tile walls as he leans forward, burying his face in my pussy. My fingers circle my clit faster and faster as I imagine the feel of his tongue against me, the addition of his fingers pumping into me as he sucks and kisses and licks me right to the edge of the known world. I'm lost in this fantasy and I don't care. All I want is to embrace the pleasure, let it build, and ride that sweetly demanding tension until I break apart. I'm close, so fucking close. I can barely breathe. My whole body feels like it's pulled into itself to the point where I can't take it anymore. That's when I hear Erik as clearly as if he were standing next to me, whispering in my ear, urging me on in words that I can't formulate. The fantasy is blurring as the tension inside me builds and I slap a palm against the shower wall to keep my balance before my orgasm explodes through me, a rush of pleasure that leaves me gasping.

I stand there for a minute under the shower spray to just enjoy that melty, easy, satisfied feeling that makes my limbs heavy in that good way. The usually invisible handfast mark encircling my wrist is glowing and warm. It doesn't burn, exactly, but there's a tingling sensation that's more than a buzz and less than the pain of trying to walk when your foot falls asleep. I trace my fingertips over the line that's already beginning to fade as I catch my breath. My thighs are a little shaky and my pulse erratic, but I get back to what I was supposed to be doing in the first place and grab the tiny bottle of inn-provided shampoo.

Chapter Fourteen

Erik . . .

I'd spent most of the night with a hard dick trying not to imagine what LeLe looked like on the other side of that ridiculous pillow wall. Sure, one easy iustus velox vultus spell could have given me a peek, but I'm an asshole, not a creep.

So instead I contemplated a cerebri torpet spell just so I'd numb my brain enough to stop remembering how she looked when she slept, when she came, when she danced around the room in only my white button-down shirt singing the wrong song lyrics that she'd argued with complete conviction were the right ones.

No, she hadn't been on key.

No, she hadn't been even *close* to getting the words right.

No, I had not spent the last year singing the song with *her* lyrics whenever it came on. I might have thought them though. Don't fucking judge. Sometimes things are so wrong they're right.

That's not the point though. What is? That last night was the longest fucking seven hours of pretending to sleep of my life and this morning is beginning to feel even longer. Why? Oh, I'll tell you exactly why—because some asshole invented the shower.

You see, I'd thought I'd made it through the worst of it when LeLe disappeared into the bathroom. But then she'd turned on the water and all I could picture was her standing naked under the spray as the air from her four-million-degree shower grew thick with steam. I didn't have to cast a spell to see the droplets cascading down her body, traveling over her shoulders, gliding over her full tits, and dripping off of her hard nipples. My imagination and memory, the shitbirds that they are, teamed up to make that happen.

Her red hair is probably piled on top of her head, thick with shampoo bubbles that smell like sugar cookies fresh out of the oven. She's got that closed-eye dreamy look she gets whenever she is surrounded by heat. I swear the woman has to have Hyperion in her ancestral line somewhere. Only someone related to the Titan god and personification of the sun could stand the boiling-hot showers she takes. It's like she finally unwinds and lets herself go whenever she's surrounded by steam and heat— man, does she let herself go. Her hotel room in Vegas had a massive walk-in shower with heads on each wall and a rain shower up above and two well-placed teak benches. We'd had some good times in that shower, some really fucking good times—my favorite being when I was eating her out and she came hard enough to almost crack my skull between her thick thighs. Yeah, that had been worth the not-quite burn on my back from the water she'd set to lava temperature.

And that's why, for the past ten minutes, I've been all but trying to suffocate myself with this damn feather pillow, getting scratched on the cheek by what was left of some golden goose in the process. At this point, I'm not even sure death would change the state of my cock. It's just tenting up the sheets like a giant fuck-you to my dumb ass for thinking I could be this close to LeLe and not want to keep her naked and orgasmic for the rest of eternity—or at least until she discovers what I'm really up to and turns me into a slimy, log-sitting vodyanoy complete with algae hair and a smoking pipe.

That image alone should have killed my hard-on. That it didn't makes me reconsider that brain-numbing spell.

Chapter Fifteen

Leona . . .

*F*ifteen minutes and a clean head of hair and shaved legs later, I get out of the shower, my mood post-orgasm improved. Erik is singing in the bedroom, his smooth bass coming through the thin bathroom door. K-pop? Erik? That is not what I was expecting, but weirdly enough, there is a lot of the unexpected from him. The old-fashioned car when he could have a Ferrari. The way he talked with Eustis as an equal as opposed to a care-taker who was beneath the Svensen family. The way he'd made me giggle despite everything.

Since he can't see me, I mouth along to the words of the latest catchy dance tune as I dry off with one of the small but superabsorbent fluffy towels stacked on a shelf above the toilet. It isn't until I'm squeezing out the last of the heavy wet from my hair that I look around the bathroom and my stomach drops. That's when I realize I failed to bring new, clean clothes into the bathroom. Sure, there are the clothes I wore in, but there's no way in this lifetime that I'm putting on dirty panties after taking a shower.

Fuck. Fuck. Fuckity fuck.

Taking a deep breath, I weigh my options.

I could magic an outfit. Easy. Efficient. Explicitly logical.

I could go out with just the little towel almost wrapped around me. Daring. Unexpected. Very breezy (because there's no way the small swatch of material could encircle all of me).

I could ask Erik for help. Uncomfortable. Not like me at all. A little bit thrilling.

There's only one reasonable choice. I gather my magic, picture my favorite outfit, and—

CRASH!

A loud clatter scares the ever-loving shit out of me, and I let out an involuntary squawk of surprise as I whirl around. The heavy wooden shelves that had been holding the folded towels are now on the floor. I'm a good two feet away from them and nothing knocked into them, so what in the world made them fall?

"LeLe," Erik hollers as he starts to open the bathroom door. It gets a quarter of the way before he jerks to a stop and yanks it almost closed again. "Sorry. I should have knocked or hollered or—" He lets out an annoyed breath. "Are you okay?"

His voice is muffled through the door, but there's no missing the concern—or his stage-and-screen-worthy imitation of it.

"I'm fine," I say, pressing my hand to my chest above my fast-beating heart. "The shelves just came down."

"Did they hit you?" he asks, his voice pinched.

I will not get a warm, gooey feeling in the pit of my stomach because he sounds like he cares. I will not.

Too late.

"I think I'd know if I'd been whacked in the head," I say. "It missed me completely."

I glare at the wall where the shelves had been as realization hits me. Sentient houses love to play tricks on their guests. First the bed, and now the shelves when I am all but buck naked? I flip off the wall. The house really has an agenda.

"You could have a concussion and be confused." Erik pauses for a beat. "Do you need me to come in and check you over?"

I clutch the sorry excuse for a towel tighter against my chest, closing it as much as I can, but I'm fighting back a smile. "You are not coming in."

"Why? Are you still naked?"

Oh, fuck it. He can't see me anyway. I let the smile out. "That's what you're thinking about at a time like this?"

Why are you even asking that? Tell him to fuck off and then shut up. He's the husband you're divorcing, not the one you actually like. Don't let that I'm-not-a-good-guy spiel from last night get to you. Do not be suckered like you were in Vegas.

I wish I could say I'm going to take my own good advice. We both know I'm not—or at least I don't want to.

"You said you were fine."

I barely stop my chuckle. "You're incorrigible."

"Does that mean devastatingly handsome, irresistible, and so fucking amazing in bed you haven't been able to stop thinking about me for the past year?"

"You're deranged." Now I'm just grinning like a fool, and my hold on the towel is getting looser by the second.

"Ooof. I'm heartbroken," he says, making it sound like I'd landed a physical direct hit before turning back to being serious again. "You sure you're okay?"

No. Not at all. But not for the reasons he's thinking.

"I'm fine."

And horny all over again. And a little giddy. And doing that big-eyed mooning thing with my face while staring at an almost closed door. What in the world is wrong with me?

"Okay, good. I'm going to go find Eustis and find out how far we are from a gas station."

I hold my breath and listen to the sound of his footsteps fading as he walks to the door and then the firm click of the room door being shut. I wait a couple of beats and then crack open the bathroom door and peek out. The room is empty.

I hustle over to my side of the bed, where the suitcase labeled "Mrs." is sitting and pop it open. Inside, there are a handful of sweaters, my favorite pair of jeans, and the best selection from my special lingerie drawer—you know, the one that only has your for-sexy-times bras and panties (most of which are more about the idea of underwear than actual underwear).

This is what happens when a guy magics your clothes for a road trip. There's not a single pair of comfy granny panties.

Of course, the lingerie is better than wearing one of the miniature towels in the bathroom—especially when I am about to spend the rest of the day riding shotgun next to the man I never should have married.

And not flirting. I'm definitely going to spend the day not flirting. I won't even imagine Erik naked.

Not once.

Not a single time.

The only problem? I already am. Again.

I flop down on the bed, landing on my back with enough force that the suitcase clatters to the floor.

I am so screwed.

Chapter Sixteen

Erik . . .

We've been on the road for three hours, and LeLe is looking at me like I've grown a second head. (For the record, that only happened once, and it was because I agreed to let Cy try out one of his new spells on me. Trust me, that will never ever fucking happen again.)

"This is a classic," I say, taking a break from singing Johnny Cash's promise to walk the line. "How do you not know this song?"

LeLe finishes adjusting the elastic band she's using to keep her hair back as we fly down the highway with the top down. "Because I wasn't born a million years ago."

"Good thing we've got a few days to educate you, wife."

LeLe opens her mouth as if she's going to tell me for the

billionth time not to call her that, but there must be something in the air as we drive through flyover country, because instead of saying anything, she just shakes her head and relaxes back into her seat. And because I'm a smart man who knows when to accept small victories, I don't push it but instead start singing along with Johnny again.

The sun is out, the weather is unseasonably warm for the early fall, and the traffic on the back road we're traveling is sparse. The last car we passed was a tractor with a bright green hay baler attached to the back. There have been a plethora of red barns, field after field of corn bracketing the two-lane highway, and a limited number of stoplights in the towns we've driven through. That means there's no one but LeLe looking at me strangely as I belt out the lyrics to a song that was released the same year Bessie came off the assembly line in Detroit.

Normally I wouldn't be singing along to the radio when anyone besides my sister or brother is in the car. I learned early on in life not to show that I enjoyed anything, because that would always be the first thing Dad would take away when he decided I needed to learn a hard lesson.

But singing (badly) in front of LeLe makes her smile even if she still isn't talking to me. Finding that crack in her icy facade is pretty much worth any kind of personal embarrassment.

We make it through Patsy Cline's greatest hits and are just starting on the brilliance of Dolly Parton when we pull into another one-stoplight town. This one, however, has a mom-and-pop ice cream shop that promises the best soft-serve cones in three counties right next to a gas station.

"Are you a vanilla or a chocolate?" I ask as I pull into the small parking lot and find a spot.

She looks over at me and grins. "Swirl."

Of course. LeLe is rarely what I expect.

She hops out of the car as soon as I cut the engine. I'm about to open my door when my phone vibrates. My dad's face fills the screen and my good mood evaporates in a flash. It rings a few times and then stops—not that the old man has given up. He'll keep calling until I pick up.

"I gotta take this," I say, letting my hand fall from the door latch. "You go ahead and get a cone."

She cocks her head in question. "You want one?"

Not anymore. "I'm good."

"Your loss," she says before setting off across the lot, her hips swaying.

The phone stops buzzing while I watch LeLe go, unable to look away. I should have been more specific about the packing spell. I'd requested her favorite jeans; I hadn't realized they'd be my favorite too, considering how they fit her phenomenal ass like a glove. Looking away isn't an option, not even with knowing who had called and would definitely be calling back.

She joins the short line in front of the ice cream shop window and immediately starts chatting with the mom holding a baby on her hip in front of her. It takes all of about five seconds before they're chatting like old friends and LeLe is making funny faces at the kid.

She looks so relaxed and happy. I try to remember the last time I felt like that, and the only thing I can come up with is last year in Vegas with her when I was pretending to be someone else.

Well aren't you a sad sack, you fucking chump.

I'm tempted to say fuck it and join her in line, but my phone starts up again. Putting off Dad will only delay the inevitable and give him time to work himself up into a narcissistic rage at being kept waiting.

I tap the answer icon.

"You got her in the car or what?" my dad asks without pre-amble.

"Got who?" I ask as I watch LeLe playing hide-and-seek behind her hands with the baby.

"Don't play dumb with me, son. You give chase to those thieving Sherwoods who stole The Liber Umbrarum from us, magic that idiotic car of yours in from where in the fates knows, and then you message your sister that you're gonna be gone a few days. Even your sorry excuse for a brother could have figured out what was going on. You better be making that move on the Sherwood heir that you should have made in Vegas."

When he'd found out I was late to that meeting with the Kiehls, I had to make up a story quick so he wouldn't devote any time to thinking about what I could be up to. So I stuck to part of my truth—I was in Vegas on LeLe's trail to try to get her to marry me for access to her family's money—and his truth—I am a failure who fucks up everything. As far as my dear old Dad knows, I rolled snake eyes with LeLe. I can't let him know about the handfast until everything else is in place for my plan to work. I need him a little more desperate, a little more on edge, a little more willing to do whatever it takes to save his own skin, his family be damned.

Not to mention that if Dad knew the truth that LeLe and I were married, he would have been at the Sherwoods' house faster than the twitch of his nose to make his demands. He probably would have siphoned off half of their money by now. Not that I give a shit, but this isn't about him, it's about me getting my revenge.

"I'm working on something," I tell him, keeping my voice steady so as not to betray just how much I hate him.

If I don't, he'll lash out at Cy and Sigrid, making them pay the price for my slipup. He's done it before, and I'll do just about anything to make sure it can't happen again.

"Good. The clock is ticking. We've got a payment due to the bank at the end of the week. I don't have time for you to fuck this up again." He pauses, and I can picture him in his study. He's probably sitting behind the huge mahogany desk that has been in the family for generations. It sits on a platform that's a few inches higher than the rest of the floor so that he's always looking down at whoever is sitting across from him. "So I repeat, is she with you?"

There isn't any purpose in lying on this point. The man has spies everywhere. He probably already knows the answer. "Yes."

"Then use that supposed charm of yours and woo the homely chit," he snaps. "Once our houses merge, our debt becomes Sherwood debt, and they'll have to quietly pay it all or face societal censure themselves—something they really can't afford with the Council gunning for control."

In Witchingdom, image is everything. You are powerful because you look powerful. Once that is no longer the case, though, that's when your enemies come for you—and our family has nothing but enemies. It's happened before. The Peks had it all one day and lost everything the next when it turned out their family accountant was embezzling before disappearing without a trace. When the checks started bouncing, the invitations stopped coming, the opportunities dried up, and avoidance spells became the rule, not the exception. For the Peks, it was all over in a matter of weeks. Witchingdom is like that; the only ones the witches look out for is themselves. At least we Svensens are up-front about it, unlike the rest of the families.

"And we won't stop with them paying off our debts. Fuck no," he says with a cruel laugh. "We'll bleed those sanctimonious Sherwoods dry."

"What's your endgame here? Why not just use The Liber Umbrarum to get what you want?"

"Because I'm not a complete idiot," he says, his tone making it clear that he thinks I am. "Right now the Council thinks the Sherwoods have the book, and they're wasting all of their time trying to figure out how to get it back from them without causing a war out in the open. The last thing I want is to turn the Council's attention to us. I haven't been playing both sides of the divide for the past ten years to have it blow up in my face because I was shortsighted enough to use the most powerful spell book in Witchingdom to pay off a few debts."

I glance over at Bessie's glove box with its magical wards

carved into the shiny walnut surface protecting the book inside. "Then what are you going to do with it?"

"Nothing that you need to concern yourself with. What you should be worried about is what will happen to Cy and Sigrid if you don't do your job and marry the Sherwood heir."

Heat rushes through me, making it feel like I'm boiling from the inside out. "I'm well aware of what's on the line."

"Are you sure? You're not going soft, are you? We don't have time for you to turn into your mother."

Everything fades into the background. The ice cream shop, the parking lot, and the baby LeLe has been charming, they're all gone. I swear I can hear my heart beating in my chest, feel the electric pulses of my brain synapses firing, and hear the sound of my own hatred simmering in my gut. "I told you not to talk about her ever again."

"Don't like to be reminded how you fucked that up, huh?" he sneers.

I know what he's doing. He's been goading me like this my entire life, poking at any perceived emotional weakness and exploiting it. The bastard knows exactly where to land the sucker punch.

It takes almost all my control, but I manage not to give him the reaction he's looking for. Instead, I keep my voice ice-cold as I tell him, "Consider your message delivered."

"I sure hope so, otherwise Cy and Sigrid will pay the price for your failure just like your mother did."

Dad hangs up and I just sit there white-knuckling my phone and staring out at nothing. That's a lie. It's not nothing. I'm seeing my mother's face the night the Council came and took her away in the dead of night. I know it's not happening right now, but as the memory plays in my mind, everything tightens and I can barely breathe. Her eyes are red-rimmed and she's begging my dad to help her. He just stands to the side, his face stony. Then she's gone.

I'm not sure how long I stay like that, trying to get my pulse to settle and my jaw to unlock while I'm banishing the echo of the worst day of my life. It's not until I hear LeLe's cheerful "It was great to meet you" that I manage to pull my shit back together.

She strolls over to the passenger side of the car and pauses, her hand resting on the door handle.

"Did you change your mind?" She holds up her half-eaten swirl cone, the bottom of which is wrapped in about a million bright purple napkins. "I can go back and get you one."

Something inside me shifts as I look at her. She's got a huge grin on her face, the tip of her freckled nose is starting to burn, and there are enough golden highlights in her red hair that the sun going through it looks like she's standing in the middle of a spotlight. All of a sudden it's a little easier to breathe, and some of the tension ebbs out of my shoulders. Finally, I unwind my fingers from their death grip around my phone and shove it into the center console.

"Hard to drive and eat a cone." I put my sunglasses back on before looking over at her. "Unless you're going to hold it for me?"

She scoffs. "Not a chance."

"You've done it before."

It had been our second morning waking up together in Vegas. We were having breakfast in bed, both of us naked, and I kept getting distracted by the sounds of absolute unrestrained pleasure she made when she ate a strawberry dipped in whipped cream. She noticed and said she wanted to share her breakfast, so she dipped a strawberry in the whipped cream and then used it to draw a line of cream around her hard nipple and told me to have some. She hadn't had to ask twice.

"I'm not the person I was in Vegas," she says, her harsh tone yanking me back to the present. "Neither are you."

She's right, of course. The guy she'd thought he'd been was a fucking paragon. He was a stand-up guy. He didn't lie and cheat. He didn't do whatever was necessary to do what needed to be done. He got to fall for the girl and have her fall for him. He got to be happy.

I'm not that guy and I never will be.

I've really fucked things up. Usually, I'm better at minimizing my dad's plots, but he pulled out the big guns this time by putting Cy and Sigrid into the line of fire already. I'd figured that would be his last-ditch effort once he realized my plan to force him to give up the family power, but he did it early, which only means he's got more bad shit looming over his—and therefore my—head than I even know about.

I pull out onto the highway and after a few miles sneak a glance over at LeLe. She's given up on fixing her ponytail, and strands of hair are flying in the breeze as we head down the highway. We have another day—maybe two—of hard driving ahead of us before we get to the secured facility and LeLe realizes this has all been an elaborate con, so I might as well enjoy the view.

Yeah, like I said. I'm an asshole.

Chapter Seventeen

Leona . . .

*F*or the past two hundred miles, I've been getting smacked in the face by the strands of hair that escape my ponytail and are twisting around in the wind as we drive down the highway. It should have me in a foul mood—but it doesn't.

I could tell you that's because of the late-in-the-season blast of warmth making it possible to drive with the top down.

I could tell you it's because the ice cream was that damn good—when the chocolate-vanilla swirl hits just right, it does change your perspective on things.

I could tell you it's because being with Erik, I'm that much closer to getting exactly what I want—a divorce.

I could tell you all that, and I'd be lying my ass off and we both know it.

The truth of it is that what has me fighting off the giggles is the man in the driver's seat chair dancing like he is getting paid for it.

There are dramatic facial expressions as if he's the main character in a video.

There are exuberant arm motions, made possible by the fact that he magicked Bessie to drive herself.

There is the absolute no-fucks-to-give joy of singing all the lyrics to a song released before either of our parents were born.

I shouldn't be trying to hold back giggles as I watch him out of the corner of my eye, as if he wouldn't realize I was paying attention—he does, but we're both pretending that I'm not looking and he's not noticing.

This is the Erik I met in Vegas. The one with the goofy-ass sense of humor and a book addiction. The guy who kissed me like he'd been waiting his whole life to do it. The man who made me believe that I wasn't locked in to a life I had been born into but had never chosen.

And like it was in Vegas, the show he's putting on is probably just an act so he can pull another con. He can try all he wants, but I'm not going to fall for it this time, and that's all there is to that, so what's the big deal if I sit back and enjoy my soon-to-be ex-husband's antics while riding in a classic car with the top down and the wind blowing through my hair?

Nothing.

And that's the story I'm sticking with, so don't even give me that raised-eyebrow look of *oh yeah, sure.* I have this. Trust me.

Erik jams on the brakes, making Bessie's tires squeal, and pulls to a stop in front of a closed iron gate on the side of the road.

Hair ruffled from driving with the top down, he turns to me, an excited grin on his face. "Do you know where we are?"

I look around at the old-growth walnut trees behind the iron fence that seems to go on forever in either direction on one side of the highway and the great expanse of cornfields on the other side. "The middle of nowhere?"

He puts Bessie into reverse and stretches his arm across the back of the seat as he looks behind us at the deserted highway and then hits the gas. "We're at The Overlook."

My pulse quickens as I take a closer look at the gold sigil of the hippocamp (a half horse, half fish hybrid) on the gate and pretend I do not notice the brush of his fingertips on my shoulder. Yeah, the mind is willing, but the flesh is weak. Even this barely-there touch has electric currents of awareness sizzling through me. I swear, at that moment I am so tuned in to Erik that I can feel every ridge of his fingerprints as my lungs tighten because I'm too turned on to remember to breathe. From his fingertips on my shoulder! What the hell is wrong with me? This man is my kryptonite. I just need to focus on getting through this road trip and then divorcing his fine ass. Of course, the first thing I need to do is lean forward and break contact.

And I will.

In the next second.

Or maybe the following one.

Definitely the one after that.

Yes, you're guessing what happens next correctly.

My pathetic self stays right where I am, and it takes everything I have not to let out a shaky breath when Erik strokes his thumb against my skin in a smooth motion that leaves me breathless. The sizzle of attraction, the anticipation that has my pulse skyrocketing, and the heady lust whipping through me is exactly what I don't want to be happening. Mostly. Kinda. Oh my God, just let me get through this road trip without orgasming all over Erik's fabulous fucking dick, because my duty to my family outweighs any want I may have. My nipples don't get the don't-react message, though, and they tighten into hard buds desperate for his touch.

"You know what I love in life? A win-win. And this is exactly one of those. We get a break from the road to stretch and the Council goons trailing us would never think to look for us here." Erik turns to me and winks, either completely oblivious to the chaos he's stirred up in me or way too aware of it. "Ready for an adventure?"

My body screams yes. My mouth—thankfully—stays shut.

He keeps his arm slung across the back seat, his fingers resting against my suddenly overheated skin, and puts the car in drive, pulling right up to the closed iron gate.

He can't be serious. This is not the kind of adventure I signed up for. I am only here to return the spell book, divorce the man currently giving me way too many hurry-up-and-get-naked ideas, and then go home to live my predetermined future. Seeing a hippocamp doesn't fall into that. They're completely mercurial wild creatures who are as likely to bite a chunk out of a swimmer as they are to let anyone climb on their back for a once-in-a-lifetime ride, which is why every witch is warned early on in life not to mess with a hippocamp.

Barter with a troll? Fine.

Make a bet with a fairy? At your own risk.

Get spotted by a hippocamp? Not even on your best day.

My gaze lands on the stark black-and-white warning sign next to the gate, and I latch on to it like a life vest after a water crash landing. "It says no trespassing."

"Come on, live a little," he says with a wink.

Then he whispers, "Aperta sesamae," and the scent of freshly brewed coffee skates along the breeze. The iron gate swings open under the power of magic.

He looks over at me as he draws tiny little circles along my bare shoulder. "It'll be worth it," he says, pulling his hand away and shifting the car into drive. "I promise."

I wish I didn't care about lying to you, because that would make it easy to say I didn't still feel the delicious tingle of his touch on my shoulder. Really, if I could lie with a wink and a grin like some witches in this car, that is exactly what I'd be doing right now. But I'm not, and so I won't. Fuck. I swear my life wasn't complicated at all until that girls' weekend in Vegas.

I push all that out of my brain (because Vegas equals Erik equals bad decisions and naked blissed-out post-orgasmic bliss) and take in the scenery as Bessie's tires kick up a cloud of dust behind us while we drive through the orchard. The walnut trees go back as far as I can see on either side of the road. The branches of the stately trees are bare, which makes it easier to spot it when the knot in the trunk opens, revealing the eye inside it. Staring at the unblinking bright green eye, a shiver that's more of a premonition of danger than the anticipation of dread makes its way up my spine. In the next heartbeat, my palms are clammy and my gaze is ping-ponging from one tree to another in the seemingly never-ending orchard. That's the thing with the trees in Witchingdom—they're always watching and listening and ready to report back to whoever they're willing to recognize as the head witch in charge.

Unnerving? Oh yeah, most definitely.

"Erik," I say, my voice wavering just the slightest bit. "I think we should go back."

"If they wanted to keep people out, they would have put a protection spell on the gate."

"And because they didn't, you think the no trespassing sign is just something to ignore."

"When you have the chance to see that"—he jerks his chin upward, toward the spot ahead of us where the dirt road seems to disappear into thin air—"most definitely."

I turn back to face front right in time to see the view

change from looking like we are about to drive off the face of the earth to the vast expanse of Lake Avernus. The lake is a dark blue color that promises deep waters, and it surrounds a large island plopped down in the middle of it. There's a trio of walnut trees on the island that have to stand three hundred feet in the air. They form a kind of triangle around a stone fountain with water shooting from the tipped pitcher of a human running away from a large silver hippocamp. And as if that wasn't frighteningly beautiful enough, on the west side of the island is a pair of hippocamps galloping through the water.

The sight makes me forget about the trees' glares, the warning for trespassers, and the danger that comes with catching a hippocamp's attention. All I can do is stare in awe as they change colors depending on how the light from the setting sun hits them, going from blue to purple to pink to silver as they chase each other. Erik pulls the car to a stop near the edge of the lake and we both sit there, silently watching as the one creature in Witchingdom that everyone is warned about from birth frolics in the water.

It's not until they dip down under the water that the spell breaks enough for me to realize we've been parked for only the fates know how long enjoying the show. Erik has a look on his face that's about as far from his usual smirky, I've-got-everything-a-witch-could-want expression as possible. There's a sadness in his eyes and his jaw is clenched tight enough that he's going to have to make an appointment with the dentist if he doesn't ease up. If I didn't know any better, I'd think he wasn't one hundred percent pure jerk.

But I do.

And he is.

Yet I'm half a second away from giving him a damn pep talk like the chump I am whenever I'm around him.

Scrambling to figure out something to say before I ask him about his feelings or something just as idiotic, I blurt out the first thing that comes to mind. "Have you been here before?"

He nods. "My mom brought me here once."

That stops me cold, because that's when I realize that hardly anyone ever talks about the Svensen matriarch—and I can't even begin to imagine what that's like. In my family, Izzy Sherwood is the queen bee. She and my dad share power and lead our family together, but when people talk about the Sherwoods, it's usually about my intimidating, maddening, and absolutely wonderful mom. But for the Svensens? The talk is always centered around Erik's dad. If anyone talks about his mom at all, they do so in hushed tones. Before I can ask about his mom, though, Erik snaps back to his normally annoying self. It's quite the trick. His posture relaxes, his eyelids lower just enough to give him a look of arrogant insolence, and that mocking little smile of his is back in place.

He gives me a wink as the smell of fresh-brewed coffee floats around us, and chants, "Cibum quoque, et potum," three times.

A red-and-white-checked tablecloth floats in on the breeze coming off the lake, landing on a grassy spot. A giant woven basket drops down out of thin air, followed by a bottle of wine, two goblets, and even a dozen ants that start marching across the blanket as if they have no clue why they're here or where they're going, but they are going to do it together.

Erik gets out of the car and strides around Bessie's hood, coming to a stop at my door, which he opens with a practiced flourish and an exaggerated bow. "Picnic time."

Sure, I could stay in the car and glare at him from my seat, but I can already smell the eye of newt muffins, and ice cream is only going to hold a woman over for so long.

My stomach growls.

Erik lifts an eyebrow.

The hippocamps neigh in the distance.

Fuuuuuuuuuck.

I already know what's going to happen next, but my brain is rationalizing anyway. After all, how often does a witch get a chance to see the horse-fish hybrids and not end up with a chunk bit out of them? Not very often. My aunt Calliope is missing part of her right butt cheek and she still says it was worth it any time she starts telling tales while sipping her third werewolf-blood Negroni. (Don't worry, it's made with Campari—at least it is *now*. You do not want to dive into the family recipes from a few centuries back. Trust me.)

I glare up at my soon-to-be ex. "I still don't like you."

"Fine," he says with a shrug. "You can keep on hating me on a full stomach."

Solid argument.

I unlatch my seat belt and get out of Bessie. Erik closes the passenger door gently behind me and lays his hand on the small of my back as we start toward the picnic blanket, setting off enough sparks of awareness that it could be an entire fireworks show. Heat from his touch radiates through me, making my breath catch because I know what he can do with that hand and those fingers. He teases and tempts and drives you right to the brink of losing your ever-loving mind. It's awful and amazing all at the same time, and it's not for me. Never again.

I quicken my steps, pulling away from him before I forget that I'm already breaking too many rules.

"And you always follow the rules?" Erik asks from half a step behind me.

Shit fuck. That was not supposed to be out loud.

"Some of us have to." Oh yeah, that snotty tone covered up my idiocy. Definitely. For sure. Fuck me. Why does being around my soon-to-be ex mess with my head so much?

"But don't you ever want to fudge them a little?" he asks, catching up with me.

He doesn't put his hand on my back, but it doesn't matter. I'm so tuned in to him that I can practically hear his heartbeat. Yeah, we've got a few vampires in the family tree, but that doesn't mean I normally pick up on another witch's blood pressure. Anyway—I suck in a deep breath and force the thoughts running around in my head like squirrels after falling in a vat of meth to stop. I am better than this. I am in control. I am the iciest witch to have ever iced (recently literally after Tilda glitched Effie's spell, but you already know that story). No one gets to get me this discombobulated—not even the guy who gave me my first (and, sadly, only) five-orgasm night.

"You've never tried to waltz through a loophole?" Erik asks, oblivious to my inner monologue of desperate denial. "Find the out that lets you get what you want?"

"Spoken like a true Svensen," I say as I sit down on the picnic blanket on the opposite side of Erik.

He doesn't sit down. Instead, he curls his lips in a slow smile and crosses his arms. (No, I did not notice the way that made his biceps bulge under the waffle weave of his Henley. Fine. I'm lying. I did notice, and it made my mouth go dry.)

"Look, my family has problems, that's for sure," he says as he joins me on the blanket and looks out to where the hippocamps are splashing in the water. "But being sticklers for Witchingdom's rules about how a witch needs to act—or be seen to act—isn't one of them."

"*Not always?*" I scoff. "Have you *ever* done what polite society expects of you a day in your life?"

"I'm sure once or twice." He rolls over onto his side and props his head on his hand. His gaze settles on my mouth, and his grin fades as his eyes darken.

Something shifts in the air, the kind of crackle you feel sparking against your skin and seems so loud even though you don't hear it. The hair on my arms is standing straight up as if

I've been blasted with a frigid gust even though I'm way too hot for it to make sense, considering it's fall.

"Aren't you ever tempted to break the rules?" he asks, his voice rough and growly. "Do you ever want to do what you want just one time?"

Chapter Eighteen

Leona . . .

T reach into the picnic basket, grab the first food item I touch, and shove it in my mouth to stop myself from saying a single solitary thing, let alone yell out yes. And I might have gotten away with it if what I'm eating weren't a fistful of extra-spicy wasabi peas that were in a cute little bowl that appeared out of thin air. My eyes are watering and my tongue is on fire, but I silently crunch my way through. I am a Sherwood. I am not about to admit that I'm pervious to pain.

(Yeah, I know that sounds like a fake word, but Bea used it to beat me in a loser-takes-rooster-pickup-duties-for-a-month-without-using-magic Scrabble game with stakes that I agreed to once and will never agree to again. That's not the kind of thing a witch is ever going to forget. Barkley is nasty and has been obsessed with me ever since.)

For his part, Erik doesn't say a thing. He just watches with that whole I-know-why-you-did-that smirk on his face as he plucks a bottle of water out of the basket, unscrews the cap, and holds it out to me. A better Sherwood would ignore the offer and suffer in superiority and silence. I, however, have just swallowed a mouthful of atomic-level wasabi peas and could probably breathe out lava at this moment, so I take the bottle and drain it.

While I'm doing that, Erik says, "Mensamque," and the plates float out of the open picnic basket, followed by blue napkins decorated with ants doing the conga while carrying a whole watermelon, and silverware that gracefully lands on the blanket in the perfect place setting in front of each of us. That's when the food comes—fried chicken and potato salad, watermelon slices and deviled eggs, brownies, and eye of newt muffins that still have steam coming off of them, which land in perfectly portioned amounts on our plates. Then the wine bottle levitates before tipping forward to pour a generous amount of chilled rosé into our wineglasses. And as a final flourish, there's a click from the depths of the picnic basket and the scratch of static for a few seconds before some mellow yacht rock starts playing. It's quite the floor show.

Yes, I know it's just a distraction or an attempt to set me up for another bit of flimflam, but my shoulders lower from being way too close to my earlobes and my breathing eases anyway.

"So tell me, LeLe Sherwood Svensen," he says, "what is it that you want to do—besides kick my ass to the curb?"

"Just Sherwood," I say as I swipe a muffin, because it is turning out to be a dessert-before-dinner type of day. "I'm the heir, I don't have that option."

He picks up a slice of watermelon and says with a too-neutral tone, "What about Vegas?"

"That was a mistake. Obviously." Did that sound like a lie? Because it sure feels like a lie with how clammy my palms are all of a sudden, and there's a giant ball of you're-full-of-shit stuck in my throat making it hard to swallow.

Erik cocks his head and looks me dead in the eye. "I'm not sure it was. Admit it, being with me isn't all bad."

Orgasms. Giggles. Rambling conversations in the middle of the night tucked up against him in the dark. Hearing his stories and telling him mine over room service before we fell into each other and ended up naked again.

Everything is fluttering on the inside as I fight to keep it all icy bitch on the outside. Thank the fates I have practice with this. It's impossible to grow up with four sisters and not have the ability to keep your emotions under control—or at least be able to pretend you do until you can enact your well-deserved revenge.

Using my decades of experience, I level a superior look at him. "It's completely awful."

"Even when we—" He pauses, his gaze going smoky.

I can feel my face go sitting-in-front-of-the-fireplace-in-August-at-your-vacation-home-on-the-sun hot as I'm bombarded by images of the two of us in various compromising positions. Really, what we did in the elevator at the resort was beyond risky, but I seem to make a lot of bad decisions around this man. This trip alone would be exhibits one through a million in the court of have-you-lost-your-ever-loving-mind.

"When we played poker in Vegas?" Erik continues, the smug expression on his face showing that he knows exactly what I was thinking about. "You didn't have even the least bit of fun then?"

I shake my head, not trusting my voice to not give away the game.

He bends forward over the picnic basket between us and drops his voice to barely a whisper so I have to lean closer to hear him say, "And when we used an invisibility spell to watch the fountain show from the middle of the Bellagio's pool?"

We'd had to stay in constant physical contact not to break the spell—a fact that meant he either *really* liked the show or the feel of my ass against his cock.

"That was mildly enjoyable." I cringe before I can stop myself, because that didn't sound even the littlest bit believable. I swear, I need to become a better liar.

"And that second time in the elevator?" He inches closer so that we're so close all I need to do is move a little bit more and our lips would touch. "As I recall, you liked that so much we missed our floor and you lost your panties."

AVERY FLYNN

Oh yeah, I'm hot all of a sudden. And breathing? Who needs to do that? Not me, not when it's taking everything I have to just keep my ass planted firmly on the picnic blanket instead of leaning forward and closing the distance between us.

"I guess I remember that," I say, not even trying to put any truth into the words.

He chuckles softly as his gaze dips down to my mouth. The air between us sparks with electricity as he focuses so completely on me that it's like there's no one else in the world but the two of us—or at least he wishes so. He's not looking at me to see if I'm going to make the right decision, if I'm going to do what is expected, or if I'm the Sherwood heir. Instead, he's looking at me as if all he wants to see is Leona—and he actually does. It's almost too much to process. Desire, warm and slick, envelops me as need practically vibrates through me. I wish I could blame it on some kind of spell, but there's not even a hint of magic in the air between us. Just want and the heady memory of what it was like between us when we were naked—or at least naked enough.

"And the night we fucked against the hotel room window," he continues, his voice as tempting as a forbidden touch, "when you came so hard you couldn't even talk?"

Sort of like now, because forming a thought is an impossibility when my head is so full of images from Vegas and my body is primed and ready to repeat every single glorious naked moment.

That's when the bastard has the audacity to wink at me

and then lie back on the blanket before closing his eyes and intertwining his fingers over his chest. "What, no response to that one?"

All the air whooshes back into my lungs and reality smacks me right across the cheek. Why that little—giant—pain in my ass. He knew! He knew the whole damn time what he was doing to me. How he was making me feel. What he was making me think about. I squash the napkin in my fist.

I want to smother him.

Or kiss him.

Or—okay, fine, I want both, but the kissing is winning out at this moment. I know. I'm disappointed in myself too. I should make better life choices—and I usually do—but when it comes to Erik Svensen, everything always goes sideways and against the wall and over the couch and—

Oh my fates, Leona. Get your shit together!

"Wife," he says without opening his eyes, self-satisfied amusement thick in his tone, "is there something you want to ask me?"

"I'm not your wife," I grumble.

He takes a peek at me and then closes his eyes again. "Go ahead and ask if you can kiss me."

I let out a cleansing, calming breath and release my stranglehold on what had been a perfectly good napkin. I will not let this man get to me. Again. For the billionth time. I. Will. Not.

Squaring my shoulders, I shoot him a withering glare that is completely wasted since he still isn't even looking at me.

"I don't want to kiss you." Something that would have sounded a lot more convincing if I actually meant it. As it is, I'm all fluttery insides, quick breaths, and heat—so much fucking heat—that I should be levitating at this point.

Erik still doesn't look at me, but his mouth curls into a crooked grin. "And here I thought the Sherwoods were all too noble to lie—especially the always-follows-the-rules heir."

Always rule-following? I grab the goblet of rosé and down half of it. If only I was. Then I wouldn't be stuck on the road with the most frustrating man in all of Witchingdom. Erik doesn't say anything. He just stays lying there with that smug, hot-jerk face of his. And the second half of the glass of rosé tastes like the possibility that bad decisions really could be good ones. Really good ones. Great bad ones. The kind that you'll remember years later when you're eyeball-deep in re-sponsibilities as you dutifully sit next to the husband your mom picked for you because it made political sense to join your families. And that man will never make me feel like I do now with Erik—like there's electricity running through my veins, like anything is possible, like if I don't lean down and kiss him I'm going to implode.

"Oh, fuck it." I shove the picnic basket to the side and cross over to where he's lying, stopping just shy of climbing on top of him. "Can I kiss you?"

He turns and looks at me and fists his hands as if he's having to fight the urge to reach out and touch me. "Abso-fucking-lutely."

"This doesn't change anything," I say as I straddle him, leaving an inch of space between our bodies. Am I talking to myself or him? A little of both? "It's just scratching an itch." I lower my face until my mouth is a hairsbreadth from his. "As soon as we get The Liber Umbrarum safely tucked away, we do the divorce spell."

He tenses underneath me for a fraction of a second—a moment so short I almost think I've made it up in my head—and then relaxes before planting his hands on my hips and pulling me down so that I'm pressed right up against him. Pleasure shoots through me at the contact, and it takes everything I have not to rub myself against him. Even with layers of clothing between us, there's no mistaking how much he wants me too.

"Erik," I say, his name coming out like a plea.

He answers—but not with words. He lifts his head and closes the distance between our mouths, kissing me like a man making a promise that he intends to keep. It starts with a brush of our lips that sets off a cascade of sensations like a waterfall of want sweeping through me. Then he parts his lips, inviting me for more. It's not an invitation I'm going to pass up. I deepen the kiss, teasing his tongue with mine as I cup the sides of his face. His day-old scruff tickles my palms and the phantom feel of that prickle against the inside of my thighs as he eats me out makes my core clench.

The man is so fucking talented with that tongue. Even now, he's working it to take the kiss from just-scratching-an-itch to guaranteeing so much more. This is dangerous because it is oh-so-tempting. We both know exactly what could—would—happen next. It's in the way he knows the precise right moment to slip his hand under the bottom of my lightweight green sweater and settle on the small of my back. He spreads his fingers and holds me not with pressure but with that unspoken knowledge that when we're like this, everything just works.

Like, works really, really well. My nipples are hard and aching for Erik's fingers or mouth. My breasts are full and heavy as I press them against his chest, and I have the urge to stretch so my tits, accessible by the V-neck cut of my sweater, hang in his face, and the only thing stopping me from doing just that is the fact that I'd have to break this kiss. I'm not ready to do that. I'm not sure I ever will be. Seriously. The man is simply kissing me, letting me take the lead, and I'm ready to go sexy whirlwind on his ass. My skin is electrified, every nerve is tuned in to him, and time is slowing down even as it speeds up while I try to hang on to every sensation and reach for the next oh-fuck-yes at the same time.

I rock against his hard cock as I keep kissing him, trying to ease the lust burning through me. If I had the brainpower for words right now, a get-us-both-naked-stat spell would be in the works. As it is, it's all I can do to remember to breathe. Hey, maybe there are women out there who wouldn't just melt into a kiss like this. That's not me. I cannot get enough and it's too fucking good for me to pretend otherwise.

"Hey! This is private property." A man's voice cuts through the lust enough to make me raise my head.

A farmer in denim overalls with a head of hair that looks more like a chestnut mane is rushing toward us. He waves the pitchfork he's carrying in the air and fire sparks off of the tines.

"That doesn't look good," Erik says.

The farmer tosses his head back and lets out a loud neigh that sets off a cacophony of responses from the hippocamps, yanking my attention over to the lake to see them racing toward the shore near us. Yeah, they'd have to cross the sliver of beach and climb up the slope to our illegal picnic area, but stranger things have happened in Witchingdom.

"Can the hippocamps run on land?" I ask.

"I don't know," Erik says, jerking his chin at the farmer, "but he sure can."

The other man is gaining ground, and flames are shooting out of the pitchfork. The mental image of getting toasted shoves out all thoughts of the hippocamps and pretty much everything else but white noise and panic. This is not how I expected to go out.

Erik clamps his hand on mine, jerking my attention to his face and the sexy smirk of his that makes it seem like we're having a normal one when the reality is we're about to be turned into roasted marshmallows.

"Effugium," he says.

I barely have time to translate the word into "escape" before we're flying through the air just above the trees, which are using their branches to try to snatch us out of the sky. A skinny, gnarled limb wraps around my ankle, the rough wood scratching my skin, but it can't hold me, and we fly onward, dropping down into Bessie's welcoming leather seats with a soft thud.

Erik turns the key in the ignition as he grins at me like a kid who got away with snagging the last snickerdoodle in the cookie jar. "Still not having fun?"

I don't say anything, because what's the point when he can see the truth on my unable-to-stop-grinning face?

He laughs and sends a cloud of dust into the air as he does a fast reverse and spins Bessie around before shifting into drive. The wind is whipping through my hair and the giggles are back as I throw my arms up as we speed down the road and turn onto the highway with a squeal of Bessie's tires, leaving the scent of burnt rubber in our wake.

It's like being back in Vegas with that feeling of exhilaration and absolutely fucking joyful freedom rushing through me, making the blood rush through my ears. Erik must feel it too, because his dimples practically have dimples, he's smiling so hard as Bessie eats up the miles. I close my eyes and take in a deep breath, doing my best to cement this core memory in my heart so I can access it later when all of this seems like a dream or a nightmare or just unreal enough that I'm not sure it happened at all.

"Shit," Erik says.

That exclamation is my only warning before he slams on the brakes, flinging an arm out to block me from flying forward as if I'm not already wearing a seat belt. That's when I look up and see the snaggletoothed grin of a ten-foot-tall bridge troll standing smack-dab in the middle of the highway in front of an interstate overpass.

"Walter!" The troll rubs her hands together with glee. "Don't worry about ordering from Broom Dash. It looks like dinner has arrived."

Chapter Nineteen

Erik . . .

*F*uck me—and not in the good way.

Keeping my gaze focused on the troll's face, I shift into reverse and hit the gas, but the troll grabs Bessie's bumper and lifts the front end of the car off the ground. The back tires try their best, but there's not even a drop of sweat on the troll's wide forehead, making it more than obvious that we're not going anywhere.

The troll grins. Her pointy teeth are a particularly disturbing shade of puce. Then she waggles her bushy dark green eyebrows, dislodging a twig that had been stuck in them and sending it falling to the crunchy, leaf-covered ground.

I'm already halfway to casting a silent vanquishing spell

when the sun catches on the gold amulet hanging from a chain looped around her neck.

Shit.

Next to me, LeLe—whose eyes are closed in concentration—takes a deep breath, and the air around us starts to smell like warm cake donuts fresh out of the oven. It's one of the best smells in the world, but the scent of her magic means nothing but certain disaster in this situation.

Heart hammering in my chest and adrenaline rushing through my veins, I reach out to her before everything goes pear-shaped. "LeLe—"

Either she's concentrating too hard to hear me or she doesn't want to, because she starts her hex in motion. "Quod electrica inpulsa—"

I grab her hand and yank her out of spell-making mode before we both end up on the dark side of the moon or exiled to The Beyond.

"She has a presidium," I holler.

LeLe's eyes snap open and her wide and wild gaze goes straight to the amulet around the troll's neck.

"Shit," LeLe grumbles.

I couldn't say it better myself.

"Well, it takes the fun out of things when a witch notices my little prize." The troll pouts as she strokes the gold amulet. "It's always so much fun to watch a know-it-all witch's magic bounce off me and land on them. If you ever see a witch with an ear for a nose and noses for ears, tell Mick that Frieda says hi."

That sucks for Mick, but the fact that he survived means there's a way out of this situation. If there's anything that growing up as a Svensen teaches you, it's how to find the loophole. And I am going to find it. I have to. The alternative is getting doused in Devil's Horn BBQ sauce and squished between two halves of a witch-sized hamburger bun.

Sure, there are fates worse than getting eaten by a bridge troll—for instance, you could agree to be a test subject in one of Cy's magical experiments that leaves you with a tiger's tail and the inability to enjoy a cold beer on a hot afternoon ever again. That said, this is pretty shitty. Like, fuck me, how in the hell am I going to talk my way out of being dinner? We can't outrun her since she'd catch up to us within two strides. We can't hex her, because she has the amulet. Her little trick with the bumper showed that we can't speed off in Bessie and leave her in our dust.

I shoot LeLe a reassuring look while everything I know about bridge trolls rushes through my brain at warp speed.

Average height nine to eleven feet.

Likes: campfires, riddles, and eating witches.

Dislikes: rules, regulations, and backing down from any kind of challenge to their sense of honor or hospitality.

All the synapses in my brain spark at the same time, illuminating the perfect loophole. *That's it.*

"We request passage under the old rules," I say as I give LeLe's hand a squeeze to let her know I've got this.

Her sideways glance and eye roll tell me she has her doubts. She's probably already working up a plan of her own.

With a huff of disgust, Frieda lets go of Bessie and the car bounces once before settling. Even from the driver's seat I can see the set of brand-new troll-sized finger indents in her chrome front bumper.

"You lost the option of safe passage when you tried to hex me," the troll says as she flexes her arms, showing off biceps the size of Bessie's very generous trunk.

Locking my most charming grin into place, I relax back against the leather seats, willing my jackrabbiting pulse to calm the fuck down. Just like when I've faced off against my father, there is no benefit to letting anyone see how I really feel. Forget never let them see you sweat. Try never let them think you are anything other than a bored rich guy with absolutely nothing invested in the outcome.

"We *would* have," I say, picking a nonexistent piece of lint off my sweater. "However, LeLe did not *finish* the spell."

Frieda narrows her eyes and crosses her thick arms, revealing a large tattoo of three vines climbing up her sinewy forearm. "Only because you stopped her."

There's something about the tattoo that seems familiar.

"Tonor vine," LeLe whispers, her words barely perceptible.

That's it!

About ten years ago, Tonor the Troll successfully campaigned for the trolls to go vegan. A few trolls remained carnivores, but the majority became herbivores and, as part of their pledge to stay the vegan path, got a three-vine tattoo. Oh sure, all trolls still threaten to eat witches and other magical creatures for breakfast, but for most trolls it's all talk. Instead, they just spend hours tormenting and teasing their prey before extracting a gift and sending them on their way.

I give her a discreet nod in acknowledgment and then relax back against the seat, keeping my body loose. Sure, they may not eat us, but that doesn't mean we're out of danger. When it comes to trolls, you gotta play the game or you could be stuck under their bridge for a while, and we have a spell book to return to the secured facility before the Council catches up with us.

"There's nothing in the Knoxville Accords that states a partial spell negates passage," LeLe says, her tone chipper.

"There's nothing that says it doesn't either," the troll grumbles.

"So you'd like to appeal to the full tribunal?" LeLe asks, bringing up the group of twelve magical creatures that pretty much no witch or troll wants to deal with.

I don't bother to keep the grin off my face. There is something incredibly sexy about watching LeLe meld a situation to her liking.

"Those stiffs?" Frieda grimaces. "No one wants to leave their fate up to a bunch of anal-retentive bureaucrats." Frieda contemplates for a second, watching a red-tailed hawk fly toward the setting sun before letting out a long sigh and focusing back on us. "I'm not conceding it's a loophole. You're just lucky I'm in a good mood because Walter got a line on some pixies, and nothing goes better with peanut butter cookies than deep-fried pixie wings."

LeLe flinches and I barely manage to cover the automatic

gag caused by the mental image of de-winged pixies. "Understood."

"So we do this the old-fashioned way—with a riddle." Frieda narrows her eyes at us. "You only get one chance to answer the riddle correctly. Fuck it up and I'll be picking my teeth with your bones after breakfast."

LeLe lets out an offended huff and says, "The Accords grant us three answers."

Frieda grins, showing off the remains of whatever breakfast had been in her teeth. "You wanna go appeal it to the tribunal?"

When neither of us says anything, Frieda plucks us out of Bessie—so much for there being no downside to a convertible— and then uses her foot to nudge the car onto the shoulder of the road. I have enough time to double down on the protection spell keeping The Liber Umbrarum safe while we deal with the troll.

Frieda holds us tight and heads deeper into the forest on the side of the highway. "You can bunk up at our place tonight, but in the morning you'd better have the right answer."

"Why not just give us the riddle now?" LeLe asks.

"Because it's more fun to watch you squirm," Frieda says as she clomps through the trees toward a campfire's light by an old bridge. "Plus y'all are going to have to tell Walter that you're not for dinner. He's going to be disappointed."

Once we get to the clearing, there's a huge bridge troll wearing a backward ball cap, jorts, and his own presidium amulet leaning against what remains of a rusted-out suspension bridge that probably hasn't been used since Bessie hit the highway for the first time. The road on the other side of the bridge is covered in forest overgrowth. On the side closest to the campfire, vines and tree limbs have been bent and shaped into a house complete with a wraparound porch, bay windows, and a second story, all of which lead up to a thatched roof. Even in a world full of magic, the troll's home looks like something out of a fairy tale. Frieda sits us down on a wooden platform covered in intricately carved wards that's attached to a pulley system hooked to a tree.

"Wow," LeLe says, her eyes round with amazement as she peers closer at the house's second-floor bay window. "This is amazing craftsmanship."

"Oh yeah, Walter has a true talent," Frieda says, her chest puffing up with pride. "We have a DIY WitchyGram account. You should give us a follow—*if* you make it past breakfast."

Chapter Twenty

Erik . . .

The threat would carry a lot more weight if it weren't for the fact that the trolls in question are more likely to eat their phones than a pair of witches. Not that I am going to point that out. Frieda and Walter may not eat us, but that doesn't mean they wouldn't squash us.

As LeLe and I sit on the platform, Walter dishes us up small—for a troll—plates of biscuits drowned in white gravy minus the sausage with a side of crispy roasted Brussels sprouts. Then they start telling us stories of all the travelers they've stopped—all of whom they threatened to eat and yet none of whom they actually did. There was the satyr who taught them how to play the electric flute during his five-night stay, the pair of pixies who told jokes for the solid week they were here that had the pair laughing so hard they were crying, and the tatted-up unicorn shifter who played Texas Hold'em until the wee small hours of the morning during the single night he was at their camp. We are about halfway through the story of the witch who made them newt muffins when LeLe shoots me a knowing look. You don't have to have the Graeae sisters' shared all-seeing eye to understand that despite all their talk, these trolls kidnap for company.

After that, LeLe ends up telling them all about her sister's rooster familiar Barkley that has it out for her. By the time we're eating peach crumble, we're all laughing. All in all, for being witch-napped, it's a pretty enjoyable experience.

Finally though, Frieda gets up from the log she's sitting on and does a full-body stretch. "Well, not that hanging out with you isn't better than watching the bark peel off of a river birch, but it's time for us to head in."

"What about the riddle?" LeLe asks.

Frieda grabs a huge glass Mason jar with a sticker on it that says "Riddles" in perfect cursive script and flashes us her toothy grin. "What, you think we have them all memorized? Do you have any idea how many witches and gnomes and werewolves and other magical creatures pass through this way on a regular basis?"

"Too many, and I hate it," Walter says, not sounding believable in the least.

"Exactly, and there's no way we could make up a riddle on the fly for that many folks." She pulls a piece of paper out of the jar, unfolds it, and then reads aloud. "What disappears completely as soon as you say its name?"

Fuck. What I wouldn't give to have Sigrid's brain right now. My little sister loves two things most in life: reading and word puzzles. Me? I do my dad's dirty work and keep his cruel attention pointed away from my brother and sister. Yeah, not helpful at all in this particular moment.

"That's it, folks. No clues," Frieda says. "Now, not that I don't trust you, but I don't trust you, so . . ." She takes out a huge bowie knife, its edges as sharp as her teeth, and cuts through a rope tied to the tree with one bold swipe.

The severed rope zips up the massive trunk of the old-growth tree faster than Bessie when I hit the Nitro boost switch. I barely have time to grab LeLe's hand and brace myself before the platform flies up into the air before stopping with a jolt once we are up in the highest branches.

"And don't go getting ideas about making spells," Frieda hollers from the ground. "We paid extra for the wards to be carved into it. But don't worry. Walter will pull you down in the morning."

"Sleep well, but not too close to the edge," Walter adds. "We lost a leprechaun once that way. Poor little fella rolled off the edge. When we woke up, all that was left of him was a rainbow splat and three gold coins."

And on that note, Walter and Frieda lumber into their troll-sized fairy house. I glance over at LeLe. Her mouth is pressed so tightly closed it looks like she doesn't have lips anymore, and her shoulders are shaking as she fights to hold back her laughter.

There's only one thing I can or should do at this moment. I shoot her a stern look and say, "They're very frightening trolls."

She loses it. The laughter escapes. It's full and joyful and one hundred percent real. Damn, I've missed it. She wipes the tears from her eyes as she tries to catch her breath, which just makes me start laughing—and that's when the actual trouble starts.

The platform starts to rock and then dips on the left side. LeLe's giggle changes to a squeal of surprise and an image of a rainbow splat flashes in front of my eyes. Without the ability to cast a spell because of the runes, neither of us could stop her fall. She tips backward, gravity tugging at her as one corner of the platform sinks, and I'm not laughing anymore. There's no way I'm going to let LeLe end up like that. I reach out and yank her to my chest and roll us so we're in the middle of the platform. While she's underneath me, I lock my forearms in place on either side of her shoulders and my legs on the outside of hers to block her from rolling as the platform pitches this way and that in slower and slower waves until it finally stops.

Pulse as erratic as a coked-out finance bro witch, I ease my way onto my back next to her. Neither of us says a thing, but she reaches out, and the backs of her fingers touch mine, and I let go of the breath I was holding. The muscles knotted in my shoulder unwind, and that hypervigilant part of me that's always gauging the other person shuts the fuck up.

"Do you think the answer to the riddle is Bloody Mary?" I ask, because that is exactly what someone should say after almost rolling off a platform hanging twenty feet up in the air.

"Nah," LeLe says. "You have to say her name three times and then she appears."

We stare up at the five billion stars as the quiet wraps around us. Well, almost—an enchanted forest is never really quiet. There are the raccoons and the owls on the hunt, their triumphant calls filling the air. The sound of twigs snapping under the feet of goblins and dark elves who must be gathering in a clearing come with regularity. And every once in a while, the galloping of centaurs sends flocks of nightingales rushing out of the trees as they take to the sky. There are a million other sounds too. LeLe's steady breath. The soft sigh she lets out when a falling star goes by.

I'm way too aware of her, and I swear I can still taste her on my lips after that kiss in the meadow. Every part of me is completely tuned in to her, and a dozen memories of being with her are flashing before me, but one in particular stands out. She's naked and sitting in the middle of the hotel bed, eating the chocolate-covered strawberries and drinking the champagne that had come with our breakfast. The sheets are wrapped around her waist. I cannot stop looking at her tits. They're fucking perfect. Her pale pink nipples are hard and tempting and I've got my hand wrapped around my hard cock just admiring the view. That's when she accidentally-on-purpose spills the small amount of champagne she has left in her glass all over her tits and winks at me. My cock goes from hard to granite and I'm sweeping the plate of strawberries off the bed on the next heartbeat, licking up the sweet droplets as slow and fast as I possibly can.

"Rumpelstiltskin?" LeLe asks, yanking me back to the here and now. "Nope," she answers her own question as she snuggles closer to me, resting her temple against my shoulder as if it's the most natural thing to do. "He has a temper tantrum and stomps off, but doesn't disappear."

"My uncle Lars disappears whenever the check appears at a restaurant," I say while my brain runs at light speed trying to memorize this moment so I can remember it for after the power transfer ceremony, when she hates my guts again.

She giggles and gently turns on her side to face me. "You are no help."

"Incorrect," I say as I roll to face her, our mouths so fucking close that it would barely take any movement for me to kiss her. "I'm the one that saved us from being a rainbow splat. We are twenty feet up in the air."

"And you caught me." Her gaze drifts over me, hot and hungry. "Why? When letting me fall would knock the Sherwoods down a peg or two?"

I should confirm it. Give her the answer she thinks is true. But I can't. Not when we're this close. For some probably horrible reason, I can't lie straight to LeLe's face like I can to anyone else.

"No, I didn't do it to put your family in their place."

She gnaws on her bottom lip as if trying to put puzzle pieces together that just don't fit. "Was it to make a fool of me?"

I shake my head.

The platform sways as she inches closer, so near I can smell her shampoo and feel the soft kiss of her breath.

"So why did you save me? Letting me go splat would make it easy to just declare yourself my widower and get access to whatever it is that you want from this marriage without having to deal with me."

It's probably—no, definitely—what I should have done. It's what my father would have done. It's what I would have done if it had been anyone other than LeLe.

What a fucking mess you've made for yourself, numb nuts.

I'm halfway to confessing that truth when old habits kick in. I'd walk in front of a renegade flying carpet that would knock me into next week for my siblings, and I've never once told them. It isn't possible, not with my dad and his spies seemingly everywhere. Never admit you care is as close to a personal code as I have.

"I did it because it amused me." I drop my hand and fall onto my back. "Don't worry. I'll probably let you fall next time."

She gives a little harrumph, but she doesn't argue.

Why would she? I'm a selfish, unethical bastard, and all of Witchingdom knows it.

"You know what we need to do to solve the riddle?" she asks after a minute.

I keep my gaze on the stars overhead because I'm not sure what will happen if I look over and see that sexy I-have-a-plan face of hers. "I'm sure you're going to tell me."

"Forget about it," she says.

I turn and look at her before I can stop myself. The woman looks smug and way too happy with herself. It's all I can do not to reach over and kiss her, high likelihood of us both going splat be damned.

Instead, I roll back and lace my fingers together behind my head, as if that can help stop me from reaching out to her. "What do you mean, forget about it?"

"Have you ever lost something and you find it as soon as you stop looking for it?" The platform swings gently as she rolls over and lays her palm on my chest. "It's the same thing. We just need to forget about it and the answer will come to us."

I would give her an answer if I could form thoughts. All I can do at the moment though is feel the tips of her fingers as she traces random shapes over the spot where my heart would be if I had one. Each soft touch steals a little bit of my breath, all of my concentration, and my determination not to give a shit what happens to her or her family after the power exchange ceremony.

The only way this ends is badly, and yet, I can't find it in myself to care.

"Are we going to talk about it?" she asks, her voice barely above a whisper.

"The way I just saved you from certain death if you'd rolled off?" I respond, even though I can tell by the uncertainty in her tone that she isn't talking about that.

Her fingers still and she lets out a tiny sigh. "No."

All I want in the world right now is for her to start tracing circles and triangles and octagons across my chest again, but I can't ask for that, so I say, "How we're going to sweet-talk the recipe for that crumble from Walter?"

"Very funny," she says with a chuckle. "You know what I mean."

I do.

I turn my head so I can see her face. Her eyes, one blue and one green, almost glow in the moonlight. No doubt it's because her dad's a shifter. The little upward tilt of her nose? The same as her mother's. There's a bit of her sisters in the freckles and the crooked nose and the ears that are just a little too big for her head. And the way she's looking at me right now as if I'm not the worst person ever? That will change soon enough.

I can't give her the divorce, not until my dad is powerless and can't fight for control of the family magic. After that, I'll do the spell and she'll be free. She'll leave after the ceremony. I won't try to stop her.

Unable to stop myself, I take her hand and roll it over so her wrist is facing up and trace my finger over the glowing handfast mark. "You mean the kiss that doesn't mean any-thing."

"It doesn't," she says.

I've never heard such a bald-faced lie in my whole life.

"Not at all." I lift up our clasped hands and kiss the mark, the heat of it making my lips tingle. "Good night, wife."

She shivers next to me and—for once—doesn't tell me not to call her that. I may not be the smartest man in the world, but

I know when to shut the fuck up so I don't mess things up. That's exactly what I do until I drift off still holding LeLe's hand against my heart like it means something.

I'm still holding her hand the next morning when we're both woken up by the platform being swung back and forth.

"Time's up, witches," Frieda calls up to us. "Time to solve that riddle or become breakfast."

Chapter Twenty-One

Leona . . .

This morning I'm as twitchy as Barkley would be in a fried chicken shop—and somehow, some way, this is all Erik's fault. Probably because he was so nice last night. That can only mean one thing. He's up to something. Even worse than that, my first thought wasn't *oh shit!*, it was *mmmm, good*.

Yes, I'm as disappointed in myself as you should be.

And in the bright light of a new day, as Frieda slowly lowers us down, all that easy connection we'd had in the dark last night feels like when you're wearing a sweater and there's a little string, so you pull it and end up with a gaping hole. It's too open, too out there, too much. I hate sensation. I'd rather have

Barkley roosting on my naked ass again than have this sickly, vulnerable unease making me queasy.

And *that* has me prickly.

"So what did you come up with?" I ask while sitting with my legs pulled up tight so I can rest my chin on my jeans-covered legs and keep my arms wrapped around my shins.

Erik lets out a snort of a laugh. "Me? You were the one who said not to think about it, so I followed your direction, wife."

So this is going to be my fault? No. That isn't gonna fly, not even with a volare spell.

"I only said that because you're so stubborn that I knew that you would probably just sit there and think about it the whole time."

It's what he always does. I say left, he goes right. I say divorce, he says stay married. Just because he looks especially hot all sleep rumpled and bleary eyed in his well-worn jeans and I-know-for-a-fact supersoft navy blue Henley doesn't mean I'm going to cut him any slack.

"Well, I didn't." He shrugs. "I fell asleep just like you did, and then you snored the whole night through."

I let out a triumphant "HA!" and grin my smuggest grin. "So you were awake!"

He yawns, opening his mouth wide enough to let a full-sized pixie in. "Only because you insisted on snuggling me," he says as he rubs his palm against the back of his head.

Which is exactly why I'm curled up so tight. I woke up squeezing him like he was my own personal husband-sized bed pillow. I'd even drooled on his shoulder! That cannot happen again, no matter how tempting it is to just scooch on over and cuddle up against him.

"That was just a case of any port in the storm," I grumble.

Erik smirks his stupid sexy smirk and looks up at the cloudless blue morning, then over at the dry green leaves on the trees as we inch ever closer to the ground. Finally, he turns his attention back to me and the sweet-innocent-aw-shucks expression on his face does nothing but spike my hackles even more.

Maybe becoming breakfast for a pair of trolls would be worth it if he is served on the platter next to me.

"You know you really are a jerk."

He curves his lips into a pout, obviously having the time of his life poking me. "And here I thought we really had a breakthrough husband-and-wife moment last night as we chatted under the stars and I saved your life."

"We're not talking about that." I glare at him even as the butterflies in my stomach start doing warm-up stretches. "We need to either figure out the answer to that riddle or we're going to become breakfast."

This time his laugh is genuine, and the way his whole face softens when it does makes my breath catch.

"Frieda and Walter are not going to eat us, and you know it," he says. "They're vegan."

"Yeah, but they could keep us here as forced guests," I sputter, "and as you yourself said, we've got to get the spell book to the secured facility. It's only a matter of time until the Council figures out that we're the ones with the book and sends someone after us."

His smile fades at that reminder. Good. We are not on a delayed honeymoon. This little road trip of ours has two purposes.

One, secure The Liber Umbrarum in whatever magic-resistant fortress Erik's super paranoid family has created.

Two, get Erik to perform the dimitto spell with me.

Neither of those is going to happen though if we end up spending the rest of our lives under a rusted-out overpass with Walter and Frieda. The pulley and rope squeak as we pass below the tree line and the roof of the trolls' supercute house appears.

I have to come up with a solution. I'm the Sherwood heir, it's kind of my thing. And by "kind of," I mean completely, utterly, and without fail, not even a single solitary time, because everything I do is for the family.

My palms are clammy and my stomach is a jumbled mess that has nothing to do with how good Erik looks before he magics off his morning scruff and everything to do with the look of disappointment that will be in my mom's eyes when she finds out that I failed not only to get The Liber Umbrarum put away where the Council can't touch it but also in her power marriage plans for me.

My lungs get tighter the closer to the ground we get, and then my nose starts cramping. Yes. Cramping. My right nostril is hitched upward in a weird Elvisy-type snarl, and I can't get it to relax, and it's starting to really hurt.

Erik scoots closer to me, the space between his eyes squished in concern. "Why are you doing that?"

"I'm not trying to," I say, my voice cracking. "I can't stop."

We're on the platform that's warded out the wazoo, so it's not because of a spell. I've never had this happen before. I mean, sure, occasionally my knee jiggle gets out of control or I start squeezing one butt cheek and then the other in a quick beat until my ass is burning, but that's only under times of great stress and—

Ooooohhhhh.

Fuck.

I try to take a deep breath to do some breathing exercises and take my heart rate down. It works out about as well as you'd think considering one half of my nose is cranked up halfway to the moon.

My left glute pulses.

Then my right.

I'm halfway to Freakoutville, population me, when Erik cups my face, forcing me to look at him. His eyes are softer than they have a right to be at that moment. They should be hardened, and his mouth should be twisted in a gotcha-loser smirk, but they aren't, and it isn't. Instead he looks . . . serious, concerned, empathetic.

"Two dragons walk into a bar," he says. "The first dragon says, 'It's hot in here.' The second one tells him to shut his mouth."

Of all the things he could do at this moment, sharing a dumb joke didn't even make the first billion. I'm still trying to process what in the hell he's doing when he launches into another one.

"Who granted the fish a wish?" He pauses a beat. "The fairy codmother."

Oh, that one is bad. Like bad, bad. But I start giggling anyway.

His hold on me eases, but he doesn't break contact. "What do you call a fairy who forgets to put on deodorant?" He lifts an eyebrow as if inviting me to answer, which I am very much not going to do. "Stinkerbelle."

All the tension whooshes out of me when I let out a sort of snorty chuckle. "Those are the worst jokes I've ever heard."

"Yeah, but your nose isn't doing that thing anymore."

He's right. Yes, it nearly kills me to admit it, but I'm no longer about to put on my blue suede shoes—something that almost makes up for the fact that he drops his hands and, like a complete dork, I miss his touch.

"It would be easier to hate you if you were just a jerk all the time," I say, the truth slipping out before I can stop it.

"I'll work on that," he says, his voice soft as his gaze drifts to my mouth.

And for a second I think he's going to kiss me, and I'm already leaning in toward him when the platform lands with such a solid and hard thunk that I swear some of my teeth jiggle.

"Time's up," Frieda says in a singsong voice.

Chapter Twenty-Two

Leona . . .

"Sorry about that," Frieda says as she plucks Erik and me off the platform and sets us down on the ground. "Walter just gets really excited at the prospect of fresh witch for breakfast." She brushes us off and smooths Erik's hair, which is sticking up in every direction, like we're her dolls or something, and then steps back next to Walter. "So it all comes down to it now. Can you tell us what disappears completely as soon as you say its name?"

What I wouldn't do to have Bea here, even if that meant Barkley came with her. She is definitely the sister who would have figured this out within twelve seconds.

"Oh, come on, don't say we need to get the barbecue going; I don't think I cleaned the grill plates from last time," Walter says, sounding about as sincere as a toddler holding a cookie, swearing they never took anything.

I look over at Erik, the Svensen heir who should have found about twelve loopholes or been able to lie his way out of this. He's just staring at me with a whatcha-gonna-do look on his face. I glance over at the barbecue. It's humongous (it's made for trolls), but the vines covering it have grown vines, so there's no way it has been in use for decades. Being breakfast is not in our future, but there's no way we can afford to spend another night here. One, there's the Council to worry about. Two, I'm not sure I can go another night on the platform without making a fool of myself and/or getting naked with Erik.

Looking up at Frieda and Walter's house, my gaze lands on the trophies crowded onto shelves that line the wraparound porch.

That's when it hits me.

The only thing that trolls like more than company is winning.

That is it. That's what we need to do. We have to offer the trolls a little competition, a contest so easy for them to win that they can't even imagine it going any other way. Then all we have to do is beat them.

Easy, right?

Not really, but I'm all ears if you have any better ideas.

I do my best to settle my nerves with a deep breath and then give the trolls my most accommodating smile.

"Frieda," I say, "we have the answer to your riddle." My ears heat at the lie, but I power through. "However, we've enjoyed your company so much that I'm hoping we could come up with another way for us to pay passage to go under the bridge."

"Oh yeah, sure you know the answer." Frieda's laugh booms so loudly that a whole flock of crows take flight. "We're not giving you any new riddles until the first one is solved."

Glancing down at my feet, I force out a disappointed-sounding sigh. "Oh yeah, yeah, I totally get that, it's just I thought we could do something together so we could all have fun. Maybe like a game of Monopoly or Trivial Pursuit." I pause, letting possibility hang in the air. "Or we could have a foot race. I don't know. I was just trying to think of something we could all enjoy, because the riddle just seems like fun for only Erik and me."

Walter crosses his massive arms as he shakes his head. "Do you think your puny little witch legs can take one of *us* in a race?"

"Of course not mine," I say as I turn toward Erik, giving him a please-play-along lift of my eyebrows. "But his?"

Erik, being about as helpful as a wart on a newt's chin, looks down at his legs as if he hadn't realized until this moment that he had any. Why does he have to be such a pain in my ass? Can he not just go along with things?

"I know he's scrawny and has never really worked for anything in his life," I say, and yes, I'm venting a little, "but I think he could do it if he actually tried."

Walter busts out into giggles. Frieda just shakes her head in disbelief.

I mean yes, the idea that Erik could outrun him or Frieda

is ridiculous, but Erik isn't helping by starting to do stretches—or at least attempting. He bends down to touch his toes and his fingertips barely get past his kneecaps.

"Now I know Erik and his family have a bit of an unsavory reputation for *finding loopholes*." I put as much emphasis on the last two words as possible while Erik starts doing a pathetic imitation of a backbend. "So I'm willing to put my honor as a Sherwood to guarantee that Erik will in no way, shape, or form break the rules that you set."

This last bit gets Frieda's attention, as I'd hoped.

She makes a humph sound and pulls a few sticks out of her eyebrows that she uses to clean between her teeth, and she contemplates her next move. "So I get to set the rules?"

I nod. "Three rules you pick."

"He can't use magic to impact Frieda's performance," Walter says.

Frieda shoots him a dirty look. "I am the one in charge of making the rules here."

He shrugs. "Then make them."

While she thinks, Erik continues to act like a fool by running tight circles around me and then stopping directly between me and the trolls to do a set of jumping jacks. I'm more than half tempted to knee knock him.

"Okay, got 'em," Frieda says. "One, he can't use magic on me. Two, there are no do-overs. Three, there are no double-or-nothing opportunities after it's over."

Utilizing my years of practice at not showing my true emotions, I stuff the "yeah, baby" way down deep. I couldn't have asked for better rules, but I know I can't give in right away if Frieda and Walter are going to take the bait. I hem. I haw. I pace around a little.

"I don't know, Frieda, those seem like awfully tight rules." I rock back on my heels. "I mean, no do-overs? What happens if, like, lightning strikes? Or a bunch of pixies fly straight through the race path? Or the earth stops turning?"

"Then you are shit out of luck," Walter says, his huge smile practically showing off every one of his sixty-eight yellowed teeth.

"So those are your rules?" I let my shoulders drop a few inches as I mentally prep to seal the deal. I hold up one finger. "No using magic on Frieda." I hold up a second finger. "No do-overs." I hold up a third finger. "And no double or nothings. Do I have that right?"

Frieda and Walter both nod yes and give each other a high five.

"And there's no changing the rules now that we've all agreed?" I ask, cementing things in place. "And they apply to us all?"

"That's right, little witch," Walter says. "You cannot use magic on Frieda to help your boyfriend there."

"She is my wife," Erik says as he hops around doing one-leg quad stretches.

Now he speaks up? Well, it's a little late for that, because I learned at the feet of a master when it comes to getting the most out of every interaction.

"I'd like to add a rule of my own, if that's okay with you," I say, putting all the sugar I can muster into my smile at the trolls.

Frieda narrows her eyes. "Depends what it is."

"When we win—"

"If," Frieda interjects.

I nod and take a deep breath to prep for what I have to do next, but even a Sherwood has to play dirty every once in a while—nothing in life or love is fair. Not that this is love. It's not. Not even close. "Sorry, *if* we win, my husband has to participate in the dimitto spell immediately after the race."

Erik doesn't stop the hands-on-his-waist windmill stretches he's doing, but there is a definite flinch in his movements before he recovers. Yeah, this is a risk. He could throw the race, but he won't. When it comes down to it, Erik will always put his own self-interest and survival above everything else, just like a Svensen. It's not a question of if the Council will figure out we have The Liber Umbrarum but when. And when they come for it, they won't leave witnesses.

Walter lets out a low whistle. "You wanna divorce *that* bad? That is not an easy spell."

"Do you find that additional rule acceptable?" I ask Frieda and Walter, purposefully ignoring Erik.

They nod.

"Great," I say. "Let's do this."

Five minutes later, Erik and Frieda are lined up underneath the rusty overpass facing the split tree a quarter of a mile in the distance. Seeing Frieda next to Erik is like looking at a hundred-floor skyscraper next to a one-story bungalow. She is that much taller than he is.

"A kiss for good luck?" Erik asks.

I roll my eyes. There is no way I'm going to fall for that.

"Oh, come on," he says. "If this all happens, then we do the divorce spell. Don't you think a little kiss goodbye is warranted?"

I'm not even thinking about it. Kissing Erik is not even the beginning of a possibility of an idea that I maybe could have someday in the middle of a weak moment. I'm too smart for that. I know what he's like. This is obviously some kind of trick.

And yet my feet are moving.

Before I know it, I'm standing in front of him, tilting my head upward and parting my lips. My heart is speeding, the butterflies are butterflying, and the anticipation of the moment is about to kill me.

"See," he says, brushing a strand of my hair behind my ear. "I knew you couldn't wait to kiss me again."

His gaze drops to my mouth, and desire, hot and tempting, flashes between us. He leans down and comes within millimeters of my aching lips before he switches his direction and kisses me where my jaw meets my earlobe.

"Gotcha," he whispers before taking a step back.

Heat blasts my cheeks.

He really is the absolute worst.

I'm all hot air and frustration when I spin around, ready to march off, half hoping Frieda will kick his ass, when his fingers encircle my wrist. He whirls me around and tugs me back. I land with a thunk against his hard chest. His lips are on mine before I can even register what's happening.

The kiss is everything. It's hard and soft, promising and demanding, the best and worst of this maddening man all at once. And like a complete fool, I never want him to stop.

But he does, breaking contact completely as if he's afraid if he touches me at all—even just his fingers around my wrist—he won't be able to stop.

"You know," he says, "if people realized how devious you really are, they would go into shock. But I see it—and I like it." He dips his head down and kisses me again.

This time it's a quick sweep of his lips against mine and he still manages to thrill me all the way down to my toes and jumble my brain before I can untangle his words. Devious? Me? Not a day in my life.

"Don't worry," Erik says with an evil grin, "I get it. You left me a big enough loophole in those rules to ride a dinosaur through. I've got this."

My knees are all shaky as I walk over to the sidelines and stand beside Walter, who is sitting crisscross applesauce in the grass and still towers over me.

He gives me a head-to-toe look-over. "Are you sure you want that divorce after that kiss?"

No.

Yes.

Maybe.

I'm not sure about anything right now except for one thing.

"Want has nothing to do with anything when you're the Sherwood heir," I tell the troll.

Walter doesn't say anything in return. He just pulls a whistle made out of the wheel from a semi-tractor trailer and blows.

Frieda doesn't hesitate. She takes off running. The ground shakes beneath my feet as her feet pound on the path from the overpass to the tree. She doesn't just have a lead on Erik, she's blowing him away. She reaches out to slap the split tree. But before her palm hits the bark, Erik poofs from the start line and reappears leaning against the tree with a shit-eating grin on his face while her hand is still in midair.

"You cheated!" Frieda says, sucking air into her tired lungs with enough gusto that the leaves shake on the trees as if they are about to fly off.

Erik lifts a shoulder in that absolutely annoying blasé way of his and says, "There was nothing in your rules about me using magic to help myself, only that I couldn't use it to interfere with *you*."

Frieda snarls, the lowest, scariest sound I've ever heard.

Walter jumps up from the grass and sprints over to the tree, his hands curled into fists.

My stomach drops. Okay, I did not mean for this. Erik is awful, but that doesn't mean I want a couple of trolls to pull him apart like he's a chicken wing.

Yes, I do look good in black and I could definitely work the whole widow thing, but we still have to get the spell book to the secured facility to keep it out of the Council's hands, and I can't do that without him. I have an obligation to get that book back.

And that's why I am hustling across the clearing to stand between Erik and the two trolls who are already gnashing their teeth.

"Okay, I hate to be this person," I say, putting as much Sherwood heir ice into my tone as I can muster, "but you did make the rules, and Erik stuck to them." Frieda lets out another growl. "However, just so everyone walks away happy"—and alive—"how about if I spell one wish for each of you. Right here. Right now. No hesitation."

"What," Frieda says, not sounding mollified at all, "like you're going to give me my dream fruit and veggie garden that never stops growing even in the winter?"

"Done."

I wiggle my fingers, and the smell of warm cake donuts fills the air, and then a troll-sized container garden of tomatoes and zucchinis and cucumbers and potatoes and carrots, watermelon and peppers of nearly every variety, shape, and color appear next to their absolutely adorable house.

The troll claps her large hands together and, giggling with glee, takes off for the garden, the ground shaking underneath her feet.

I turn to Walter, who has a pink tinge to his cheeks and is nudging a massive blackberry bush with his foot.

"I've always wanted a puppy," Walter says, his voice quiet. "But they're just usually so scared of me that I gave up. It sure would be nice to have a dog come on my walks through the woods with me when Frieda doesn't want to."

Okay. That one makes me a little sniffly, but I blink back

the sudden wetness in my eyes, wiggle my fingers, and an Irish wolfhound puppy appears next to Walter. The dog is shaggy as can be and its paws are the size of dinner plates.

Walter sinks to his knees and the puppy gallops over to him, not in the least bit frightened. The dog yaps happily and licks the troll's face as he laughs.

And then it's my turn to have my biggest wish fulfilled.

And it is.

It really, really, really is—because it has to be.

I flick my wrist and a copy of the dimitto spell appears out of thin air and flits this way and that as it slowly sinks to the ground in front of Erik. Like before, when I sent the spell to him via flying monkeys, all he needs to do is chant his lines, and poof, we're divorced. His post-win grin doesn't flicker as he picks up the spell I spent the past three months weaving.

"It *is* what we agreed to," I say, surprised my voice isn't shaking with nerves as I remind myself over and over that this is what I want.

"Absolutely." He glances around at the clearing and points to a small hill at the other end. "That seems like the best place to do this, don't you think? And you know, if divorce means you can't take The Liber Umbrarum to the secured facility with me, that's okay. I promise you can trust me to get it there without me using any of the spells in it for my own benefit."

For a second his words don't click, and then his Svensen duplicity reveals itself like a zombie hand popping out of the ground on All Hallow's Eve. Fury blasts through me like a wind gust from the sun.

That.

Low.

Down.

Dirty.

Husband.

Of.

Mine.

That whole time while I was setting up the race so we could, you know, get out of here right away and therefore keep The Liber Umbrarum out of the Council's hands and save Witchingdom, he was working out a loophole that *only* benefited him.

I really should have just let the trolls turn him into toothpicks.

Chapter Twenty-Three

Erik . . .

LeLe is definitely going through a mental list of murder spells right now. Maybe some gelding spells too.

Yeah, this might be the end of me, but getting to see her go all evil adjacent without even realizing it while setting up that race was pretty fucking hot. Then watching her fight to keep her cool when all she wanted to do was fillet me was melt-your-brain sexy. Add in the fact that she always knew how to use those perfect pink lips of hers to say just the right thing at the right moment? Sexy redheads that are occasionally evil adjacent, have iron wills, and are excellent purveyors of competency porn is definitely my kink.

Don't make that face. It's not like your turn-ons are all one hundred percent non-weird either.

"We cannot get to the secured facility fast enough," LeLe says through gritted teeth. "We. Are. Leaving."

I want nothing more than to pull her close and kiss her breathless again, but I have to satisfy myself with watching her hips sway as she marches over to Frieda and Walter to say goodbye. I'm a risk-taker, but not a complete idiot. The woman really is slicing and dicing me in her head, The Liber Umbrarum and Witchingdom be damned.

So I make the smart move and don't move at all.

"Can't wait to get back on the road with you either, wife."

Okay, fine, my mouth moved. Sue me.

LeLe's only response is to raise her right arm straight up in the sky and flip me off.

Damn, that is one hot witch who knows how to keep a man on his toes.

Take this morning, for instance. I knew the moment I woke up that there would probably be some pushback on last night. I could have forged ahead, or I could accept her mood and figure out how to work around it—a decision that took all of two seconds to make. One thing growing up Svensen teaches you is to always be moving. Why? Because a moving target is harder to hit, and more importantly, as long as you're moving, you have time to find a loophole. Sitting back and waiting for things to happen to you is for suckers. So, I played LeLe's game, and while she was manipulating Frieda and Walter into gaining our freedom, I used her distraction to my advantage to get what I wanted—her.

The fate of Witchingdom doesn't mean shit to me, but

staying married long enough to inherit my family power so I can get Cy and Sigrid away from the Svensen shitty influence? That's all that matters.

And if I keep repeating that to myself, I will block out the little voice in my head saying some really stupid shit about finding a loophole that will keep LeLe from getting hurt in the process.

Sure, that would be nice, but come on, we all know this is going to end ugly. I told you from the beginning that I'm not the good guy. I look out for mine and that's it. The rest of Witchingdom—including my dad—can sit and spin.

Speaking of the world's worst DNA donor, my phone vibrates in my pocket. It *could* be Cy or Sigrid, but it's not. I swear the buzz is different—angrier, nastier—when he is calling.

I pull out my phone and, no shock at all, it's dear old Dad. "Father."

"What is taking you so long?" he snarls. "Can't you get one stick-up-her-ass girl to fall for you? Do I need to do this myself? The Sherwoods gave us the perfect opportunity when they stole The Liber Umbrarum from us, and we're going to seize it and kill two birds with one weird-eyed witch."

He is definitely a shit father, but he's damn good at pivoting when he has to. The second he realized the Sherwoods were the ones who took The Liber Umbrarum, he knew the Council would assume they'd keep possession of it and stalk them for it. Meanwhile, he'd have it in the family's secured facility and without the Council being any the wiser could carry on with the original plan to sell it off spell by spell to the highest bidder—minus the iron to gold alchemy spell that hadn't worked and had given Dad a third nipple. That was bird one.

Bird two? The family debt that would be erased by the access to the Sherwood money. Dad would drain them dry as fast as he'd done my mother's family's bank accounts—at least that's what he assumed. I wasn't so sure it would work that easy with the Sherwoods even before I met LeLe. Afterward? My chips are all in on her winning that hand.

"You there, boy?" my father bit out. "Or am I talking to an even dumber witch than I sired?"

The edges of my phone bite into my palm because I'm gripping it so tight. Usually I'm better prepared for my father's vitriol, but being around LeLe and the lack of constant cruelty is making me soft.

My jaw is clamped tight enough to crack a molar, but otherwise I manage to keep my reaction on lockdown. What he wants is to get me to explode. It's what brings him joy. The fact that I know he's doing it to provoke only makes it sweeter for him if I break. So I don't.

"I have everything under control," I say, managing to keep the fuck-you out of my tone.

Dad goes on as if I hadn't said a thing. "Technically your mother and I are still married, but no one's seen her for decades. You can do the same with the Sherwood heir. They'll just assume she's dead or something."

Red swirls on the edges of my vision.

Or something.

I close my eyes and let all that dark nothing fill me. "I said I've got it."

"You better, boy," he says, his words sharp. "The Council has already been through here looking for you and The Liber Umbrarum. It would break my heart to have to sacrifice my heir to them in order to keep the family safe."

I don't bother to hold in my laugh at that ridiculousness because by "family" he only means himself. Never mind that I filched The Liber Umbrarum in the first place because he ordered it. Supposedly he'd had a fence who'd sell it, but they decided it was too hot and reneged on the deal.

I glance over at Bessie's bright yellow tail fin, the only part of her I can see from here, and let my magic reach out to push against the protective wards I put on the car, letting out a breath when I can feel them still in place.

"Like you," I tell my dad, "I am devoted to doing the best thing for the Svensen family."

"Then marry the fucking ginger twat and bring home her money and family protection before she meets with a horrible and very convenient accident, or I don't know what choices I'll be forced to make concerning your siblings," he says, and then hangs up.

No, his threat wasn't specific, but it didn't need to be and he knew it.

I could stand here and stew about what a giant asshole he is, but that isn't going to get me anywhere. I have to keep moving. I follow LeLe's lead and go say goodbye to the trolls.

They've already given LeLe a basket of food from the new garden to eat on the road.

LeLe is still pissed enough to not even look in my direction as we walk with the trolls—as much as physically possible considering the size difference—to Bessie, where she's parked just off the two-lane road. We're almost to the car when a bone-chilling wind whips through the trees on either side of the highway.

The birds go silent.

The deer scatter.

Every single squirrel that had been gathering acorns on the forest floor scurries into the closest hiding spot.

Every oh-fuck nerve in my body goes on instant alert.

"Get in the car, LeLe."

She shoots me a questioning look and starts to open her mouth, no doubt to tell me off, when a low hum reverberates through the air.

All four of us look east to where the highway rises up with the land and then dips down and disappears. The air starts to waver at the top of the crest of the hill, and another icy blast of wind—the Council's calling card—blows through.

"We gotta go," I say, yanking open Bessie's driver's side door and ushering LeLe in, following behind as she scoots across the bench seat.

Bessie starts on the first try, and I let out a breath I didn't realize I was holding.

"I really hate those assholes," Frieda says, glaring at the shimmering air in the distance.

Walter grunts in agreement.

"Go back through the woods the way we came," Frieda says. "Follow the clearing under the overpass and take it past the cornfields. It meets up with the highway again, but you'll have at least ten miles between you and these goons."

Walter fishes a glass Mason jar out of his front overalls pocket. It's labeled "Extra Hard Riddles." "We'll buy you some extra time with one of these," he says. "Everyone has to stop for us, and these idiots take forever to solve a simple riddle; they'll be here for a lot longer trying to figure out one of these."

Their behavior is making my head ache because it doesn't make sense. They're not going to get anything out of helping a pair of virtual strangers avoid the Council. In fact, it's far more likely they end up paying for it. Yet here they are, grinning at the approaching air waver that always precedes the Council enforcer's arrival as if they can't wait.

Frieda and Walter wouldn't make it a day in the Svensen compound.

When I put the car in gear and we start down the path, LeLe twists in her seat and rises up on her knees to wave goodbye.

Then she hollers out, "So what does disappear as soon as you say its name?"

"Silence," Frieda and Walter answer at the same time.

LeLe gives them one more wave and then sits back down, a determined look on her face.

The chances are slim to none that this plan to ditch the Council works, but it's the best we've got, so I hit the gas and

Bessie speeds down the path, kicking up a cloud of dust in our wake.

The dirt path twists and turns and is pockmarked with holes where rain and wear have washed the ground away. I should have both hands on Bessie's wheel, but instead I reach over and rest my palm on the seat between us right next to LeLe's. She glances down at it and then returns her focus to the path ahead as we speed through the forest.

"I'm still mad at you," she says, not looking over at me.

But she takes my hand anyway, and I get the oddest feeling in my chest. It's tight and fizzy and completely unfamiliar.

I can't explain it.

I can't identify it.

But I'm holding on to it just the same.

Chapter Twenty-Four

Leona . . .

Sure, we're both riding high on adrenaline when we finally pull out onto the highway after racing down Witchingdom's bumpiest dirt road, but that doesn't explain why I'm still holding Erik's hand.

Sure, he's got great hands. Strong and slightly calloused, they aren't the hands you'd expect from someone whose last name is Svensen and who gets by in life by doing the least amount of honest work—or anything else—ever.

I'm not saying my extra hand-holding means I'm wrong about him.

That crap he pulled about the dimitto spell after the race pretty much proves that society and I are right about him—but maybe we're not *all* the way right.

And the fact that I'm even considering that possibility means I'm in so much trouble.

Also? I'm still holding his hand.

Erik breaks the silence after an hour on the road with no sign of the Council's goons. "We're not going to be able to get to the secured facility on schedule."

That tingling rushing through my body at his announcement? It's not excitement or happiness or va-va-voom anticipation. It's disappointment—major disappointment.

"But you said we would," I say, while not staring at our joined hands.

"That was before we took a detour through the woods and ended up off course." He checks the rearview mirror for the billionth time. "We have to find a room for the night."

I pull my hand out of his and straighten my spine, pulling up my best ice princess attitude from wherever it hides when I'm around Erik. "Two rooms for the night."

"Whatever you say, wife," Erik says with a grin as he leaves his hand right where it was next to me, palm up, just waiting for me to reach out.

I clasp my hands together on my lap and focus all my attention on Bessie's side mirror, watching for sights of the Council. I don't even notice how close his fingers are to my thigh.

It's nearly dark when we pull into the parking lot of The Nysa Inn on the edge of a small town that's so quiet it's like they've already rolled up the sidewalks for the night. The inn is a four-story neoclassical limestone mansion with a red tile roof that looks like it's from the early 1900s. There is a massive two-story front porch and balconies that wrap around the third floor. In front of the steps leading to the porch is a Greek statue of a man holding a bunch of grapes and a wood sign that says "Vacancy" in fancy script.

Erik puts Bessie in park but doesn't cut the engine. "What do you think?"

"It's gorgeous." Just looking at the place makes my shoulders a little lighter and my mood a little mellower.

He rests his head against the leather seat and lets out a tired sigh. "So that's a yes, we stay the night here?"

Guilt gets me right in the chest for not stopping earlier when he had to have gotten exhausted hours ago. Long-haul driving is about as tired as you can get just sitting on your butt.

"Yeah." I give his hand a quick squeeze and then open my door and get out before I'm tempted to hang on. "Let's go check in."

He turns off the engine and does a quick protection spell to reenergize the car's protective wards. Then we get our "Mr." and "Mrs." suitcases out of the trunk—once again Erik ignores my logical point that I can carry my own bag—and we climb the stairs and walk through the massive wood doors decorated with intricate carvings of flutes and wine goblets.

We make it two steps inside before we both stop to take it all in.

In the center of the inn's huge foyer is a large round fountain, big enough to host a small pool party. Surrounding it is an oasis filled with broad-leafed plants next to detailed statues of people embracing. Wide chaises upholstered in velvets of deep plum and gold are scattered about, and the walls are decorated with oversized oil paintings showing off revelers celebrating on lush green hillsides. Dotted around the circular foyer are small but sturdy tables of various shapes that all stand about hip-high, topped with bowls of figs, plates of oysters, towers made up entirely of chocolate squares, and baskets of scones accompanied by little jars of strawberry jam. The ceiling is open all the way up to the fourth floor, and while the air isn't perfumed, there is a hint of the woody, sweet, earthy scent of musk and ambergris teasing my senses.

"Wow," Erik says.

I've never agreed with him more.

I'm still gawking at it all when the bearded innkeeper walks through an arched doorway holding a tray bearing two glasses and an unopened bottle of red wine. The innkeeper is wearing a loose hooded kaftan of a gauzy, flowy material that looks light enough to feel like nothing at all. It's sexy and comfortable and easy all at once.

What I wouldn't give to swap outfits. Well, maybe not trade. After spending the past twenty-four hours in the same clothes, the material is a wrinkly mess and starting to smell a little ripe. No one should have to put my outfit on, and honestly, I cannot wait to take it off.

However, the idea of slipping on the kaftan—and only the kaftan—after a long, hot shower and then lounging on a chaise eating strawberry jam–covered scones and drinking wine floats into my thoughts like a feather on the wind. I'm about to ask if they sell the kaftan here in town or if the inn carries extras for guests when the innkeeper smiles at us and gives us a devilish wink.

"Welcome to The Nysa Inn. I'm Silenus, but everyone calls me Sil, and I go by they/them pronouns," they say as they set down the tray with a flourish. "You must be tired; please enjoy refreshments on the house while we get you checked in."

They wave their hand and the bottle goes up into the air, the cork pops out, and then it tips over, letting the wine flow into the two glasses, which rise up from the table and drift over to us without spilling a single drop.

"You weren't expecting us, were you?" Erik asks as he sets our suitcases down.

"No, but I can pretend to if that works better for you two," they say as they press a button hidden under the table. The sound of a jaunty melody played on a flute comes out of speakers that must be hidden among all the greenery. "Or are you expecting another or more who should have alerted me to your arrival?"

"It's just us," I say as two burly, bare-chested assistants in voluminous pants made out of the same material as the kaftan come through another doorway.

They strut over to our suitcases, each step easy and confident, and each take one bag and look back over at us. Muscular in the thick way of a lumberjack or one of those men who participate in the strong witch competitions, they watch me with unabated interest. It's the same look they give Erik and the innkeeper and maybe even the statue of a group of frolicking water nymphs in the middle of the fountain.

Erik lays his palm on the small of my back, sending a hot sizzle of desire across my skin, as we follow the innkeeper to a square table near a marble statue of a man in a low-dropped toga holding a wine goblet. That reminds me I'm holding a glass of wine, and I take a sip. Even if I wanted to, I couldn't hold back my groan of appreciation at the taste of ripe strawberries, raspberries, and black cherries. It's absolutely delicious.

Sil gives me a smile of approval.

"Once this tantalizing couple is all checked in, please take them to the Barberini suite," they say as they take Erik's credit card and input the information into a computer that had been hidden behind a voluptuously-leafed lemon balm plant.

"We need two bedrooms," Erik says, putting in the request before I can remember I'd insisted on it.

"Not a problem," the innkeeper says. "The suite has two bedrooms, a large bathing area, and a lounge area where you can recuperate as needed. I believe you'll both enjoy your stay immensely." The innkeeper snaps his fingers and a leather-bound guestbook appears. He opens it and holds out a fountain pen that looks like it was carved into a grapevine. "If you'll just sign here, you'll be all checked in. Cissus and Orestes will show you to your two-room suite."

I sign my name in gold ink and hand the pen to Erik, who does the same.

"Thank you so much," I say, noticing for the first time the hint of curled horns underneath the innkeeper's hood.

"Of course. At The Nysa Inn, our only goal is to ensure you

have a wonderful time. If there is anything you want during your stay, all you need to do is ring this bell and whatever you desire will be yours."

Erik offers up a thanks and takes my hand, intertwining his fingers with mine as we walk through the foyer to the winding staircase that I swear wasn't here moments ago. All the stress of being chased by the Council and the exhaustion of driving hundreds of miles must be getting to me, because as we go up the stairs, I swear the gold figures of witches, gnomes, pixies, trolls, and more on the dark purple wallpaper turn their heads and watch us. If that was actually happening, you can bet I would be freaked out. However, I'm as relaxed as I've ever been as we climb upward. By the time we're on the last set of stairs to the fourth floor, the figures no longer seem to be watching but have gone back to doing other things, which I realize as I look closer all involve sexual activities.

I'm gonna be truthful here. I'm not sure the staring or the fucking is more disturbing or fascinating or inspiring. Yeah, I don't know how to respond to that either.

We follow the bellhops to the double doors at the end of the hall. They open the doors and place our suitcases just inside before stepping back out.

"Is there a key?" I ask because I didn't notice a keypad outside or any kind of lock on the door.

"No need," one of the bellhops says, his voice thick and sweet like warm honey. "No one can or would ever violate your boundaries at the inn."

Then he closes the doors with a firm click. Still holding

Erik's hand (I'll let go eventually), I turn around to take in what Sil described as the suite's lounge room to recuperate. My breath catches.

I've seen a lot of things in my life. Witchingdom is as deep as it is wide when it comes to creatures, people, and tastes. However, I've never seen anything like the Barberini suite.

The same interior decorator who designed the foyer worked their magic in this suite too. The color scheme is all dark greens and blues with touches of gold and dark walnut giving it a luxurious vibe. There are a trio of low backless couches with cushiony, rounded armrests at each end that form a spacious triangle around the room. Piles of oversized jewel-colored pillows are artfully scattered about the floor. In the middle of the room is a life-sized marble statue of a man—no, a faun—with thick, curly hair and beefy muscles. He's lounging on a chair with his eyes closed, an arm bent behind his head, and one hand wrapped around the thick girth of his cock, the muscles of his forearm straining with activity. His bare legs are splayed open, one leg draped over the chair's arm and a foot next to a floor cushion that still has divots in it from where someone had been kneeling. It is immediately apparent that the artist had been very devoted to their craft—and the model for this statue.

Letting go of Erik's hand, I take a few steps forward to get a better look at the faun and realize it's not the only statue in the room. The rest are displayed on shelves or in decorative nooks. Like the faun, they are highly detailed with loving devotion paid to what they're packing between their legs. I'll have to tell Effie all about the decor next time we talk. She's going to want to book this room for sure.

In addition to the solitary statues, there are paintings depicting fauns and humans and witches and shifters and vampires and gnomes and pixies and trolls and even hippocamps in every sort of combination engaged in any sexual practice you could imagine and a few I never had and really want to think about in depth next time I am alone with twenty minutes to spare.

"They're satyrs," Erik says, his voice low and rough as he comes up behind me and rests one hand on my hip. "The *Nysa* Inn? I should have realized."

I'm trying to think about that revelation while I'm being bombarded with a million sensations from Erik. The light yet possessive feel of his fingers on my hip. The way he almost but doesn't quite brush up against my ass. The wisp of his words brushing against my neck. The fact that my clothes don't feel right being on my body anymore. The tension in my scalp from having my hair pulled back into a too-tight ponytail. All of it is almost more than I can or want to stand.

"I thought they only acted as matchmakers for profit," I say, knowing I should put some distance between us even as I don't move an inch. "Did you slip Sil money?"

"We are already married, wife." Erik chuckles as he glides his hand from my hip across my stomach, his fingers spread wide across the thin cotton. "There's nothing to matchmake between us."

When did him calling me "wife" start sounding so good? I don't know, and I can't think about that right now. I really can't think about much. Not when the air is so thick with want and need and gotta have that it's nearly impossible to breathe. I don't plan to step back, but I do. His hard cock presses against the top of my ass and a shiver of anticipation goes through me.

Erik lets out a harsh hiss of breath and his body tenses behind mine. "I need to go to my room."

"You've got to be tired after everything," I say as I take his free arm and wrap it around me too because the urge to be totally surrounded by him isn't a want, it's a need.

He groans, and it's the sound of someone trying—maybe for the first time—to do the right thing even though it's wrong.

"Not in the least. I feel fucking fantastic, that's the problem." He tightens his hold on me, locking me in place as he dips his head so his lips are only millimeters from my ear and says, "You're right that the satyrs matchmake for money, but what do they do for fun?"

I bite down on my lip and give in to the urge to relax against his hard chest. "Orgies."

"And?" He kisses the spot behind my earlobe.

It's not fair that he knows just what to do to make me feel this good, to make me forget everything else but him. I am the Sherwood heir. I don't get to have who I want. I—

"Oh shit," I gasp as my heart races. "The inn is covered by Nullam Inhibitionis."

"That's right." Erik nods, the day-old scruff on his chin grazing my neck and making my breath catch. "The spell guarantees nothing you don't want and everything you do without fear of consequences or judgment or others' expectations. It's just you and what you really want deep in your heart."

Tempting doesn't even begin to cover the possibilities. Under every satyr's roof, the Nullam Inhibitionis spell is sacred in Witchingdom, protecting everyone and granting them their lusty desires. It's not that it makes you do anything—it definitely doesn't. It's just that it gives you permission to allow yourself to have what you want. It's freedom. It's safety. It's letting go of everything outside the front doors.

In a lot of ways, it's beyond my comprehension and an opportunity that is completely overwhelming. So I retreat back to what I know, my role as the heir only concerned with my family.

"What I want doesn't matter," I mean to sound firm, but it comes out as a wavering whisper.

"It does here," Erik says, letting me go and putting a sliver of space between us. "It does with me. So tell me, LeLe, do you want me to say good night now and then disappear alone behind that bedroom door, or do you want me to stay?"

Chapter Twenty-Five

Erik . . .

*J*ust having that inch of air between us is fucking killing me. Unlike her usually put-together self, LeLe is all unwound. Her red hair is coming loose from her ponytail and the humidity has curled some of the loose strands at her nape. There are a few small pieces of leaves caught in the weave of the torturously thin green sweater she's wearing, the one that doesn't hide just how hard her nipples are right now. I wish there was something off about her jeans, some reason why I should recommend she get rid of them, but they are as perfect as the round ass they're covering. There's not a stain from a drop of her ice cream. There's not a smudge of dirt from our wild drive through the woods. There's not a snag from sleeping on the trolls' platform in the sky. And that perfect denim is the exception that proves the rule that Leona Sherwood is—maybe for the first time ever—letting herself go.

Her plushy curves fitting against me like this is just what should happen naturally every time we're together. The mix of hard and soft, good and bad, anticipation and satisfaction—the perfect combination.

"Is all of this some kind of spell?" she asks without turning around, sounding like a woman fighting against what should happen and what she wants to happen. "Is it magic making me feel like this?"

"It's worse, because Nullam Inhibitionis isn't a spell at all. It's a sacred treaty between the satyrs and the rest of Witchingdom guaranteeing that in their spaces, the only thing that matters is what you want." Giving in to that near-constant urge to touch her, I curl one of the spiraling wisps of loose hair around my finger, tightening just enough that LeLe can't hold in her soft moan of pleasure. "It's not a spell. It's freedom. This is just us with our layers of responsibilities, obligations, and inhibitions loosened."

"More like unbuttoned, half off, and slipping down quick," LeLe says as she melts back against me. "I shouldn't want this."

That makes two of us. It'll only be harder to do what I know needs to be done at the power exchange ceremony and betray her if I give in to this feeling to hold her, protect her, make her feel good any way I can. I'd fight it if I could, but I can't. No. That's a lie I can't even tell myself. I don't want to fight it. I want to give in. I want LeLe to give in. I want us to be in our world, not the one outside.

I want it all.

And unlike LeLe, I'm not above being selfish. I'm gonna tease and tempt to get my way, to make her want me as much as I've wanted her since the first moment I saw her at the hotel pool.

Yeah, I'm a bastard and I don't care.

"So I shouldn't do this." I reach around and slip a hand underneath the hem of her soft sweater. Her quiet exhale nearly undoes me. "And you don't want me to do this." Light, so fucking light it nearly kills me, I trail my fingers over the rise of her belly, up toward the valley between her heavy tits as she rocks her ass against me. "And this"—I slide my fingers under the cup of her bra, and the air around us begins to spark as I roll her nipple between my finger and thumb—"is definitely a non-starter."

Her only answer is a needy moan as her eyelids flutter shut.

Watching her face in the huge mirror across the room as I pinch and tug her nipple is almost more than I can take, especially when my dick is pressed against her full ass. Her lips are parted slightly and her eyes are closed as she lets the sweetest, hungriest, most desperate sounds escape.

"I don't think Leona Sherwood is allowed to make that sound. She has to just close her eyes and think of Witchingdom." I pull her nipple almost too hard, and she melts into me with a lusty sigh of pleasure that goes straight to my aching dick. "But you're not just the Sherwood heir tonight." I need to hear her make that sound again, the one that says all she can think about is us, so I tighten my arm around her waist, locking her in place against me in a firm hold she could break with a whisper, but she doesn't. "*Who* are you?"

"LeLe," she says, her name riding the wave of that needy moan.

"So close, but not quite," I murmur as the ribbon of control starts to slip through my hands, and there's nothing gentle about the way I'm holding her against me. "Let's try it again. Who are you tonight?"

She rocks her ass against my hard cock and starts to repeat, "Le—"

I stop toying with her nipple.

I loosen my hold around her waist.

I'm nearly wild with this need I can't explain, this have-to-have that overwhelms almost everything else. I'm ready to roar, to demand, to insist; it's building up in me, rushing to the surface like an epic wave that will wash away half the earth, but when I open my mouth, what comes out isn't any of that.

"Tonight, LeLe," I say, the raw request giving her an exact map to deliver a death blow—something a lifetime of experience as a Svensen taught me to never *ever* do. "Who are you *just for tonight*?"

Empires rise and fall in the silence as it stretches and winds around us until it is squeezing me so tight I couldn't move even if I wanted to—which I don't. Ever. I can stay like this for as long as it takes.

Without meaning to, I let the question slip out again, a bare whisper that's nothing more than a live wire of desperate want. "Who are you?"

"Wife," she says without hesitation.

The last threads of control slip past my fingers and I don't even try to hold on.

I spin her around and my mouth comes crashing down on hers. I want to imprint this night on her, make it part of who she is so that later, when she hates me again, when she wants nothing more than to see me banished to The Beyond or—more probably—from existence completely, she still remembers tonight.

And I'll remember it all. The way she fits against me. The way she's just as demanding as I am when she kisses me back. How she buries her fingers in my hair and tugs to force me closer and holds me there—as if she needs to.

"Erik," she says, coming up for air from that kiss that has both of us breathless. "I want you to stay."

If I wasn't so fucking hard, I would melt with relief. "Whatever you want, wife."

Her fingers are on the hem of my sweater, just resting there, as if she's still making up her mind deciding if I'm worthy. I already know the answer to that, and I'm more than half tempted to magic all our clothes off with a quick spell to distract her from the truth—but like always, LeLe is one step ahead of me.

One soft whisper from her and my sweater is gone. "This doesn't change anything," she says as she traces her fingertips across my chest, setting off a literal line of sparks in their wake as the scent of our magic mixing together begins to fill the air. "Tonight is tonight. When we leave the inn tomorrow, it's back to who we are on the outside."

Done fighting the urge to touch her, I tuck a strand of her silky hair behind her ear, relishing the way her eyes darken with lust even from this small gesture. "What, me being my usual bad self and you only being evil adjacent?"

Both of her eyebrows go up. "Excuse me?"

"You, LeLe Sherwood Svensen," I say, marveling at how she can even make my last name seem like something good, "are a naughty girl surrounded by nice-girl wrapping."

"I am not," she says, the flick of her gaze down to the floor giving away the fact that even she doesn't fully believe her words.

"So how do you explain what happened with the trolls?" I ask, fighting the urge to kiss that knowing almost-smile of hers. "You set that race's rules up with loopholes you knew I could make my way through blindfolded."

"Don't forget it was to trap you into completing the dimitto spell," she says, her full cheeks turning pink.

"And yet you didn't hold me to it." I lean in a little bit closer, unable to stop myself from teasing her just to see her pretend not to be affected. "Doth the heir protest too much?"

She shrugs one shoulder with practiced indifference. "That was just smart maneuvering."

"You mean manipulation." I put my knuckle under her chin and tilt her face up. "It's okay to be a little bad, wife." I drag the pad of my thumb over her bottom lip, leaving it to rest there. "You don't have to pretend with me."

"I don't, huh?" she asks before nipping my thumb and then kissing it all better.

"No." Even with the brush of her lips, the sting of her bite and the look in her eyes promising trouble goes straight to my aching dick. "You can let that evil-adjacent witch come out and play tonight. Put your wants first for once."

She takes a step back and looks me up and down. One side of her mouth goes up in a smirk almost as dangerous as the look in her eyes. The air sizzles around us, and I have half a second of oh-shit-what-have-I-unleashed hesitation before the scent of coffee swirls around me. LeLe's magic surrounds me, touching and caressing as it lifts me from the floor, and when I come back down across the room, it's without my clothes in front of a mirror that takes up half the wall.

She strides toward me, her hips swaying with each step. "I'm going to arrange you just how I want, and then . . ." She pauses for a second to give me a confident, sexy smile. "I'm going to do just what I want with you, so don't move unless I tell you to."

A soft gust of her magic presses me back into a wooden chair softened with cushioned velvet. She stops by one of the chaise lounges, her fingers trailing over the small pillows on it, and doesn't even look over at me as she says, "Your leg."

I'm trying to work out what she means when she finally picks out a pillow and slides her finger over the silk brocade pattern before it disappears. A second later it reappears at my feet and I understand.

I relax back into the chair, letting my butt slide to the edge of the cushion before lifting my leg and positioning it so it hangs over the arm of my chair. I put one arm behind my head and wrap a hand around my cock, which might as well be made of stone by this point. The last thing I see before my eyelids close is LeLe's clothes falling away as she walks over to me. The air shifts when she stops in front of me and every single nerve in my body is focused on my wife, the anticipation of what she is going to do next burning inside me like a breath I can't exhale. Then her hand is on my splayed leg, pushing it open wider.

Maybe it's my horny imagination, maybe it's the magic thick in the air around us, but I swear I can feel the heat coming off her full, pillowy tits on my cheeks as she leans over me. It's taking everything I have to stay still with my eyes closed so she can arrange me just the way she wants.

Then she's gone, standing close enough that even with my eyes closed I can feel her presence, but too far away for me to feel the heat from her body or smell the sweet scent of her arousal. The loss has me wanting to squirm in my seat, open my eyes, search to the ends of the earth for her—my muscles tense, but I manage—just barely—to be still.

"Oh, Erik," she says, her sexy, teasing tone tempting my resolve. "You're very good for being so bad, Erik."

"You could say I'm properly motivated not to move." Even though staying like this just might kill me.

"But for how long before you break?"

"I could stay forever for you." Lie? Me? Yeah, it's kind of what I was raised to do.

"Pretty to think so," LeLe says, "but let's test that theory."

The magic crackles the air between us as I fight to keep my

eyes closed even as I feel the strands of her red hair brush against my inner thigh, meaning she's settled down between my legs. Is she kneeling on the pillow? Is she reaching down to stroke that swollen wet clit of hers? Is she tweaking her nipples, pleasuring herself, as the torture of not being able to watch her makes a bead of the pre-cum pooling on the tip of my aching cock slide down the shaft?

"Now that's a sight I'm going to remember when this is all over," she says, her voice thick with desire. "I could just lick that right up."

I'm all for that, but LeLe has other plans. The hard edge of her fingernails press against the sensitive skin of my inner thigh close enough to my balls to send a breath-catching shock of pleasure straight through my whole body like a lightning bolt of fuck-yeah. I let out a gasp of surprise half a second before her soft mouth comes down on that very spot and my shock turns into a harsh groan of barely controlled want. Forget just moving my leg or twitching my shoulder, I'm literal heartbeats away from breaking. I'm already mentally throwing her over my shoulder and taking her to one of the beds so I can taste just how wet she is and make her as desperate as she's making me when she cups my balls. All sense of time, place, and self fade away as she squeezes and rolls them, all while resting her cheek against my inner thigh so close to the action that her breath is tickling my dick.

There's a fine line between letting go in the moment and losing your fucking mind, and I'm right there. My grip on the base of my cock is so tight at this point that under normal circumstances I'd be worried about doing damage. But these aren't normal circumstances.

She may not realize it, but my LeLe put a spell on me in Vegas that's only grown in strength since then. And fool that I am, I don't want to counter it or fight against it. All I want is to go where she's taking us while pretending tonight will never end—that's my Nullam Inhibitionis.

Chapter Twenty-Six

Leona . . .

*E*vil adjacent?

Erik couldn't be more wrong about me on that point, but I have to say it's fun pretending. The man is so close to snapping. The muscles in his thighs strain with the effort not to move. And when I tilt my head just enough that my eyelashes brush against the skin of his inner thigh while breathing a little more, let's say, emphatically than normal so that he feels it exactly where I want him to? It's a thing of absolute beauty.

Maybe I am kind of adjacent to adjacent to being evil adjacent. I'd label it as being bad in a good way—and the power of it is delicious.

I bend one finger and drag the knuckle up Erik's thick

shaft, following the line of pre-cum to the swollen head. The sound he makes—half groan, half muttered plea to stop or keep going, I can't quite make it out—makes my core clench.

Fine. I'll go as far as saying I'm adjacent to being evil adjacent. After all, we Sherwoods didn't become the deciding influence on governments and markets by being nice all the time.

"You win," he says.

"What was that?" I ask as if I hadn't heard him correctly.

"You heard me."

"But I want to hear it again."

He smolders down at me. "You. Win."

They are two of my favorite words in the English language already, but coming from Erik Svensen, the man who's been the bane of my existence since I foolhardily married him? There really is nothing better—not that I'm going to let him go so easily.

I give his thigh another soft kiss and stand up so I'm looking down at him as he sits. He still has one leg splayed open, the other draped over the chair's arm, and one hand wrapped around his cock. I was so wrong. Erik doesn't look like a guy who just lost, not even close.

Matching his smug attitude, I cross my arms under my boobs to give the girls a little lift and ask, "So what's my prize?"

If I'd expected the answer in word form, I would have been sorely disappointed. Lucky me, Erik doesn't blather on about the bizarre attractiveness of my two-colored eyes or the way my hair is so bright it looks like a chemical fire at sunset, or that all my curves give so much more cushion (yes, I've heard each one of those before and worse). Instead, he moves so fast I would swear he's part vampire. One moment he's lounging in the chair and the next he is standing with his hands on my hips and whirling me around. I land with a soft thwump, sitting on the smooth velvet chair cushion, my brain trying to catch up with my body. Before it can, his hands are on my thighs, pushing them apart as he drops to his knees on the floor pillow. Then he slides his hands around to my ass and tugs me to the edge of the chair so my more-than-ready center is just millimeters away from his very talented mouth.

"I should torture you like you did me."

"That doesn't sound like much of a reward for me."

"So you just want all the orgasms right now?"

"Yes."

"No waiting? . . . No buildup? . . . No sweet, delicious anticipation?"

"Exactly." I run my fingers through his hair, tugging just enough to make his jaw tighten with the effort it must be costing him to tease me like this. "You think you can make that happen?"

"Wife," he says with a grin, "you know I can."

He barely has the words out before his face is buried in my wet core, taking slow, deliberately maddening licks that come oh-so-close to my clit without ever touching it. If it were any other man, I'd magic him up a map, but I know this is just payback from Erik. Oh, he'll give me the orgasms—probably more than I can take—but first he's going to make me really, really want them.

"You taste so good." He takes another long swipe with his tongue, the tip just barely brushing my clit and making my whole body tense. "You like that, huh?"

As if he doesn't know—which is exactly what I would have told him if he hadn't followed up by doing it again and again and again before changing tactics and swirling his tongue around my clit in lazy circles as I make sounds I don't recognize.

"What was that?" He rolls back onto his heels and looks up at me, his mouth slick with my pleasure. "I didn't quite catch it."

I open my mouth to answer, but on the next heartbeat I'm floating, not too high—there's only a few inches between my bare ass and the velvet cushion—but it's enough to bring me mouth level with Erik. Not that the damn man uses his mouth. No, that would be too expected, and Erik is anything but.

Instead it's his thumb pressing against my opening, rubbing the sensitive entrance and then moving up and down along my slit, taking the time to press against the side of my clit once, twice, three times before going back and starting the whole process over again. My thighs are starting to shake as the pleasure pulses in my core, but I can't stop watching him as he plays with me. The expression of absolute fucking promise on his face as he sees what he's doing to me, how his touch pushes me closer and closer, just adds to the hedonistic thrill of the moment. Here we are in a satyr's orgy room, surrounded by sex everywhere we turn and the scent of our magic combining, and all I can see is Erik just living for the moment when my orgasm hits. It's not because he wants to get that done so he can get his or because of some weird power trip, but because it's plain as the thin, pale scar on his chin that he just wants me to feel good. The realization hits like a mini orgasm, and Erik must take this as his cue to lean in and get his whole mouth in on the action. My ass is in the air and I'm gripping the carved ends of the chair's arms like they're the only thing keeping me from flying into the atmosphere, and he continues to feast on me. He slides two fingers inside me, stroking in and out as he centers his mouth on my clit. It's more than I can take. My orgasm crashes into me, making the lights in the room flicker and buzz from the power surge.

Body slack and eyes closed, I hover above the chair, held up by Erik's coffee-scented magic, too blissed out to make a fuss about the fact that he's kissing his way down my thighs, massaging my ass with his strong hands, and just in general making me a boneless mass of a sickeningly satisfied woman.

"You're smiling," Erik says, sounding way too sure of himself.

I don't even crack open an eyelid—honestly, I can't yet. "It's an illusion spell."

He snort-chuckles against the inner curve of my knee. "You're so full of it."

"I'd rather be full of something else."

"Is that your way of asking me to fuck you now?"

"Asking?" I lift an eyebrow. "I thought tonight was all about me being selfish and demanding what I want."

"Yes, wife."

The layer of rough want under those two words sends a delicious shiver through me. And when he stands up and takes a few steps back from the chair, it's all I can do not to magic the doors locked forever. It isn't just the way Erik looks—the man is fucking gorgeous—but it's the way he's looking at me as if he's seeing through all the layers of practiced Sherwood heir bullshit right to the actual me. It's enough to steal my breath and make my heart stutter as every single thought I have in my head scatters like crisp yellow leaves in a fall breeze.

He wraps his long fingers around his cock and strokes its hard length. "Tell me who you are."

"You know who I am," I say, needing to draw out this game even though we know how it's going to end, because each time I say it, the words increase in power like an ancient spell.

Erik makes a tsk-tsk sound as he shakes his head at me and continues to jerk off to the sight of me spread out before him. "Say it."

My heart is beating so hard in my chest I can't believe he doesn't hear it. "Why?"

"Because hearing you say you belong to me and I belong to you is the hottest thing in the whole damn world." His hand stills and his jaw hardens as if he's forcing himself to step back from the edge. "Who are you?"

Pushing away his magic so I stop floating, I land softly in the chair and grasp the curved wooden ends of the chair's arms, knowing that what's coming next is going to make it hard to remember that this is only happening because of the Nullam Inhibitionis. Yeah, the fates help me, I want Erik Svensen, but I can't keep him. I can't stay his. I can't fail my family by putting my wants first when keeping Witchingdom safe from the Council's control lies in the balance—that's not how life works when you're the Sherwood heir.

But tonight?

Here?

Under the auspices of the Nullam Inhibitionis?

None of that matters. I can be who I want to be.

"I am Leona Sherwood Svensen." I stand and cross over to Erik. "I am your wife."

Magic thunders in the air as a blast of warm donuts and fresh-brewed coffee sweeps through the room, knocking over the smaller statues and knocking me off my feet. Maybe it's the lingering power of that last orgasm, but I don't worry for a second about what is going to happen next, I just know it's going to work out. And when Erik catches me, drawing me to him as the wild wind curls around us both, part of me is absolutely one hundred percent certain he always will.

Am I a fool?

Without a doubt, I'll get all angsty about that tomorrow, but as soon as Erik's lips come down on mine, there is no way to think about anything else except what he's doing to me right now.

Our hands are everywhere, desperate to touch and memorize every inch of each other. The dark scar on his shoulder. The hard plane of his chest. The way his ass tightens when I grab ahold of it with both hands while we make out like our lives depend on it. And that dick? Fates have mercy, it's the perfect amount of thick and hard and long to make me consider using two hands when I reach down between us to stroke him off right to the edge of coming. Before I can make him spend, though, he's back down on his knees, working that tongue of his against my clit as I fight to keep my legs from giving out. It's not fair that this man can play my body like this, and as much as I am tempted to let him keep feasting on me, there's something else I'm desperate for.

Holding on to the last threads of my sanity, I manage to get out a quick spell on the end of a desperate moan because he's got three fingers in me and his mouth on my clit.

In the next heartbeat, Erik's on the pillow-covered floor on his back. Now it's my turn to be between his legs. Wrapping my hands around his base, I suck his cock into my mouth, taking him deeper with each stroke. He lets out a lusty groan that makes my core clench as I continue to work him, using my hand and my mouth. And when I feel his hands in my hair, I relax and let him dictate the speed as I take him in over and over again, pushing him as I reach between my legs and slide my fingers across my slippery clit.

"LeLe," he groans, his hands tightening in my hair. "I need to be inside that pretty pussy of yours."

Not that I'd admit it out loud to him, but that is the best plan ever. Doing a quick self-scan to double-check my contraceptive spell is still locked in, I let his cock go with a kiss before moving so I am straddling his hips. I guide his hard cock into me and slowly lower myself onto him. The feel of him filling me up steals my breath and I have to stop, staying like that as I adjust to him, to this feeling of completeness. Then Erik's fingers bite into my hips as he urges me to move, lust dark in his eyes as he holds his jaw tight.

"Is that what you want?" I tease, holding myself still. "You want me to fuck you?"

"Fuck. Yes."

It is exactly the right answer. "Whatever you want, husband."

My handfast tattoo glows hot and bright, and I can't get enough of touching him, kissing him, being close enough to feel him everywhere as I undulate my hips. I'm drunk on him and all I want is more—which is exactly what he gives me. He lifts me up on his cock and slams me back down, driving deep as he fucks me from below. It's all I can do to hold on as the pleasure intensifies. Still together, we go higher. My whole body feels electrified and our handfast tattoos are blindingly bright as I ride him faster and faster. Then he reaches between us and presses his thumb against my clit, rubbing it in circles as the vibrations start in my legs, building and building. A lightning bolt flashes in the room, followed by an ear-splitting crack, but I'm too far gone to care even if the inn is coming down around us. I hold on to Erik and ride the wave after wave of pleasure as it takes me higher and higher until I come so hard around his cock that it blocks out the rest of the world at the same time as he surges into me, crying out my name.

When I come back to myself slowly, a little at a time, my lungs are burning from breathing so hard. Erik, his hands still grasping my waist to hold me in place, watches me through half-closed eyelids, a sated grin curling his lips.

The last thing I want to do is pull away from him, which means it's the first thing I have to do. Getting up, I realize the room is a wreck. Pillows are tossed everywhere. The chaise lounges are on their sides. The small statues have all fallen from their shelves and are resting on the floor. Only the massive stone faun remains untouched, but there is a one-inch-wide crack going through the thick marble chair he sits on—and I swear his impressive endowments weren't quite so large before.

"We're definitely going to have to leave a large tip for house-keeping," Erik says from behind me.

I whirl around and start to walk backward at the same time, the reality of what just happened nearly overwhelming me—not because of regrets, but because I already want more of the same again.

I am so screwed. The Liber Umbrarum cannot get deposited in the secured facility fast enough.

"Good night, Erik," I say, trying not to step on a downed statue in my haste to get away from my should-not-be husband before I do something even more foolish than I already have—like, oh, I don't know, have the best sex of my life again with the

AVERY FLYNN

last man in the world I should be with. "I'll see you in the morning."

He moves with that vampire-like flash of speed again.

"I don't think so," he says, picking me up and tucking me against his chest. "You can decide on the room, but it'll be both of us in whichever bed you choose, wife."

I could fill my eyes at his audacity.

I could magic his ass out into the hall, where he could spend the night naked and alone.

I could banish him to the other room with a simple no and he'd go.

The only reason I'm even at this inn with him is because I couldn't trust him to get The Liber Umbrarum to the secured location on his own. Erik Svensen is the husband I do not want.

I don't.

Even if I could have him—which, despite everything I know and all that's expected of me as the Sherwood heir, is starting to sound sadder and sadder the more time we're together.

It has to be the Nullam Inhibitionis's effect on me. So I shake it off and open my mouth to do what I should, what's expected of me—but my heart shoves my brain into another dimension.

"Fine." I relax against his broad chest. "You win."

"I do love hearing those words from you." He shoots me a cocky smirk that just makes him look sexier than should be legal. "Blue room on the left or green room on the right?"

Like it even matters as long as I'm snuggled up next to Erik. "Green."

He turns and starts toward the bedroom on the right. "My favorite color."

"Really?" I ask, figuring the fates must have guided my decision.

He gives me a wink. "It is now."

And, at least for tonight, now is all that matters.

Chapter Twenty-Seven

Leona . . .

$\mathscr{B}$ecause the satyrs don't do sex dens halfway, the bedroom is a decadent pleasure palace of a room. There's a soft glow coming from the motion-activated candles placed around the room that burn brighter when anyone comes close but remain at a low, gas lamp–style flicker while Erik and I are cuddled up in bed. That's where we've been for the past hour, wrapped up in each other and dark, nearly black silk sheets underneath a mirrored ceiling. The columns of the four-poster bed are decorated with detailed carvings of fauns and other magical creatures frolicking and fucking that I swear move positions and groupings when I'm not looking. Then there is the fact that the bed is somehow cool enough that you want to stay forever while at the same time too warm to use the covers. And then there's the mattress that isn't exactly tilted, and yet it seems like an uphill battle to roll even an inch away from Erik—not that I want to.

Yes, I realize *that* is a problem.

"You're still awake," Erik says.

Busted.

Not bothering to swallow my groan, I pull the comforter up over my head and snuggle deeper under the covers. Am I avoiding him even though I can't stop touching him?

Yes.

No.

I don't know.

What I do know is that sleep has not been an option. Instead, I've just been lying here in the almost-dark, cataloging every noise Erik makes, how he looks in the mirror above us, and, yes, how much I'm starting to feel like maybe the Vegas Erik is the real Erik that's hiding under all the Svensen reputation— or at least there's more of that Erik that's real than isn't.

Now, I am not excusing what he's done.

It's been a lot.

It's been bad.

But I just can't get the jerk Erik who everyone in Witchingdom knows is responsible for the flock of ravens who snatched every ceremonial diamond hairpin from the debutante ball last year to mesh with the Erik who is next to me in bed. Would the guy with the bedhead and the pillow-wrinkled face really steal millions in diamonds? To be honest, it's not a question I want to answer right now and probably not ever.

"So are you going to tell me what has your mind going a million miles an hour, or should I guess?" he asks. "You're trying to figure out just how far Bessie can go on a tank of gas, aren't you?"

I snort a giggle, because the answer is obviously as few or as many miles as Erik wants his beloved car to go. "I've been wondering how in the world they got that gigantic faun statue in here," I say, my lie coming out as smooth as if I really were a Svensen.

He traces a finger across the curve of my bare stomach, managing to tease without tickling. "You don't think they just got the local neighborhood moving witch and had them magic it in?"

"That's a boring answer." Rolling over to face him, I prop my head in my hand and let out a dramatic sigh of disappointment. "You told much better stories in Vegas."

"Is it that you can't sleep?" He turns over, and our faces are only inches apart. "Do you need to hear a bedtime story?"

"Yes." My body is already starting to buzz with desire, and I definitely should be keeping my hands to myself, but instead I reach out and brush the flop of hair that has fallen in front of his eyes. "A story would be good."

He catches my hand before I can tuck it back down by my side and kisses the palm, sending a shiver through me, and I bite down on my bottom lip to keep from making an embarrassing sound.

"So what do you want to hear a story about?" he asks as he releases me, his cocky grin making it obvious that he knows exactly what he's doing to me. "Do you want to hear about how Sigrid had to negotiate a contract with a gnome and didn't have any red M&Ms?" He lays a hand palm down on my hip and leaves it there, making me wonder what he's going to do next. "Or maybe it's a story about how Cy's goat familiar got his horn stuck in a magic carpet and accidentally set the thing off, and it took us hours to get this idiotic bleating goat out of the sky?" His eyes grow dark with lust as he takes me in from sex-mussed hair to chipped toenail polish. "Or do you want to hear about how my cousin Hugo accidentally added dancing powder to the Midsommar celebration crepes and we were all doing the funky chicken for twelve hours?"

"No." I shake my head. "I wanna hear about you."

His gaze flicks away from me for a second before returning. "That's boring."

"I highly doubt that." Especially since the more time I spend with him, the more of a contradiction he's becoming. "I want to know what it's like to be the Svensen heir."

He glides his palm over my hip and up to my waist, brushing his thumb against the outward curve of my stomach. "Going for insider information, huh?"

"You tell me yours," I say, trying to ignore the butterflies doing the conga in my belly. "I'll tell you mine."

"You're gonna tell me about growing up as one of the absolutely blessed and beloved Sherwoods?" Lifting an eyebrow, he snorts in disbelief. "I don't think I can take that much sugar this late in the day."

The butterfly dance floor clears in a heartbeat, and I push

his hand off me and sit up, curling my legs in tight to my chest. "That's what you think, that being the Sherwood heir is all fun and rainbows?"

Erik shrugs. "Well, yeah, everybody loves your family."

It takes everything I have not to let out a loud braying laugh that would probably add another crack to the faun's stone chair. "You couldn't be more wrong. There are a lot of people who are fascinated by our family, but there's a bunch who just don't like us, and some—like the Council—who'd like to see us banished to The Beyond. My mom's been shouldering all of the pressures that come with that for decades, and next year after we complete the power exchange ceremony, I'll be the one walking that tightrope—something I can only do if I do the right thing every time. Period. Everyone's depending on me."

"To do what, be sure to eat all your fruits and veggies?" he asks, his voice light as if he's making a joke.

But it's not a joke, not for me. My jaw tightens as the light buzz of desire turns into something darker, something that I shove down the darkest hallway to the darkest room to the darkest corner.

"No," I say, barely recognizing the resentful voice coming out of my mouth. "Like memorizing family beefs—even the minor ones—so I always know who to put together or keep apart at events to keep everything smooth and easy for everyone else." My breath is starting to come faster, and I can feel my pulse in my cheeks. "Like spending my every spare moment reading the background of every single political figure and attending meetings so I know where their loyalties lie and what I'll need to do to keep them on our side." I adjust my arms around my legs because my palms have gone all clammy, making holding on to my shins difficult. "Like not bothering to have hopes or dreams or plans of my own because everything about my life was decided before I was even born." Every muscle in my body is tight and I'm afraid I'm going to throw up, but I can't stop. Everything I've never said before—barely even let myself think before—has had enough of being in the dark. "Like the fact that all of the elders in my family seem to think it's a great gift that my parents are letting me pick from three possible husbands as opposed to just telling me which heir I have to marry for the greatest political gain so the Sherwoods maintain the power they've grown accustomed to." I'm on fire and on ice and swirling around even as I sit perfectly still and my cheeks are wet and I know deep down in my soul that if my hands slip away from my shins again they'll be shaking so hard I may never get them to stop. "Like the fact that I have to always make sure everyone knows I can be counted on, I am dependable, that I will always make the right decision for the family, and that the family always comes first."

I'm white-knuckling the world right now and I can barely breathe. I've never said any of that before.

Never.

And the one person I told? The guy whose family is known across Witchingdom as the most underhanded witches who'll use any weakness, any hint of discord to their full advantage. That was definitely not the right thing to have done, and yet I don't regret it. Not even a little. The realization is like seeing the sun after four months of darkness. I can't quite believe it, but there's no point in denying it.

There's a whoosh of coffee-scented magic and then Erik's behind me. His broad chest presses against my back, his arms wrap around me, and his legs bracket my hips. We stay like that, neither of us speaking or moving, and then he kisses my shoulder.

"I take it," he says, his tone light, "that I am not in that list of three possible husbands."

A bark of laughter escapes along with all the tension twisting my gut. "Most definitely not."

Then we're both chuckling, because what else are we going to do? Neither of us can change it, so what else is there to do at this point?

"So that is what it's like growing up the Sherwood heir." I relax back against him. "Tell me what it's like to grow up Svensen."

His body tightens behind me, but only for a moment. Then it's as if he wills his body into being someone else as all his muscles ease even though I can still feel a ribbon of something fierce just under the surface.

"Well, unlike you," he says with a who-the-fuck-cares air that doesn't ring true, "I am expected to mess up everything every time." He reaches up and cups one of my breasts as if he's trying to distract me from the frustration he's not quite hiding. "Because, you see, my father says that I am first among what he calls his disappointments, or what others would call their children. And since I believe in living up to my potential, that is exactly what I am."

He says it with such bravado, but I can feel all that hurt just under the surface. My family might make me consider moving to the moon occasionally, but even with all the expectations they've heaped on me as the heir, I've never doubted their love for me.

"He's called you that?" I ask. "To your face?"

Erik rolls my nipple between his fingers, and his sigh brushes the side of my neck. "Only on the days that end in Y."

I don't know when, and I don't know how, but someday the Svensen patriarch is going to pay for that. Just because Erik and I can't stay married doesn't mean I'm going to stand by and watch him be hurt. Forget family rivalries, no one gets to treat Erik like that.

"Is he as hard on your brother and sister as he is on you?"

"In a different way," Erik answers, letting his hand drop to the mattress and his cheek to my shoulder blade. "You see, my father only sees them as pawns, as ways to make sure that I'm always doing what he wants—which is usually whatever's best for him and not necessarily best for the family."

Once again, we sit together alone, holding on to only each other as our disappointments and frustrations and fears flicker like the flames from the magic candles around the room.

"I'm sorry, Erik." I lay my hands on his, twining my fingers through his and squeezing. "I shouldn't have asked. I didn't expect . . ."

My words die out, because even though his dad is a complete asshole, I shouldn't be the first one to say it out loud.

"For my dad to be just as awful as expected?" Erik's laugh is hollow. "How could you have known? You're a Sherwood and therefore all that is good. We Svensens, on the other hand, are the shadow to your light."

There's something about the regret in his voice—something I'm not sure even he hears—that melts away whatever is left of the grudge I was holding on to about how we ended up here as husband and wife—no matter how temporarily. Who better to understand what it's like to shoulder the weight of your entire family's expectations than someone who's living through the same thing?

"So you're always asking me what I want." I pick up his hands and move them so his arms are wrapped around my waist. "What is it that you want?"

"If I told you, you'd hate me," he says. "Well, more than you already do."

"I have horrible news for you, Erik Svensen. I'm not so sure that I hate you that much anymore." Or at all, not even a little. "Maybe if we were different people from different families, there could've been something here."

He doesn't say anything in response. Instead, he magics us so we're spooning on the mattress, curled up together as if our lives could be like this.

"Did I ever tell you about the time that Cy's goat ate one of Sigrid's books when she was about to start the final chapter and find out who the serial killer was?" Erik asks.

Desperate for a way not to fall asleep so this night can be a little longer, I grab hold of his offer with both hands. "Tell me everything."

And he does while I try to forget that once The Liber Umbrarum is locked away in the secured facility, we'll do the divorce spell. Then he'll get back to doing all the bad things expected of a Svensen heir, and I'll go pick a husband who makes the most sense politically for my family.

That's the way this story is going to end, and the only way it can.

Chapter Twenty-Eight

Erik . . .

When I wake up after sleeping so hard it was like I'd gotten hit by a bag of bricks, the sun's up and there's a raven with feathers so black they almost look blue in the sunlight sitting on a tree limb just outside the window.

After a lifetime of getting five hours on a very good night, I'd slept for nearly eight, and I don't have to wonder very hard about why, because the answer is snuggled up next to me. LeLe has her head resting in the pocket of my shoulder and one leg flung across me. Her bright Sherwood-red hair is a tangled mess, she is definitely drooling a little, her eyes are cracked open just enough to make me wonder if she is faking that soft snore (she's not), and she's so beautiful I don't want to look away.

Whoever is texting me nonstop, though, has other plans for me. The insistent buzzing from the living room hasn't stopped for the past twenty minutes. Trying not to jiggle LeLe awake, I wave my fingers in a silent spell and my phone flies through the bedroom door, zings past the window where the raven is still staring, and pops into my waiting hand. My phone vibrates with another incoming text, but there's something about the raven that holds my attention. It takes me a second, but it finally hits me when the bird stretches out its wings before taking off. The vivid blue in its feathers is the exact same cobalt shade as the patterned scarf my mother always tied to the picnic basket before she magicked us away from our father's unhappy ranting to a grassy spot for peanut butter and jelly sandwiches and sparkling grape juice.

My chest tenses as I work to lock that memory back up—the usual process for anytime even the mere hint of weakness threatens to make its way to the surface, where my father can pounce on it. Unlike normal circumstances, though, I'm not alone. LeLe mumbles something in her sleep and kisses my chest and then starts snoring quietly again.

And just like that, the tension is gone. No, that's the wrong way to phrase it, because it's still there. It's just that it doesn't seem like so much of a vulnerability as it did before. Oh yeah, the woman I'm going to screw over so bad she's going to curse me for the rest of my life and possibly the next million to come after is the one person in all of Witchingdom who makes me feel fucking safe.

How perfect.

I'm never participating in the dimitto spell, no matter what I've told her. I can't. It's the only way I can finally take my father out of play and save Cy and Sigrid. I'm all they've got.

My phone buzzes again before I can delve too much into that epiphany of exactly how screwed I am, and what I see on the screen fills my veins with ice and I have to scroll back to the beginning.

CY: NEED TO TALK. CALL BACK. NOW.

SIGRID: WHERE ARE YOU? SOMETHING IS HAPPENING. DAD KEEPS HAVING VISITORS AND HE MADE ME PLAY THE PIANO LIKE SOME KIND OF WINDUP DOLL.

SIGRID: ERIK! IT'S GONE SO WRONG. CY AND I ARE PACKING. WHERE ARE YOU?

CY: I CAN'T LET HIM DO THIS TO SIGRID. I'LL BE IN TOUCH WHEN I CAN. I'LL KEEP HER SAFE.

I don't react. I can't, because that's when the voicemails from my dad start—fifteen of them. Forcing myself to be as solid and unperturbed as the faun statue in the other room, I listen to the messages.

"You better be marrying a little twat right now," my dad snarls. "Call me."

That escalates on the next message to, "I can't believe you've done this. You've ruined everything. All you had to do is marry the girl."

There is more along those lines until the final message left while that raven was watching me.

"You better get on this phone and call me with good news, boy," my father says, his voice hoarse from the amount of off-the-line raging he must be doing. "If you think this little prank your sister and brother just pulled changes anything, you're wrong. I don't need them to keep you in line. Nothing has changed. You'll do what you set out to do or you will pay the consequences—and you won't be the only one. I'll burn all of Witchingdom to ash and it will be your fault, boy."

If I hadn't grown up having to choose between shit and crap, I'd probably be drowning in my own sweat about now. Lucky me, I grew up in the jackal's den.

The strategic thing to do at the moment would be to call my father and let him know everything is taken care of; the timeline of my marriage to LeLe doesn't need to come up in conversation. Then once Father was convinced, I'd send out a covert communication to Cy and Sigrid to stay away. They've made it out. There is no reason for them to return. Anyway, after I blow up the family at the power exchange ceremony, there won't be anything left for them to come home to—only me watching until the last dying ember of the Svensen magic burns out into nothingness.

No one needs to wait around decades for that.

Of course, that's how long it will take until the handfast marriage bonds finally sever. LeLe won't get her divorce—and she'll hate me forever for that—but she will, eventually, be free of me. I can't wait for that for her, but I need her to take the family magic, and then I'll need the combined power of both families to banish my father and keep him in The Beyond until he draws his last breath. She could leave me then, and I won't fight it. What would be the point? I'm only going to stay breathing long enough to watch the Svensen magic disappear from Witchingdom.

This is my plan. I've spent years studying the masters of strategy to develop it. I've followed the rules, stayed close to best practices, and I'll stick to the plan no matter what.

I fucking hate it with every ounce of my being.

Lying here with LeLe asleep on my chest as I coil a strand of her bright red hair around my finger, I watch the fauns and other magical creatures carved into the bedposts play their games. They never make the same move twice. Each change in position, each exchange of partners is new and unexpected.

It's what makes satyrs and their like such dangerous enemies. They live by the code of fuck-it-let's-just-do-it. There are no common plots or standard plans. There is no tomorrow for them, only today, only this moment, only this heartbeat, only the now.

So what about that makes them so formidable in battle? Because how in the hell are you supposed to outmaneuver someone who doesn't know what their next move is until they make it?

It's absolute chaos.

And it's brilliant.

And maybe—just maybe—this Nullam Inhibitionis doesn't have to end when LeLe and I walk out of the inn.

Chapter Twenty-Nine

LeLe . . .

$\mathcal{I}$'m barely awake and I'm giddy.

It's weirding me all the way out.

Usually I wake up in the morning and my brain is only sort of maybe a little bit working until I've had at least three elderberry teas. This morning? I am on the ball as soon as I roll over and find the note.

GETTING SNACKS FOR THE REST OF THE TRIP.
MEET ME DOWNSTAIRS WHEN YOU'RE READY.

E

So that's how I ended up in the bathroom post-shower grinning my face off and brushing my teeth, which doesn't seem like a problem until you actually try to do it. Have you ever tried to brush your teeth with a permagrin? It's much harder than you would think. I'm finally getting into the groove of things in the mirror above the sink when the reflection gets all wavy, sending my oh-shit meter into action. The next thing I know, my sister Effie is staring back at me, scaring me out of my mind. Heart racing, I spit toothpaste all over the mirror before I realize it's just an astral reflection.

Grumbling about how it's not polite to barge in on people, I start wiping away the mess with a towel while my sister laughs her face off at me.

"Little bit high-strung, sis?" Effie asks once she can form words.

Rinsing my toothbrush off, I give her a tight-lipped smile. "I was thinking about something."

"Well, going by your aura, I don't need three guesses to figure out what that something was—or more correctly, *who* that someone is."

"You and your aura reading can go jump in a lake," I grumble.

Effie makes a tsk-tsk sound. "Oh, somebody is testy this morning. Has it been an orgasm-free road trip?"

I manage to keep my expression neutral, but my cheeks feel like they're as red as my aura. "I don't know what you're talking about."

She snorts. "Yeah, try lying to somebody who isn't your

sister and hasn't known you your entire life. So I take it that means you haven't murdered him in his sleep and become a gorgeous widow?"

"You're always so bloodthirsty."

My older sister shrugs. "Only when it involves family and somebody who can potentially hurt them."

"I am not going to get hurt." Which would probably sound a lot more convincing if I weren't pressing my hand against my belly as if I need to protect my vital organs from attack. "This is different," I go on. "My eyes are wide-open. I know who Erik Svensen is. I am under no illusions. I am just having fun."

And if I'm whacking my toothbrush against the faucet to get the last of the water drops off of it before I snap the travel cap on it, well, that just means I'm back to my normal not-a-morning-person self.

"If you say so," she says, managing to fit a whole lot of you-are-so-full-of-shit-and-we-both-know-it in four words. "I'm warning you now that if I get even a twinge that something is wrong through the sisterly SOS signal, I'll be there before you even get a chance to ask for help."

I'd like to say she's kidding, but I know she's not. I might be the Sherwood heir, but Effie is the oldest Sherwood child, and despite her wild ways, she takes her duties as big sister very seriously.

"I appreciate that," I say, meaning it wholeheartedly. "But Erik says we're about a day out from the secured facility. We should be there tonight. We'll get The Liber Umbrarum tucked away where the Council can't access it. Then we'll knock out the divorce spell and I'll come home single, ready to do what's expected of the heir and marry whichever politically expedient husband Mom wants—it's not like the who really matters to me. The important thing is that the family is taken care of and the Council never gets the chance to turn Witchingdom into their own version of a fascist utopia."

And I am not blinking away tears or swallowing past the emotion clogging my throat or clasping my hands so tightly together that my knuckles are white because I'm afraid I'll fall apart if I don't. And if I was feeling like that, I'd stuff all that frustration and sadness into that deep, dark hole where all the other feelings I am ignoring go. Judging by the sympathetic look on my sister's face, though, she doesn't believe any of that.

"Leona, I'm probably the last person in the world who should be saying this since it's not like I can do anything to change it," she says with a sad sigh, "but I think you're getting a raw deal out of being the heir. There has to be a way for you to be with who you want and be a good heir."

"Want has nothing to do with anything when it comes to my life, and that's fine. It is what it is." Straightening my shoulders, I dig deep for my best impervious Mom expression. "Anyway, all of the husband candidates come from families who are the only ones with enough power to help us defeat the Council."

"The only families?" Effie asks.

I know exactly where she's going with this, but it doesn't matter that the Svensens have as much family magic as we do. They aren't to be trusted—not even Erik, which makes me want to go back to that giant four-poster bed, crawl in, and never come out.

"Whatever you say, sis. You know best."

"Exactly." I nod emphatically even though I've never hated being right more in my life. "Give everyone hugs for me. I'll be home soon."

Ignoring the way "soon" weighs in my gut like a lead balloon, I finish getting ready and head down the stairs to find Erik. And there's no doubt about it this time, the fauns etched in gold on the blue silk wallpaper are definitely swapping partners and positions. By the time I reach the landing above the lobby, Sil is waiting for me, this time in a sage-green-and-silver hooded kaftan, their eyes lined with a dark kohl. "The wallpaper really is something, don't you think?" they ask as they link an arm through mine and walk with me down the rest of the stairs. "Our guests often tell us it's quite inspirational. I like to think of it as a reminder that there really is no end to the possibilities that life offers."

It takes a second for my eyes to adjust to all the extra light. Whereas last night the lobby was bathed in a soft, romantic candlelight, this morning it's bright with natural sunshine coming in through the three walls of windows that had not been there before. They give a gorgeous view of a massive inner courtyard that's filled with a manicured garden.

"I guess I've never really thought of that before." No need for therapy to dig deep and figure out why that is.

Sil chuckles. "Youth really is wasted on the young."

I take a closer look at Sil, and there's not a single wrinkle to be found on their face. There's no way they're old enough to be making a comment like that. Then again, satyr magic is a unique vintage for sure.

"Can I ask how old you are?"

"Of course. Why would I be ashamed of that?" Sil beams at me, obviously proud of every one of their years. They stop at the check-in desk, which this morning is underneath a flowering magnolia tree. "Do you know how much experience someone can gain in 632 years? Soooo much."

Before I can ask for more details, Erik and the inn's chef come out into the dining room singing a dirty limerick about a witch, a gnome, a unicorn, and a pair of mischievous pixies, the lyrics of which would put the inn's wallpaper to shame. They are each carrying an oversized picnic basket that is so over-stuffed with edible goodies that the lid won't close.

"Wife," he calls out, and lifts his basket. "Beware of satyrs saying they just want to add one more thing to your picnic basket or you'll end up like this when all you wanted was a few sandwiches."

While he and the inn's chef pack the baskets and our "Mr." and "Mrs." matching luggage are brought out by the porters to Bessie, Sil pulls me aside on the front porch.

"I have a feeling you're going to need this; you just have an aura about you and a mother always knows," they say as they press a gold amulet in the shape of a sand timekeeper into my hand. "It's a rewinder. If the Council gets too close—or something else happens—all you have to do is turn it upside down and say the spell engraved on the bottom. You'll rewind time by three minutes, but it can only be used once, so make sure to only use it for what matters most."

My gut twists. Satyr magic is different than our witch magic. It's more ancient, and some argue more powerful—making it more coveted than even the rarest of spells. My training as heir kicks in and I'm trying to figure out what to give in return as protocol requires, but nothing I have is as precious as the amulet.

"And I don't want to hear anything about not being able to accept it," Sil says as if reading my mind—but I'm pretty sure that's just a rumor and satyrs can't actually do that, at least I hope not. "It's a gift, and I'll be highly offended if you don't take it, and no one wants a satyr mad at them."

This is true. The stories of satyrs taking their revenge are legendary. Let's just say they're very creative when it comes to getting even. Trust me, you don't want to know more than that.

Accepting my fate, I loop the long gold chain around my neck and tuck the amulet under my sweater before giving Sil a hug. "Thank you. This is a precious gift, and I appreciate it."

Sil squeezes me back tight and even though they only come up to the middle of my chest and their horns poke into my boobs, it's one of the best hugs I've ever had in my life.

They break the hug and look over at Bessie. The car looks as shiny and new as if she'd just been driven off the showroom floor this morning instead of decades ago. There's not a speck of dust on the white leather seats or a single leaf stuck in the grille after our race through the woods to stay ahead of the

Council's goons. Erik is leaning against the passenger side of the car, his arms crossed, and looking even better than Bessie. Those forearms of his really should be illegal, and I'm pretty sure wearing the sleeves of his sweater pushed up like that so I can't help but look at them is definitely against the law.

Sil lets out a sigh and when I look over, they just shake their head at me. "You better go get in that car with that good-looking husband of yours, or I might be tempted to work a little illusion magic and take your spot."

My cheeks feel like I've just gotten too close to the Fall Festival bonfire. "He's not my husband," I say right before a wistful sigh escapes. Yeah, way to really sell it, Sherwood. "Or at least he won't be for much longer."

"Uh-huh," Sil says with a snort of disbelief. "Whatever you say."

I could argue with them, or I could just pretend my pants are on fire while I walk over to Bessie.

It shouldn't take you three guesses to figure out which one I'm gonna go with.

Chapter Thirty

LeLe . . .

This is the longest road trip I've ever taken in my life.

Fine, I know that's actually not saying much, considering I usually just magic myself whenever a trip is within a few hundred miles. For trips longer than that, it's usually via magic carpet or spelled train. Either one of those options will allow you to have breakfast in New York and dinner in Sydney on the same day.

But three nights out on the road going from point A to point B? That's an absolutely unheard-of length of time just for magical travel—and it's still not long enough.

I'm not saying I'm sitting here asking the fates to give Bessie a flat tire or punch a hole in the tank so she runs out of gas or anything, but I'm not saying the thought hasn't crossed my mind.

The land grows flatter with every mile we travel farther west, and it's nothing but cornfields and the occasional farm dragon who swoops down from the clouds and lets loose with a blast of fire to clear the fields of anything left over after harvest so the farmers can start fresh in the spring.

"So you think we'll get to the secured facility today?" I ask. "Barring any more sentient houses, trolls yearning for company, or satyrs?"

Yeah, I'm going for a joke here, but it comes out flat, and I sink back into Bessie's warm leather seats.

Erik takes the exit for a highway going south. "Yeah," he says, sounding about as enthusiastic as I feel. "We're about three hours away."

"Good. That means we'll have this all taken care of and be able to go our separate ways by nightfall."

It is exactly what I want.

Or what I did want.

What I still should want.

But I don't, and I'm tired of lying to myself about it.

I am an awful liar anyway. The only member of our family who can lie well is my sister Juniper. She can get anyone to believe whatever song and dance she's selling. Thank the fates, though, she only uses her powers for good. Well, mostly. There was the time she talked Beatrice into believing that her perfect familiar was the irate rooster at the county fair—and that's how we ended up with Barkley, the bane of my existence.

Until I met Erik.

But he's not my nemesis anymore, is he?

Fuck. How did all of this become so damn confusing?

How about the moment he magicked matching "Mr." and "Mrs." luggage out of thin air and we took off in Bessie on what I thought was going to be a quick trip to the secured facility?

Sometimes I really hate it when I answer my own questions. Even worse, I am beginning not to hate the fact that I'm hoping we never get to the secured facility because being with Erik is exactly where I want to be for the rest of my life. I know, I know. He's a lying jerk and I really should still loathe him.

But fates help me, I don't.

Honestly, I'm not sure I ever did.

That little factoid, however, is not something I can deal with right now. Not that it matters. It's not like we can stay married. He's a Svensen and I'm a Sherwood. Our families are true enemies. My mother has a whole list of appropriate husbands I need to pick from and it's my duty as the heir to my family's magic to do so. That's just the way it is. The way it's always been. There's no point in trying to change it—especially not when the Council is looking to exploit any crack in the Sherwood family sense of unity.

"So what kind of spells do you think are in The Liber Umbrarum?" Erik asks, yanking me back to the here and now.

Jaw in my lap from shock, I pivot in my seat. "You didn't even flip through it?"

"No time," he says with a shrug. "First I had to steal it, then there was a rush to put it on display for a few hundred of Witchingdom's most influential people so the word would get around to the Svensen creditors that we were not to be messed with, and then your sister and her friends stole it. And now here we are, shutting it away so the Council doesn't steal it back and cause Witchingdom's downfall."

Yeah, nothing like putting my problems back into perspective. "Did you even have a plan to keep the Council from stealing it back before Tilda lifted it?"

He drums his fingers on the steering wheel as if he has to get his annoyance out somehow. "My dad planned to sell it on the black market while letting everyone think we still had it."

"That is not the best plan." Really. It is a horrible plan.

"And yet, here we are." The lines around his mouth tighten as he glares at the straight stretch of highway ahead of us. "You and I are heirs, not the power holders. We don't get a choice."

I pop open the glove box and pull out The Liber Umbrarum. "Maybe there's a spell in here for that."

"Wouldn't that be nice," he scoffs.

I flip through the spell book, and while I don't see a way to magic out of the blessing and curse of being an heir, what I do find is wild. Some spells are ridiculously specific, some are overwhelmingly complicated, and some call for ingredients that have been impossible to find for centuries.

While Erik drives, I tell him about the wackier ones, such as the one that ensures your enemy has a permanent itch on that one spot between their shoulder blades that they can't reach. Then there's the one about how to banish a whifflesnirt— neither of us has any clue what a whifflesnirt is, so the spell must have worked. We're laughing about a spell to summon fungi (really, why would you ever need that) when I look over at Erik and something inside me shifts. It's like a curtain has been pulled back and I can see—finally see—who he really is and not just the asshole everyone in Witchingdom thinks he is.

Oh, he's not perfect by any means, but he's not as bad as he seems to think he is. He's the kind of guy who does whatever he must to protect the people he loves. He tries to hide it, to pretend he really is the witch everyone assumes a Svensen is born being, but he gives himself away every time he talks about his brother and sister.

"Why are you looking at me like that?" Erik asks suspiciously before he starts patting the top of his head. "I don't have mushrooms growing out of my head, do I?"

There's no way I can answer. I don't even know how to put what I'm thinking into words that I'd actually allow to come out of my mouth. *Erik Svensen, you're a real sweetheart.* Yeah, there is no way I can say that. As a Sherwood, I probably shouldn't even be thinking it.

But I am.

And it's true.

So I do the only thing I can at that moment. I shimmy across Bessie's leather bench seat, cup his face in my hands, and kiss him like our marriage isn't on a countdown clock, like we really like each other, like we're just two regular witches without families depending on us and therefore can do whatever we want whenever we want.

For a second it's just me putting everything I've got into that kiss, but then Erik's hands are on my hips, pulling me closer, and then he's kissing me back. My skin goes electric everywhere he touches as he skims his hands over my hips and under the hem of my sweater. His fingers brush along my sensitive skin above my waistband, teasing me with little sparks that promise more. I'm getting lost in him; the only thing tethering me to the here and now is the feel of Bessie's steering wheel jammed against my side.

I'm ready to ask, beg, demand he pull over when the bench seat slides back, stopping with a solid thump in its farthest-back position. It all happens so fast that I'm jolted back enough to break contact with Erik's mouth, and that's when I realize we're still speeding down the highway. Erik's tall, but he's not so tall that he could have his foot smashed down on the gas pedal.

"I've got you," Erik says, pulling me back to him. "Always."

I have half a second to realize that he must have spelled Bessie into auto drive before my lips are on his once again and thinking about anything else becomes utterly unimportant.

Straddling him with my knees on either side of his strong thighs, I rock against him as we kiss. No, that's the wrong word for it. It's like we're each staking our claim, daring the other one to deny it. A more clearheaded me would be backing away. Last night at the inn had been one thing. But now? Here? With him? Only danger lies ahead.

But I can't stop. Not with the way he's making me feel as if I am the center of the world—or more precisely, as if the rest of the world doesn't even exist anymore. Every part of me is tuned in to him as the scent of coffee curls around me.

I have no idea how he's doing it, but even though we're both still totally dressed, I swear to the fates that I can feel his fingers on my slick pussy, rubbing back and forth before plunging in deep over and over and over again before pulling back and circling my clit with infinite—and torturous—care. It's so good and so mean at the same time, that slow path he takes around me, adding pressure here and there, building a rhythm that my body clings to, every nerve awash in anticipation as my breath catches and my core tightens.

It's too much and not enough and the best all at the same time, but part of my brain can't stop wondering, "How are you…"

He increases the intensity and the words fade before I can get the rest of the sentence out.

"Does it matter?" he asks, his own voice ragged as if he is feeling the pressure build right along with me.

When I feel like I'm already on the edge of coming hard enough to make the rest of the world disappear? No. It absolutely does not matter how he's doing this. I swear I'm about to tell him just that when he slides his fingers back inside me and steals my breath. He curls his fingers, twisting and turning them at the same time so he hits every sensitive spot practically all at once and I lose the ability to say anything at all except *yes*, *please*, and *more*.

He takes advantage of the moment, giving me what I don't even realize I need by using his actual hands to pull down my bra so my breasts spill out. I have just enough time to clock what he's doing when he starts rolling my hard nipples into impossible peaks before tugging them just right—all while he kisses his way down my neck. It's like having multiple Eriks at the same time tasting and teasing and treating me to an experience I've never even imagined. And if this is what he can do to me with all my clothes still on in a self-driving car speeding down the highway, I can't even imagine what he's going to do the next time we're naked and alone together.

Or not alone.

At this point, I'm so overwhelmed with pleasure that there's not a whole lot the man could ask me that I wouldn't agree to. Maybe that's what I've been waiting for my whole life—the man who I could be wild with, the one who saw I wasn't perfect and wanted me anyway, the witch who made magic feel new.

"Take what you want," Erik says before giving me a rough kiss that's surely going to leave my mouth bruised in the best way.

And I do. I let go and reach for the orgasm, letting it build and build and build until I break apart from the pure pleasure of it, letting it wash over me in waves until I'm nearly drowning in it, clinging to Erik because in this moment—and I have to admit, maybe more—he's become someone I can count on.

I'm too blissed out to do more than sigh like the fully sated woman I am when Bessie starts to vibrate so hard that it breaks through my post-orgasmic haze.

"Oh shit," Erik says, his tone as tight as a dress that's two sizes too small, before he moves me off him back to my side of the bench seat even as it's flying forward into its original position. "Get down and no matter what, don't look."

Yeah, like that's gonna happen.

My head is up and I'm staring at the highway straight

ahead of us before he's even done with the sentence. Up the road there's the telltale shimmer of the Council's enforcers.

I clutch The Liber Umbrarum tight enough that the metal buckles used to lock it bite into my palms like dull knives laced with acid. The same bitterness is eating away at my stomach lining because there's twice as many of the goons appearing out of the shimmer as before.

Erik throws an arm out across my chest at the same time that he slams on the brakes. The stench of burnt rubber is thick in the air as the Council witches begin to materialize. He slams the car into reverse and punches the gas.

I whip around in my seat to help navigate and my stomach drops to my toes. There's a pack of motorcycle-riding were-wolves in a V formation heading straight for us. Even worse, they're all wearing distinctive bloodred leather jackets, which gives them away as being a part of the Aetos family. What the Sherwoods are to law-abiding Witchingdom in terms of power and prestige, the Aetos family is to the criminal underbelly of Witchingdom.

We.

Are.

Fucked.

"Erik," I say, surprised my voice isn't shaking as hard as my nerves right now. "We've got more company."

He glances in the rearview and lets out a harsh breath. "Don't suppose that book has something for this situation?"

I look down at the thick leather-bound book with its five

inches of yellowed pages, each of which is covered in hand-written spells. There's no index. No contents page.

"Probably, but it would take time to find it, and that's the one thing we don't have."

He grunts in agreement as the Council comes at us from the front and the Aetos werewolves from the back. My mind is going a million miles trying to find a solution, but I just keep coming back to the realization that there's no way for both of us to get out of here, but one of us can.

One of us.

A warm certainty settles in my belly and I know what I need to do. There's not a whole lot I can control—after all, my ultimate future was decided before I was even born—however, I do have a say in what happens in the now. Erik is driving like he was born to do it, and Bessie is responding to his every turn of the wheel and tap on the pedals. But they're closing in on us. I have to do something.

As I put The Liber Umbrarum back in the glove box, I take what may be my last look at my husband and something shifts in my chest, like all the pieces that were off-kilter are finally falling into place because of Vegas, because of the last few days, because of him. Erik really is the last man I ever wanted and the only one I ever needed. I'd love to blame the wildness of the past few days, the night of no inhibitions at the satyrs' inn, or even the sentient house's insistence on just one bed, but I'm done lying to myself.

Fuck me. I love my husband.

There's no way I'm going to let either the Council or Aetos werewolves fuck with my husband.

"I trust you to get The Liber Umbrarum to the secured facility," I tell him, one hand on the door latch. "Whatever happens, you getting out of here safe is all that matters."

Then, without giving myself time for second thoughts, I grab one of the picnic baskets full of goodies from the satyrs, whisper a quick protective spell, and shove the car door open.

"LeLe," Erik yells. "No!"

It's the last thing I hear before I tuck and roll out of the car and onto the highway.

Chapter Thirty-One

Erik . . .

I'm going to keel over and die from the heart attack LeLe just gave me by jumping out of Bessie—and then spend eternity haunting her.

But first I'm going to save my wife.

I can hear my dad in my head yelling at me that I should be thanking the fates that my powerful and wealthy wife decided to sacrifice herself—like a chump—to save the husband she's trying to divorce and get the spell book to the secured facility. And no, it doesn't matter that she's got a protection spell working, judging by the scent of warm donuts lingering in the air; it won't keep her safe against the Council goons' combined magic and the Aetos werewolves' sneaky cleverness. It's a suicide mission.

The smart move is to drive away now while we're still married. When it comes time at the power sharing ceremony, I can show off the handfast tattoo to prove the connection to the Sherwoods and force their hand to back me instead of my father. It's the strategic move. It's the smart thing to do. It's the most logical choice. But we all know I'm not gonna do that. Why? Because I'm an even bigger chump than she is.

Watching LeLe pull a stupid stunt like this to save me is like having someone use a spoon to dig my heart out of my chest. I don't know how to process it—not just the giving a fuck about someone other than myself but having someone moving between me and the line of fire. It's not that Cy and Sigrid don't care—I know they do—but I'm their big brother, and therefore, standing between them and my father's rage and cruelty is in the job description. If there's one thing in the world that makes me a tiny bit less of an unsalvageable asshole (and yes, I know that's a big if), it's that I've never shirked my responsibility to keep my brother and sister out of harm's way.

Still, knowing that no one will ever try to save me is the first lesson I learned as the Svensen heir.

And yet, there she goes, doing some action-hero move to protect me.

Me!

It's at this moment that I realize two things.

One, I love this woman, and I'm going to figure out some way to keep my father from double-crossing me at the power transfer ceremony without me having to force LeLe to use her family magic.

Two, there is no way I'm letting either the Council goons or the Aetos werewolves get to my wife. Yeah, losing possession of the spell book would mean spending the rest of my life—if I'm still breathing after this is over—exiled into The Beyond, but that isn't important, because the only thing that matters is saving LeLe.

Before she even hits the ground, I'm slamming on the brakes and spinning the wheel to turn Bessie so she's parallel in the road smack-dab between LeLe and the Council goons. I can barely hear the Aetoses' motorcycles over the pounding of my heart in my ears when I look down at LeLe. She is curled up into a ball with her arms around the bright blue suitcase, really selling the idea that something valuable like the spell book is inside it.

"Get in the car, wife," I say, all the anxiety speeding through me making the words come out as a snarl.

Her head jerks up and she glares at me.

"What are you doing?" she asks between gritted teeth. "Get out of here!"

"Not without you." Then my magic scents the air and my whole body practically vibrates with the intensity of the spell brewing inside me. "Volare uxor currus."

LeLe's eyes go wide with surprise half a heartbeat later and then she shoots up in the air and lands with a soft thump in Bessie's passenger seat, still clutching the suitcase to her chest.

"That was the only way to ensure you'd get out of here," she says, fury making her eyes shine bright. "You could've gotten away."

"There's always a loophole when it comes to getting out of a jam," I say as I try to figure out what in the fuck that loophole is this time. "Always."

The Council's goons are to the left of us, gaining ground by the second with enough malicious intent wafting off of them to be a tangible force.

The Aetos werewolves are to the right of us, so close the roar of their motorcycle engines makes my teeth rattle.

The Killjoy Forest is straight ahead of us, looming like monsters found only in the kind of nightmares that make grown adults sleep with the lights on.

LeLe is about to light into me again for ruining her plan to save my sorry ass, and judging by the strength of the donut smell smacking me upside the head, that lecture is going to come with a large side of magical fuck-you.

We, however, don't have time for that, so I hit the gas and Bessie goes speeding forward, because, as I learned at my father's knee, if all the choices are bad, pick the one that will scare the shit out of everyone opposing you—and in this case, that choice is the Killjoy Forest.

What makes going into the forest such a perilous option that even the Council and the scariest pack of werewolves in Witchingdom will hesitate to follow us? Five-inch-tall, green-haired, flying pixies.

You see, pixie spells are pure chaos. The closest nonmagical comparison I can make is that witch magic is to pixie magic what skiing the bunny slopes is to doing shots of tequila while blindfolded and speeding down the black diamond slopes on greased-up skis while wearing a jet pack. They really are the kind of magical creatures who say why add a pinch of cemetery dirt when you can add a whole grave's worth just to see what happens?

Since the dawn of time, they've done what they want to who they want because they're willing to roll the magical dice with reckless abandon. And if you are foolish enough to put a toe past the edge of the Killjoy Forest where they live? Well, no witch, troll, unicorn, or other magical creature comes back the same as they went in. As for what happens when someone goes blasting straight into the heart of the forest doing a hundred miles an hour in a bright yellow classic convertible that's impossible to miss?

No one's been fool enough to try it—until now.

Chapter Thirty-Two

LeLe . . .

I'm white-knuckling the spell book and trying to remember to breathe while Erik drives us straight toward the curving line of delicate-looking white flowers in full bloom along the edge of the Killjoy Forest. I can't see the pixies, but I can *feel* them—they're like that eerie something that makes the hair on the back of your neck stand up when you walk into a dark room.

They're the reason why you feel an icy breeze on your neck when you cross through an empty room, the thing that makes your heartbeat hitch when you look down a dark alleyway, and the cause of free-floating anxiety that puts you on edge for no reason at all. Okay, maybe some of that is a brownie or a duende or a tsukumogami, but if it *is* a pixie, you are in so much trouble—even more so if you're on their territory. Just like a witch's powers increase when they're gathered around a cauldron in their family kitchen, so do a pixie's in the Killjoy Forest.

And they're out there, lounging in the branches of the evergreen trees and eating copious amounts of peacock-flavored popcorn while waiting for us to fuck up and enter their territory.

"Watch out for the primroses!" I yell, trying to be heard over the sound of the motorcycles gaining ground on us.

He doesn't hear me because he doesn't turn Bessie's steering wheel even a millimeter to avoid the clusters of small white blooms with the yellow centers. The stubborn man is driving right at the pixies' well defined and guarded border, obviously determined to play chicken with the witches and werewolves on our tail. Really, it's not the worst plan. All he has to do is make the turn away from the pixies' primrose property line in time and before our pursuers get the chance to clock what's right ahead of them.

It could work—and I can help. What good is being the heir to one of the most powerful families if I can't use it to keep Bessie's tires from touching the favorite flowers of Witchingdom's big bad scaries (who happen to be really fucking small, but that's not the point here).

Pushing the fear aside, I dig deep and call up my magic. "Nolite tangere primrose."

That should give a little bumper of space between the tires and the petals.

"Oh, we're not going to touch the flowers," Erik says. "We're going over them."

For half a heartbeat of unease, I think he means Bessie is going to smush them under her tires. But then the smell of fresh-brewed coffee mixes with my donut-scented magic, and the three-thousand-pound car rises up from the ground and flies over the row of primroses and straight into the one place in all of Witchingdom that no one goes.

And that's when my unease turns into pure panic.

Bessie lands on the forest floor with a thunk hard enough to nearly jostle the spell book out of my grasp. I have just enough time to secure my grip and then we're speeding through the forest as the shocked cries of the trees we're zipping past carry on the breeze. Erik barely flinches from the impact or the scrape of wood on metal as the trees try to grab Bessie with their limbs. He's all cool-under-pressure calm while the adrenaline pumping through my veins has me as jumpy as a gnome out in public without a hat (which for a gnome is the equivalent of going out naked on Main Street at high noon during a parade where the whole town has turned out and it's being live-streamed). Seriously. I'm nothing but internal twitches and silent screams. And one out-loud yip when a tree snags a few strands of my hair and yanks them out.

"Are they following?" Erik asks, his tone easy, as if he just asked about the weather.

Pissed-off trees, bloodthirsty pixies, and moose that aren't magical at all, just massive in both size and aggression ahead of us, and he's worried about the folks behind us?

"What are you doing?" I holler, doing my best not to freak the fuck out when every instinct in my body is screaming at me to do exactly that. "We can't be here."

"LeLe, please." He reaches over and squeezes my hand, the touch far more reassuring than it should be when the trees in front of us are winding up to hurl apples our way.

A bright red Gala apple whizzes over my head. Another misses us by a country mile, landing with a hard thunk against another tree, which turns around and unloads its apple on the tree with the shitty aim. Then in a matter of seconds there is a volley of apples being fired off so fast I can barely keep track of the flying fruit going every which way but directly at us.

"Are they following?" Erik asks again.

Sorta confident that I'm not about to be beaned by an apple, I whip around in my seat to look behind us just in time to see the lead werewolf, who is riding point, manage a hairpin turn to keep from crossing the pixies' border. The rest of his pack hit their brakes and send up a huge cloud of dust that almost blocks the nearby Council goons from sight.

"No, they're smart enough not to run straight into pixie country and certain death," I say, clutching The Liber Umbrarum tightly to my chest.

Erik grins at me as if he hasn't just jumped us both out of the cauldron and into the bonfire. "Nothing in this world is certain, wife."

"Yeah, it is—the fact that we're not out of the woods yet." I groan at my own unintended pun as I duck down in time to avoid getting nailed by one of the trees' airborne apples. "They've stopped, but it won't be for long. The Liber Umbrarum is too valuable for them not to try to figure out a way around the pixies—at least for the Council witches."

"The werewolves too," Erik says as Bessie's tires hit a patch of slick moss.

Bessie careens to the right hard enough that the seat belt tightens painfully across my chest. Then Bessie jerks to the left as Erik turns the car, his jaw tightening along with his grip on the steering wheel as another patch of moss slides into our path. Erik lets out a string of curses as he hits the brakes and tries to avoid hitting the slab of dark green as he floors it, but the moss scurries over at the last minute and we start to spin out of control.

Closing my eyes, I try to summon my magic even as my stomach lurches from the g-forces. Maybe it's because it feels like I'm about to hurl, or maybe it's because the rumors are true and the pixies' magic really does dull the abilities of every magical being who enters their forest, but instead of magic, I've got nothing but bile swishing around inside me.

Bessie runs over something hard, and the thunk makes my head jerk back. The distinctive sound of a tire popping jars me out of my worthless attempt at spell casting. Erik's nonchalant expression has given way to a grim determination as he fights to control Bessie against the constant stream of obstacles popping up from the forest floor like frozen waffles from the toaster. Of course, instead of delicious baked goodness, what's coming up are four-foot-high rocks and moss and gnarled brambles with razor-sharp thorns. They emerge in front of us in wave after wave as Erik and a hobbled Bessie swerve around them, pushing forward toward the sound of the river and the patch of blue sky in the distance that marks the end of the pixies' territory.

If we can make it across, the sharp-toothed nightmare creatures can't touch us. We'll be in the clear. Hope, fuzzy and warm and fluttery, fills my chest, and I barely notice the bright red apples being thrown at us or the rocks suddenly jutting up from the ground.

"We're gonna make it," I say with a chuckle of amazement.

"Of course we are." Erik jerks the steering wheel to the left just as a hunk of granite shoots up from the ground in front of us. "Never doubt me when it comes to taking care of you."

Absolutely everyone in Witchingdom knows that statement is the last thing I should take at face value. There's not a witch, unicorn shifter, or M&M-craving gnome who wouldn't doubt a Svensen. And if the Svensen (who's already lied his way into marrying you) says they'll take care of you? That just means they are going to screw you over so hard you won't know up from down.

Everyone knows that.

Everyone.

Except me.

Bessie barrels toward that opening between the trees and the river's edge. I'm holding on to The Liber Umbrarum with a death grip as the ground erupts beneath us. My heart is in my throat, blocking my gasp of shock as the car goes so fast that the forest is just a blur—except for Erik. He's solid. He's real. He's all I want or need.

Deep down in that part of me where lies hold no power and there are no places where the truth can hide, I can't doubt Erik Svensen, and I believe he'll always take care of me. And that's not the worst of it.

I never should have gotten in his car.

I never should have agreed to this ridiculous road trip.

I never should have gone on that picnic with him.

I never should have slept with him.

I never should have told him my stories.

I never should have listened to his.

And I never, ever, *ever* should have fallen in love with my husband.

Because even if we make it out of these woods, I can't pick my own happiness over my family's—and Witchingdom's—best shot at beating the Council.

Bessie crosses through the line of angry trees into the open grass along the river. All we have to do is get across the fast-moving river and we'll be out of range of the pixies' magic and have a massive lead on the Council and the werewolves. Erik guns the engine one last time as we hit the dirt embankment and then we're airborne.

Landing safely and getting The Liber Umbrarum locked away in the secured facility should be all I'm focused on.

But I can't stop wondering about all the what-ifs and why-nots with Erik—as if any of them could ever come true.

My future was never my choice. It was all planned out before I was born. Go to the best schools, get top grades, excel at everything, become friends with the right people, develop connections, forge alliances, agree to the most politically advantageous marriage, strengthen the Sherwood position in Witchingdom, continue the family line, and, above all else, take care of my family by putting them first—always.

That's what it means to be the heir.

The second Bessie's tires touch down on the other side of that river, all of this will be another mile closer to being over—and I'm not ready for that.

Turns out, neither are the pixies.

We're almost to the halfway point across the river when Bessie slams into an invisible shield of magic that compacts the front of her hood and sends us bouncing back toward the tree line.

"So close and yet so far," says a high-pitched voice coming from the dark center of the forest. "Nighty night, naughty trespasser."

And then everything goes dark.

Chapter Thirty-Three

Erik . . .

There's only darkness.

Well, that and a thumping pain in my head that makes me think the pixies have shrunk a German death metal band's drummer and trapped him in my skull. From what I hear about how the tricksters work, it sounds like something they'd do.

The last thing I remember before everything went black was the oh-shit look on LeLe's face the half second before Bessie's front end slammed into the pixies' security dome. I reach out for her, but the only thing I feel is the cold, slimy rock I'm propped up against.

The reality that LeLe is nowhere to be found punches me right in the nose, and I jolt upright, fighting past the gag-inducing pain to crack my eyelids open.

It doesn't help much.

Wherever I am, it's not as dark as the endless pits of Galadon, but it's close, and it smells just as bad. The stench of sulfur and sweaty socks makes my eyes water, and my stomach cramps from the kind of fear I haven't felt in years. Worse than a hobgoblin's acidic spit, it burns my gut, and I'm upright on my feet in the next instant, sliding my hand along the damp stone walls as I move, trying to find her.

"LeLe," I whisper-yell. "Where are you?"

The only response is a very deep, very growly giggle that turns into a wheeze, then a hiccup, and finally a flash of fire that lights up the whole place just long enough for me to see LeLe sitting on a boulder with a dragon's scaly tail wrapped around her like a body scarf made out of iridescent purple scales.

Did I mention the tail is still attached to the dragon? The *alive* dragon?

I start to sprint toward her and then—poof—I'm back in the dark, but still moving toward her. My foot lands in a puddle in just the wrong way, and the next thing I know the world goes tits up and I land with a hard thunk on my ass in a foul-smelling pool of slime—but there's no time to hesitate or take stock of what in the fuck just slid over my leg.

"Stay calm, LeLe," I say as I fail to follow my own advice and start to wind my magic up for a spell that will knock the dragon into the next dimension. Even with the pixies' magic-dulling powers while in their domain. "I'll get you out of there."

Somehow.

Someway.

There's always a loophole or an escape route somewhere, and when it comes to LeLe, I'm not giving up until I find it.

That's when the giggling starts again—except it's not just the rusty accordion sound coming from the dragon; LeLe is giggling too.

"Stop messing with him, Snookums," LeLe says with a smile I can see even though I can't. "Just light the candles already."

There's a deep inhale, and then a burst of flames lights up the ceiling of the cavernous space. The fire ignites the thick wicks of the three-foot-tall candles of a massive candelabra hanging from the stone ceiling. The bright light illuminates the cave, making the diamonds embedded in the stone walls glimmer and shine, but I only have eyes for my wife. She looks way too relaxed for someone who has a dragon's tail wrapped around her like a python—a dragon who's wearing a gold name tag with "Snookums" written on it hanging from a massive leather collar.

"Erik," she says, amusement teasing the corners of her full lips upward, "this is my friend."

It is an obvious cry for help. How could it not be? Every witch knows from the time they spin their first spell that dragons lurk on the edges of Witchingdom, watching and waiting to eat any snack-sized witch foolish enough to venture into their territory.

With anyone else, I would have sent out a quick feeler spell, but I don't need to with my wife. I already know. She is as relaxed as she was on that pool deck in Vegas. There isn't even a flicker of worry crinkling up the corner of her blue or her green eye. Nope, those are definitely smile lines. And is she gliding her hand over the dragon's scales as if she's petting him? There's no way. The woman is magic (literally and figuratively), but even she can't tame a beast that flosses its teeth with witches' bones.

"A *friend* with his tail holding you in place?" I ask as I inch forward, searching for any weakness to exploit as my gaze goes from the dragon's tail to its huge nostrils to the teeth the size of the trees that were flinging apples at us only minutes—hours? days?—before.

"This?" LeLe rolls her eyes as she gets up and climbs over the dragon's tail. "Snookums got scared."

Unease crawls up my spine like a murderous band of ants wearing ice picks on their feet. "What scares a dragon?"

"The dark." She puts her hand on the single pale yellow claw sticking out of the dragon's foot. "Poor thing gets scared and then he starts nervous sneezing and then he sneezes out the candles and then his ability to breathe fire gets all wonky and then he's stuck in the dark." She pats the dragon's toe claw and smiles up at him. "It's okay. A similar thing happens to one of my sister Tilda's friends. You are not alone."

The dragon—calling something so large, so toothy, and so able to breathe fire and turn us both into witch-shaped s'mores "Snookums" is too bizarre—starts purring.

Yes. Purring.

Right up until his neon green eyes land on me, and that soft, warm vibration becomes a low, growly rumble.

"Snookums, sit," a high-pitched voice calls out.

The dragon does just that as a pixie with ice-blue hair hovers in the air at the mouth of the cave, her iridescent silver wings moving almost too fast to see.

"Good Snookums," the pixie says before wriggling her nose half a second before a giant wheel of cheese poofs out of thin air and lands on the rock shaped like a giant dog bowl. "You two," she says, turning her attention back to LeLe and me after smiling indulgently at the dragon, "are coming with me. The queen wants to see you."

I have no idea what's coming next, but whatever it is, all I have to do is make sure LeLe makes it out of the woods.

We fall (literally) out of thin air after the pixie poofs us out of the cave and into a cleared circle in the forest that serves as the pixie queen's court throne room.

The pixie queen is not what I expected. Yeah, she's a pixie with wings that catch the light like dew on the morning grass, and she has that whole sweet and innocent vibe until she smiles, revealing substantial, razor-sharp pointed teeth that could easily slice through bone. Luckily, she's busy gnashing her way through a bowl of arugula and ladybugs as she watches us approach.

I never said it was lucky for the ladybugs, but better them than us.

LeLe and I come to a stop at the base of the glittering diamond staircase that leads to the queen's gilded throne. Between that and the plethora of gold reflecting the sunlight, it's hard to look straight at the queen without my eyes feeling like they're about to be burned out of their sockets. I highly doubt that's an accident.

The queen's ladies-in-waiting flutter in the air behind her, clasping their cupped hands together over their hearts. The sound of their wings and the crunch of raw arugula and ladybug shells are the only sounds in the room as we wait for the queen to acknowledge us.

And wait.

And wait.

And wait some more.

In most cases, this is when I'd pour on the sincere-sounding charm. If that failed, I'd start dropping the dirt I had on whoever was between me and what I wanted.

When it comes to pixies, though, things work a little different. Take talking, for instance. It is completely off the table because the pixies go really fucking hard for the "no speaking to the queen unless she speaks to you first" rule and enchanted our lips closed. The only thing keeping me from really losing my shit is that the queen is sitting on The Liber Umbrarum like it's some kind of throne pillow and I can see Bessie's bright yellow fins through the trees in the distance. As long as I have LeLe, the spell book, and Bessie, there has to be a way out of here. I don't know how I'll find it, but I know I have to.

The queen pops the last ladybug from her bowl into her

mouth and considers us as she crunches it into oblivion before finally speaking. "You've trespassed on pixie land and must prove you're worthy."

I try to respond, but my lips won't move. My wife, however, doesn't have the same problem.

LeLe lifts her chin and glares (or maybe squints because of the bright lights) at the queen. "Worthy of what?"

"Living," the queen declares with a smile that shows off all her pointy teeth. "You're lucky it's the slow season for mischief, otherwise we'd just feed you to Snookums and have it done with, but as it is, we're bored, so we've arranged a game to find out."

I squeeze LeLe's hand to warn her of the danger. Pixies love three things in life. One, stealing teeth from the tooth fairies. Two, singing sea shanties. And three, gambling on their games—not about which participants will win, but whether or not any of the participants will survive at all.

LeLe's gaze slides over to me, and I may not be able to actually say anything out loud, but I don't need to. The way she's clenching her jaw hard enough to crack a walnut shell and the way-too-calm-to-be-real look in her eyes says it all. Yeah, there's a little bit of I-told-you-not-to-go-into-the-forest in there too (it's the slight lift of one nostril that gives it away), but she squeezes my hand back and I know we're in it together. That really shouldn't settle in my chest, all warm and comforting, but it does.

I'm so beyond fucked, and it has nothing to do with the pixies.

It's all about my wife and how there's no way I can use her to get rid of my father like I'd planned. Somehow, someway, I have to find a loophole in my own tightly woven scheme.

But first, we have to survive the pixies.

LeLe straightens her shoulders and looks back over at the queen. "We absolutely adore games. Which ones will we be playing?"

"Before we get to that, you need to know the stakes," the queen says. "Complete the three simple challenges and you'll both go free. Fail and one of you will spend the next fifty years as my court jester while the other one does the same for our pixie cousins in Antarctica."

There's an excited tittering among the pixies, one of whom magics in a whiteboard. It's massive, dotted with gemstones, and already has the odds of our surviving for each of the three games. Going by the rush of pixies toward the line of bookies that starts immediately, they think the fifty-to-one odds of us surviving the first game are a safe bet.

"That sounds delightful," LeLe says, her tone just as icy and imperious as the queen's. "Of course, when we win, we leave here with The Liber Umbrarum."

That's my wife, eye on the prize. Always.

The queen snorts dismissively. "I don't think so."

Unfazed, LeLe asks, "What if we raise the stakes?"

The bookie closest to the whiteboard stills, and the whirring of the pixies' wings grows louder as they vibrate with excitement.

"Twenty-four hours," LeLe says with a nonchalant shrug

before giving my hand a reassuring squeeze, as if I could ever doubt she knows exactly what she is doing. "That's how long it will take to complete your challenges. Once that's done, you hand over Erik's car, Bessie, and The Liber Umbrarum, then we're free to go with your blessing—and if you renege"—she lifts her gaze so she's looking right into the bright light surrounding the queen and she doesn't even flinch—"you'll feel the force of the entire Sherwood family in this forest. Believe me, you don't want that."

A dead quiet fills the throne room as every pixie holds their breath watching the war of wills between their sovereign and the heir of one of Witchingdom's most powerful families. This is the kind of moment that they'll be telling stories about for generations. But I don't give two shits about that right now; all I can think about is how fucking hot my wife is.

Unlike most witches, LeLe doesn't throw her family power around to feed her ego or move her family up in society. If she did, she would have done so a half dozen times on this road trip—starting with getting into Bessie with me in the first place. It isn't the use of power that is so hot, though; it's the cool, calm, and collected competence on display that hits me harder than anything else. The woman knows what she is doing and how exactly to get what she wants. That is hot as fuck.

I've never seen being an heir as anything but a burden before, an anvil hanging around my neck, but watching her, I realize for the first time in my life that it doesn't have to be. All that family power, it can be used for good—even by a Svensen.

Sure, we are still most likely going to die, but we are going to do it like the heirs we are and could be.

"Your confidence is both impressive and foolhardy, but I accept your proposal," the queen says, breaking the silence a second before the squeak of a dry-erase marker on the white-board fills the throne room as the bookie starts putting up the new odds. "However, I do believe you're going to regret it. In a thousand years, only a few have ever brought me the magical stag who walks our woods, and a mere three have made it through cleaning Snookum's cave without being eaten. But no witch—and I do mean not a single one—has *ever* returned with a golden apple." The queen pauses to give LeLe an assessing look. "I accept your terms, Sherwood witch, as you accept mine. This deal is bound in magic and cannot be altered." She slides her gaze over to me. "There are no loopholes in this game."

She's wrong—she *has* to be wrong—because there are always cracks and crevices to exploit to slide through to freedom, and I'm going to use any means available to make sure LeLe is free after this. The queen smiles as if she can read my thoughts and it sends a chill through the air, making the hairs on the back of my neck stand at attention.

"There's a reason why you haven't been able to speak, Svensen witch," the queen says. "I'll abide none of your tricks here." She opens her right hand, revealing a mound of enchanted crystal dust in the center of her palm. "I'd wish you luck, but *that* would be a waste of a wish."

Then she blows the powder toward us and—poof!—we're gone into the black ether with only our wits and each other to do the impossible.

Chapter Thirty-Four

Erik . . .

Capturing a magical stag is the equivalent of reciting your ABCs backward while balancing a ball on one finger and hopping on one foot, *after* having one too many shots of tequila.

"I can't believe you talked me into this plan," LeLe says as she scans the forest floor for candlewick plants. "There's no way this will work."

Is she right? Probably.

However, if she has any better ideas about how to capture a black stag the size of a moose with a rack of silver horns etched with runes and ancient symbols no modern witch could translate, then she would have said so. The woman is not shy about telling people what to do—especially me—and she's usually right, which is a total turn-on. This time, though, she just wrinkles her nose and then starts walking through the forest with me looking for the pale yellow flowers blooming up the tall, straight stem of the candlewick plant.

I thread my fingers through hers as we make our way around great oaks with faces carved into the trunks. "Are you telling me that the Sherwood heir doesn't know her histories from the old tales?"

"Of the candlewick plant?" She scoffs and rolls her eyes at me even as she tightens her fingers around my hand. "Those are myths."

Once again, she's not wrong, but sometimes you gotta plow forward with only the possibility of getting your way. It's the don't-fight-turn-right mentality—even when you need to go left, if traffic is jammed up, instead of waiting for a few eons for a break, you turn right and then make your way back left. There's always a way. There's always a loophole. There's always a right turn that takes you left. You just have to find it.

"Myths?" I lift the back of her hand and kiss it. "That's what some people would like you to believe. If Sigrid knew you didn't believe, she'd be appalled and give you a twenty-book reading list to fix the errors in your education, wife."

That part's one hundred percent true—never mind that Sigrid gives everyone a reading list perfectly tailored to their likes and what she deems their absolutely appalling reading history omissions.

LeLe pulls us to a stop next to a tree that has a seriously realistic face of a woman with her eyes wide with shock embedded in the trunk and cocks her head to one side. "What are you talking about? I've read all of the candlewick spells. They help with inflammation, and that's not going to help here."

"Every old myth in Witchingdom started out with at least a nugget of truth. How many times did you hear stories of The Liber Umbrarum? Conventional wisdom said the book didn't exist, and yet here we are. One of Sigrid's favorite stories from the old tales is about the Candlewick Stag." LeLe gives me a blank look. "So there are these two lovers who are forbidden by their families from being together." We start walking again, making our way around the trees and large clumps of flowers, both of us scanning the area for candlewick plants. "They go to a pixie for help."

"Not the greatest move," LeLe says.

I nod in agreement. "The pixie promises she can help them for a price. They immediately agree. Then the pixie kills off both of their families in one poof of magic, turns to the lovers, and says problem solved."

LeLe gasps in surprise.

"Yeah, always lock down the details when working with the pixies or anyone under their protection," I continue, holding back a massive fern so she won't get whacked in the legs by it. "So the lovers are less than happy, to put it mildly. They beg and plead to save their families. The pixie agrees to reverse the spell while letting them stay together, but it comes at a cost. The lovers say the cost doesn't matter." LeLe mutters a curse about shortsighted fools under her breath. "The pixie does her part and poof, their family members come back to life."

LeLe stops in a patch next to a massive gnarled-up tree

while she absentmindedly rubs the handfast tattoo on her wrist that's glowing like neon, and that's the instant when realization slams into me like a train filled with dynamite.

We can't stay like this forever. It's not because of the pixies, although they are our current biggest problem. It's because it's only a matter of time before she finds out what I've done and—even worse—what I was planning on doing. I say "was" because there's no way I can do it now. Not even to save my brother and sister, wherever they are right now.

LeLe deserves more than to be my wife.

She deserves someone better than me to love her.

She deserves everything she'll never get if we're married.

I don't have to look at the divorce spell, I fucking stared at it so hard the first time she sent it that the words I need to say to complete it are seared into my brain. She's already done her part. She gathered the ingredients, wove the spell, chanted her part of the hex and, therefore, signed it in magic, so to speak. I just have to do my part and say the lines she highlighted and sent via flying monkeys months ago.

Undoing a spell takes far less magical energy than casting one, meaning that even with the pixie limitations on witchery, what I'm about to do won't be a problem. It's the worst best thing I'll ever do in my life. I'm not supposed to be this guy. I'm a Svensen. I'm a bad guy. I don't do good things.

And yet . . .

LeLe changed all that.

Looking down at the underbrush because I can't look at her when I do what I have to do next, I whisper my part of the divorce spell under my breath so quietly it's barely audible even to me.

My chest compresses like a troll is using me for a seat cushion and sucking in any oxygen isn't an option. Everything hurts so fucking bad. I glance over at my wrist and it looks exactly like a wrist is supposed to. My head pops up before I can stop myself or prepare for the worst.

The handfast mark is gone.

"But now the lovers are dead?" she asks, no longer rubbing her unmarked wrist and looking at me as if the whole world hasn't just ended.

Fucking hope. I, of all people, really should know better.

It takes me a second to remember how to speak, but being raised as a Svensen who learned from a young age to never ever show when you've just been gutted like a fish does have its benefits.

"Well, they aren't witches anymore." It takes more effort than I'll ever admit out loud, but I manage to put on that lazy grin, the one I used in Vegas, and focus on something just past her. "He's a stag and she's a candlewick plant. And, because pixie magic has its own kind of twisted logic, they're together for the rest of eternity because where you find one"—I point at the velvety yellow blooms basking in a beam of sunshine that breaks through the forest's canopy and then turn my hand so I'm pointing a few degrees farther north at a jet-black stag watching us from a safe distance—"you find the other."

My not-wife lets out a soft gasp before her whole body freezes as if she's afraid of scaring the stag off. The stag barely glances our way. His attention is completely focused on the candlewick plant as he makes his way into the sunshine illuminating the plant. He stops next to the tall stems covered with the pale yellow flowers and brushes his muzzle against them.

"What do we do?" she asks, her voice barely above a whisper.

I point to the forest floor between us and the stag, which is littered with dots of pale yellow. "We gather the candlewick petals that have already fallen and take them back to the throne room. He'll follow us there."

Concern has her gnaw on her bottom lip as she picks up the blooms. "The pixies won't hurt him, will they?"

"Even for that bloodthirsty lot, that would be beyond the bounds," I say, sounding a lot more confident than I'm feeling.

"No loopholes a Svensen can exploit?"

"Not in the pixie forest." Standing, I jerk my chin toward what looks like an ordinary spiderweb strung between two low-hanging branches. What gives it away as pixie magic is that there's still dew sparkling on it even after the sun's been out for hours. "They weave tight spells here."

The sound of tinkling laughter carries on the breeze even though there hasn't even been a hint of wind before that, and the web detaches from the tree and lands on top of us, covering us in magic. For a few seconds there's nothing but darkness, and then I'm blinking away the brightness of the pixie queen's throne room.

Once again LeLe and I are standing alone in the center as the pixies flutter around behind their queen. The stag stands by a basket of candlewick petals, a soft blue glow around him. Next to him is the whiteboard. Our odds have improved from certain to die to most likely to die.

I'll take it.

"You're not as dumb as you look, witches," the queen says as she opens her hand, revealing the crystal dust in her palm. "It won't be so easy with Snookums."

I have just enough time to grip LeLe's hand before the queen covers us in dust and we're everywhere and nowhere all over again.

Chapter Thirty-Five

LeLe . . .

Snookums has the zoomies, which is an activity that always makes me laugh when it's my sister's rooster familiar Barkley running around like a chicken with its head cut off, but I'm not chuckling now. Why? Because witnessing the zoomies, with its high rate of speed and hairpin turns, is downright terrifying when it's a dragon the size of two jumbo-sized elephants stacked on top of each other that's running in circles in a cave the size of a hunting cabin.

Erik yanks me back just as Snookums speeds over to us and drops a piece of vulcanized rubber at my feet that is more the idea of a chew bone than an actual one. It's the same bone Erik and I spent the past ten minutes struggling to heft into the dragon's toy basket. Snookums pauses in his one-dragon race, his lilac tongue hanging out of the side of his mouth, long enough to stare at me and wag his spiked tail. That motion sends another toy flying through the air and the dragon lets out a bleat of excitement before taking off after it, moving so fast from an absolute standstill that his claws leave grooves in the cave's stone floor.

"That explains why so few have managed to complete this challenge," Erik says as he wraps his arms around my waist and pulls me closer so my back is tucked up against his chest.

It's really not the time—we do have a literal countdown clock for this challenge floating in the air above us after all, and it has less than twenty minutes to go on it before our time in this forest is literally up—but I relax back against him anyway. The truth is even if we make it out of the forest, get The Liber Umbrarum tucked away safe in the secured facility, and Erik participates in the divorce spell that's all I've wanted for the past year, I'll still feel like I lost because my shouldn't-be husband won't be anymore, and right now I can't imagine a fate worse than that.

Some fucking heir I am. I have literally one job—do the best thing for my family always, more specifically divorce Erik and marry someone who could help us politically as we fight to save Witchingdom from the Council, you know, just a little inconsequential thing—and yet I'd rather be stuck in these woods forever than do it.

As the Sherwood heir I have one job.

One!

And it's *not* doing what I want, but what is best for the family.

There is no question about what I should do when it comes to the fate of my family and Witchingdom as a whole versus getting to be with Erik. Still, no matter the shame that makes my whole body flinch, if given the choice, I'd roll the dice and hope the fates could find a way to make it all work out.

Love has turned me into an absolute selfish asshole.

Grumbling under my breath, I push back all thoughts of how I ever let this happen and try to focus on how losing Erik and finally getting what I've wanted all along is the best thing ever. I suck at that even more than I do at not falling in love with my husband.

Erik gives me a comforting squeeze. "What's wrong?"

Wrong? Oh, nothing. Just that I have fallen in love with the absolute worst person for me to fall for in all of Witchingdom. Oh, and yeah, if we survive until the morning—a big if—he's soon going to be my ex-husband who I'll never see or talk to ever again. Neither of those is going to make me freak out and cry. Nope. Not going to happen. No matter how much panic is gripping my lungs so tight I can't breathe in any oxygen or how hard I'm having to blink my eyes to make them stop watering. I am the Sherwood heir, and damn it, I'm going to behave like it.

"What makes you think something's wrong?" I ask, cursing the fact that my voice cracks on the last word.

Erik brushes a kiss across the top of my head. "The fact that you went all stiff and mumbled 'fuck me' under your breath might have tipped me off."

Way to go, Leona. Way to keep your shit under wraps. Totally heir behavior there.

"We can't keep doing this," I say as I look up at the count-down clock, hoping he'll believe my play that I am just stressed about the challenge—which you know I am. "It's not working."

"Hard agree," Erik says as Snookums drops another toy at our feet and then races off. "You got any ideas?"

"No, I—" The solution hits me smack-dab in the face just as the dragon scoops up a bedraggled stuffed bear the size of a grizzly off the floor. "I know exactly what to do."

"Well, don't keep it to yourself."

"I stand over here and Snookums does the work for us."

"How?" He cocks his head in confusion for a second, then his gaze drops to where I'm pointing and his eyes go wide. He lets out a laugh that echoes off the cave's high stone ceiling. "Fucking brilliant."

"You're not so bad yourself."

I climb up the boulder behind Snookums's tall, woven toy basket and make eye contact with the dragon. "Toy?"

He lets out a whine of excitement and races over to me, the bear's butt and hind legs sticking out of his mouth.

"Drop it," I say as I point to the basket.

While Snookums stares at the basket and contemplates what to do next, I nod my chin toward a massive bouncy ball close by. Erik winks at me and sprints over to it.

"Ball?" I ask Snookums.

The dragon's tail starts wagging fast enough to kick up a serious breeze and he drops the bear in the basket.

"Over here, Snookums," Erik calls out in a singsong voice.

The dragon whines with glee and heads right for him at

light speed, stopping just short of stomping on my husband to pick up the ball and head back to me.

"Look at you!" I tell the dragon. "Such a good Snookums. Now, drop the ball in the basket."

As he's doing so, I watch Erik run over to a hard rubber femur that looks big enough to have come from Big Foot.

"Bone?" I ask Snookums. "Go get the bone!"

The dragon does, and each time he retrieves one of his toys, Erik and I cheer like our favorite team just won the Witch's Cup, which makes Snookums run even faster to retrieve the next toy. By the time he drops the last stuffy—an oversized turtle—there's forty-five seconds left on the countdown clock for this challenge.

I have just enough time to make eye contact with Erik and wonder which one of us is grinning bigger when the world goes dark around me and once again I'm sailing through the ether heading back to the pixie queen's throne room.

Either I'm getting used to the blink-and-you-miss-it form of travel or I'm just riding high on completing two out of the three challenges, but I barely want to puke my guts up when the pixie magic unceremoniously drops us off in the throne room.

"Your odds of survival keep getting better," the queen says, disgust thick in her voice. "However, there's only ever been one person to complete the final challenge and neither of you have the coordination and skills of an alpha werewolf. Do you really think you can beat an alpha?" She opens her palm, revealing the all-too-familiar pile of pixie dust. "Now get out of my sight."

She blows the dust straight at us and then we're flying in nothingness with only each other and one last challenge standing between us and what for me is beginning to feel like a bitter-sweet victory.

Chapter Thirty-Six

Erik . . .

We land in a heap on the forest floor close enough to the river's edge marking the border of the pixies' land to hear it but far enough away that we can't see it through the trees. The queen, no doubt, just couldn't help sending us a little close-but-not-close-enough reminder. The woman loves her mind games. She and my dad would get along great.

LeLe sits up and starts to pull out the crunchy fall leaves stuck in her red waves. "I'm really beginning to think the queen is betting against us."

I lean close and pull a twig out of her hair. "Tell me something I don't know."

She looks up at me, her lips parted as if she's about to say something, but the air shifts around us. The scent of her magic is there as she gathers it within herself, soft and barely detectable because of the pixie blockade, but the abilities of an heir—especially one like LeLe—aren't so easy to put on lockdown.

In the beginning, it was her warm cake donut smell that called me because of what it represented—power and the ability to wield it against my father. But now? Yes, LeLe is one of the strongest witches there is, but she's so much more than that.

She's everything—except mine, and I fucking hate that almost as much as I love her. It makes my gut twist and my chest hurt like a real bitch, and part of me wants to just give in to the pain and the bitterness. But I've had a lot of practice in my life with denial for a greater purpose, and right now that purpose is getting LeLe out of this forest.

Still, I'm an asshole who can't help but take a taste of what he can't have.

I dip my head down and brush my lips across hers. I swear, that's all I intend, but the second I touch her, I forget the shit we're in, where we are, and the rest of the world in general. There's only the two of us. And when she kisses me back, my whole body responds. Heat and want and the rush of I-can't-believe-this-is-happening slam into me. My fingers are threading through her hair and I'm cupping the back of her head before I know it, deepening the kiss and putting into action everything I can't say no matter how much I wish I could. She matches my intensity, then kicks it up a few notches because she doesn't just give as good as she gets, the woman I love always does more. Fuck me, does she ever. A more cynical me would say it's because of the adrenaline rush of what's at stake here, but I know better. It has been, is, and always will be like this with LeLe. I'm not perfect for her, but damn is she perfect for me.

A better man would stop this now, but we all know that man is not me. I'm no hero. I'm just an asshole who isn't ready to say goodbye.

Every nerve in my body is tuned in to LeLe—how she moves, the way she shivers when I yank a little harder on her hair, every little moan that escapes that sweet mouth of hers. So when she grabs my shirt and yanks it out of my jeans, I'm already ahead of her, rolling us so I'm on my back in the undergrowth and she's sitting astride me.

Eyes hazy with lust, she looks down at me and her lips curl into a smile too wicked for the always-does-the-right-thing Sherwood heir. Not everyone gets to see that grin. It's mine. Just for me. And it steals the air from my lungs. Her quick fingers are on the button of my jeans before I can recover, but believe me, I get my shit together pretty damn fast because I like the way she's thinking.

"There are other creatures about, you know," a low voice booms with enough bass to make the ground vibrate under my ass. "Why must witches be so uncouth?"

In less than a heartbeat I'm on my feet, taking LeLe with me as adrenaline surges through me. My only thought is keeping the woman I love safe as I whirl around, shoving her behind me at the same time, ready to take on whatever pixie-incited fuckery has appeared. But it's not a pair of cursed lovers or an oversized pet hyped up on magic dragon biscuits glaring at us. Instead, a giant oak tree is sneering at us.

"It's not their fault they weren't born as an oak or an elm or even," the tree next to the first one says before dropping her voice, "a weeping willow."

"I heard that," a tree wails from somewhere deep in the forest.

"And we love you just the way you are, Antoine," the second tree calls out before turning her gaze back to me. "Hello there," she says, speaking very slowly and very loudly as if I'm fifty-one cards short of a full deck. "I am Addison. This is my often peevish and occasionally cantankerous brother Asher. Don't worry, he's all whining and no flinging across the forest."

"Unless circumstances necessitate it, and then I shall not hesitate," Asher grumbles.

I take a half step to the side, putting more of myself between the oak tree's branch reach and LeLe. She snorts in response and just sidesteps my attempt at protection, moving to stand beside me as she intertwines her fingers with mine. She shoots me a quick wink as if to say, *You know we're doing this together, right?* I'd argue if there were any point, but she's right: There's a better chance of her getting out of here if we work together than if I try something completely out of character like playing the hero.

"I beseech you to ignore my quarrelsome sibling," Addison says. "He is in a mood because it is his turn to carry the orchard's curse."

"The weight of it puts your branches out of symmetry, as you well know, sister," Asher says, sounding even more annoyed with the world than he had before. He lifts one branch higher, making all his leaves shake, until his left side is an exact replica of his right—except for the shiny golden apple hanging from the end of one limb.

Jackpot.

LeLe lets out a soft gasp of surprise and squeezes my hand. I slide my gaze over. Her lips are still kiss swollen, but the desire in them has been replaced by a singularly focused determination. It is, without a doubt, so fucking hot to see her go into get-my-way mode. When she takes over as head of the Sherwood family, the Council isn't going to stand a chance—especially now that the dimitto spell is complete and she isn't a Svensen anymore. She doesn't have to worry about my family's stain tarnishing her. I won't let it. And The Liber Umbrarum? There's a whole world out there for her to hide it from the Council. She'll find the right place. It's what she does. She makes things—and people—better.

"It really is such an annoyance whenever it appears," Antoine continues in his haughty tone. "The songbirds try to impale their beaks on the impenetrable surface with disastrous results. The raccoons try to nibble it and end up with broken teeth for their efforts. Then there are the pixies, who are absolutely obsessed with it because it is a shiny prize to be won, as if they need anything else to gamble on. They are quite committed to living a wastrel lifestyle."

"I can take it, if you want," LeLe says, giving the tree a charming smile as she steps forward. "We could trade for it, anything you want. Just ask."

Antoine crosses his branches and peers down at her. "You've traveled a lot?"

The instincts honed from being raised in the vipers' den otherwise known at the Svensen family buzz to life, making my skin crawl with unease. Antoine might look like your everyday magical tree complete with a surly attitude and strong branches strengthened by tossing witches around, but there is something more to him. Just how many rings does his trunk have? No doubt enough to hide a whole lot of intelligence behind a wooden exterior. And for all the brains and negotiating skill LeLe has, she didn't get it from growing up knowing that you were completely and utterly on your own.

I shoot Asher my most charming dumb-fuck grin and answer before LeLe gets a chance. "I've been all over Witchingdom and beyond."

The oak's attention zeroes in on me. "And you've got stories to share?"

There it is. Everyone wants something. My dad covets power and money. LeLe wants to make Witchingdom the kind of place it can be, the kind we tell ourselves lies about that it already is. This tree with its roots planted so deep it can't ever leave wants to know what the world is like beyond the forest.

And me? Well, what I want doesn't matter.

That's why it is barely even a sacrifice to pay the oak's

price—and there will be one—for the golden apple that will get LeLe free. It's not a sacrifice. I'm not a hero, remember. I don't do that shit.

"I've got so many stories about trolls and witches and dancing gnomes that glow in the dark," I tell Asher, putting everything I can into selling it. "The spells that went wrong and the curses that went right. All of the stuff they keep off of WitchyGram when they post about it. The good, the bad, and the too interesting to share with the general public."

The oak takes barely thirty seconds to consider my offer before the leaves hanging from his branches nod in agreement. "Then it'll be you."

"What do you mean, 'it'll be him,'" LeLe asks, her voice tight.

"Our newest member," Addison says, her voice filled with excitement as she does a pretty identifiable jazz hands impression with her leaves.

"Not everyone gets this opportunity," Asher says. "Usually we just mulch the creatures—witches especially—who annoy us."

Next to me, LeLe practically hums with righteous indignation. It's exactly why she'll be such an amazing matriarch; she really does care what happens to people—even the ones she shouldn't.

"I have one condition," I say before LeLe gets a chance to let loose with some well-intentioned fury on the oak.

"You think you get to make demands?" Asher asks, bending at the trunk and leaning in close to me.

Under normal circumstances, this is when I'd find the

loophole to jump right through and get myself the fuck out of this situation. But these aren't normal circumstances. This oak holds the fate of Witchingdom and—more importantly—LeLe in its gnarled branches. A loophole is the last thing I'm looking for; in fact, what I want is the exact opposite—an agreement so tight there's no space to slip between.

So I let the protective menace I usually only experience when my dad's threatening Cy and Sigrid bubble to the surface. "We're here on the orders of the pixie queen to take the golden apple and bring it back to her."

Asher scoffs and shrugs his limbs. "Do I look like a pixie to you?"

"No, but you do look like an oak who wants to know exactly what a satyrs' inn looks like, how a sentient house in love behaves, and what it's like to wake up in the morning next to the witch who made you see everything in a whole new way," I say, my voice as cold and steady as I feel. "I'll tell you that and so much more about my travels and the people I've met, but she gets to take the golden apple to the pixie queen, fulfill the challenge, and take The Liber Umbrarum out of the forest. Even if you can't use the Svensen safe house, you'll figure out how to keep it safe, I know you will. That's who you are, a witch who gets shit done."

"Erik," LeLe exclaims. "I can't leave you beh—"

"You have to," I cut her off, keeping my focus on Asher, because if I look at LeLe, the woman I love, I can't guarantee I won't give in out of pure selfishness to finding some way to stay with her even if that means the worst happens. "The Council can't get The Liber Umbrarum. And don't worry about the dimitto spell. We're already divorced, just like you wanted. Look at your wrist."

There's a few seconds of silence before she asks in a quiet voice. "How?"

"There's always a loophole, remember? There's nothing in that spell that said we have to recite the magic words at the same time, only that we each had to do our part, which you'd done before you'd ever sent it to me via flying monkey." I narrow my eyes at Asher. "We have a deal? I become a tree. LeLe takes the golden apple to the pixie queen, thus completing the queen's challenge and receiving The Liber Umbrarum and Bessie as her prize. As we both know, the queen will try to wiggle out of the deal. You and the rest of the trees, however, will do whatever it takes to make sure the pixies uphold their side of the agreement and ensure that LeLe leaves here unharmed and unhindered with The Liber Umbrarum. Do you agree to those exact terms?"

"No, it's too much," LeLe says. "I can't let you become a tree while I go free."

"Everyone in Witchingdom would tell you that turning into an oak is better than being a Svensen."

Her hands cup my face and she turns my head so I have to look in the tear-filled eyes and watch her chin tremble as she says, "Not everyone."

Even knowing it's not an I love you, a warmth fills my chest as if it were. And for a second I let myself believe, let images of what could have been fill my mind and believe just for a second that a guy like me could ever have a life like that.

I take her hands away from my face and kiss her palms before giving her a wink and a smile as if everything since that pool in Vegas has just been a meaningless game. "And they say no divorce is ever amicable."

She flinches—just barely, but I catch it. That old familiar sense of being the biggest asshole in the room fills me and I grab ahold of it with both hands, relishing the way it numbs everything else so all I feel is nothing.

I look back up at Asher. "Do you agree?"

"I give my word and the strength of my forest." The oak closes his eyes and a wind that smells like the first day of fall rustles through his leaves. "Let it begin."

At first there's nothing and then there's everything. The air cools. I can hear not just the birds in the tree but the sound of each individual feather beating against the air. I can feel the seeds buried belowground begin to split and the first sprout of growth pushing upward. The colors around me become more vibrant and varied as if instead of only a dozen shades of green there are now a million. And the sun streaming down through between the limbs of the tall trees is peace and joy and the pinnacle of all that has ever been or could ever be. In other words, exactly like when LeLe looks at me and smiles.

"So it's settled—or at least it will be by morning when the magic firms up," Addison says, bringing her branches together and clapping.

"I just need to take care of one thing first." I look up at Asher and shoot him a cocky grin. "I don't suppose I can borrow the apple and make a quick phone call before I turn into a living lumber."

The whole forest goes silent for a second as even the squirrels tucked into the tree trunks' hollows stick their heads out to see what the oak who loves to mulch witches is going to do next.

"Can you believe the acorns on this guy?" Asher lets out a genuine chuckle, then shrugs his branches. "Fine. Make your call."

Chapter Thirty-Seven

LeLe . . .

This should be the absolute best day of my fucking life.

One, I'm coming out on the right side of a pixie challenge, which almost no witch ever does.

Two, I'm officially single again without my family ever finding out I married a Svensen—the one thing I want more than anything.

Three, the heir of my family's nemesis house is about to be turned into a tree.

That's about as close to the ultimate happiness trifecta as a witch can hope to get.

And yet?

And yet, I've never felt more miserable in my life. My body aches with a million discomforts—the stabbing pinch making the arch of my foot cramp to the uptick in acid sloshing around in my belly to the bitter taste of six-day-old burnt coffee coating my tongue. Everything feels too full to the point of bursting except for my chest. That's weirdly empty, like completely scooped out so there's nothing left but this cavernous open space.

It's the same story between my ears because all I can do is stand by with white fuzz buzzing in my brain so I only catch about every third word as Erik uses his last phone call to bring his dad up to speed with most of what has happened. Why? I have no fucking clue any more than I understand why it feels like the world is about to end when everything is finally how it is supposed to be.

Erik reaches out and takes my hand, sending a soft tease of awareness skittering along my skin and bringing me back to the here and now.

"The Sherwood twit is going to be turned into a tree?" The Svensen patriarch lets out a roar of happy laughter that I would have been able to hear even if he weren't on speakerphone. "That means no Sherwood heir, which decimates their family magic, which leaves a power vacuum. And as everyone knows, Witchingdom abhors a vacuum, so I guess we Svensens will just have to step forward and pick up the slack. The Council will think they're running things, but they'll be wrong, thanks to the fact that I'll be the one with The Liber Umbrarum."

Wait, what?

I jolt back, confusion running smack-dab into me. How does Erik's dad have it so wrong? Confusion swamping me, I open up my mouth to clear up the misunderstanding, but Erik shakes his head at me.

"This is perfect for us," his dad goes on. "I couldn't have planned it any better myself. And to think I ever thought an elf had swapped you out for another child. You are most definitely my boy. You have no idea what a relief it is to know that I don't have to go with Plan B—not that you need to know what that was—and that our family's magic will be safe with you, that our legacy and standing will continue for generations to come. Come home, son, and bring the spell book. Now that we don't have to worry about the Sherwoods, Witchingdom is mine."

My gut clenches and I run everything back in my head since I got into Bessie. Has the whole thing been a con, like Vegas?

I can't breathe. My mind goes blank. The world starts to dim a little at the edges as panic grabs ahold of me and squeezes me like a dog with a squeaky toy. Then Erik looks over at me and smiles. It's not a smirk of can-you-believe-this-guy or a mocking grin, it's a real true expression, as if no matter what else is going on with the world, when he looks at me none of it matters. And in that instant all the anxiety and fear melts into a kind of certainty I can't explain, I just know it. Erik Svensen loves me, and I love him.

"I never said LeLe was the one becoming a tree," Erik says as he sets his phone down next to the golden apple resting on a flat-topped boulder. "I'm not coming home."

"What in the fates are you yammering about?" his dad yells, his tone filled with unbridled bitterness. "You best remember that you're still just the heir. You do what I say. You jump when I order it. You speak the words I put in your mouth. You don't belong to you. You're mine, do you hear me, boy?"

I'm about to start yelling in Erik's defense when I smell the warm comfort of freshly brewed coffee in the air. He winks at me and gives my hand a quick squeeze as if to say that his dad isn't worth the oxygen I'd use up hollering at him.

"We've got this," he whispers so only I can hear. "Trust me. Just do your thing. Let's cook."

I have no idea what exactly we've got besides an asshole Svensen patriarch on the phone, Erik on the verge of becoming a tree unless we find a loophole, and the Council on our ass if we ever make it out of this forest, but I do trust him.

Closing my eyes, I let out a deep exhale until there's no oxygen left and I hold it there for a moment, calling that deep Sherwood magic. It bursts forward, sweet and sugary the way only a donut straight out of the oven can smell. Our magic intertwines around us, the power of the combined force making it take an airy form, like steam that glimmers in the sunlight. Even when the entire Sherwood family gathers in the kitchen to create a spell together, the power stays invisible, and the shock of seeing my magic, his magic, *our* magic like this nearly snaps my concentration.

Erik shoots me a quick wink and mouths "trust me" before nodding his chin at his hand on top of the golden apple. It's gone from dull gold to glowing bright with an orange, almost lava-looking texture. Our magic may not be in top form in these woods, but with the golden apple, he has the power to complete almost any spell. And our magic together with the apple? Nothing can stop us.

He lifts his hand and our magic flickers in the sunlight before becoming invisible. Then he puts his hand back down on the once-again dull gold apple. It takes a second, but the glow returns, as does our magic in visual form, swirling around us as it gathers strength.

"I hear you. I've always heard you," Erik says, his voice deadly cold. "Every plot, every scheme, every plan to make sure you ended up on top—no matter who had to be sacrificed to make it happen, I've been right there hearing it all. But you haven't been listening. If you had, you'd know what was coming next—the end of the line."

"Are you trying to bullshit a bullshitter, son? Because it's not gonna work," his dad says, each word getting louder and more strident. "I'm here today. I'll be here tomorrow. I'll be here when the Council catches up to you thanks to me tipping them off to your location yet again. The end of the line? It's only the beginning for me."

"There you go, thinking it's only about you, but it's not, it never was." His hold on my hand tightens as he mouths "now" at me. "It was supposed to be about the family. It was supposed to be about taking care of the people you love."

I cover his hand lying on the apple just as he finishes, closing the loop.

Power surges through me, a hot blast of magic in its purest form. The air around us sparks with electricity and it feels like the earth stopped rotating but Erik and I continue to circle again and again and again, whirling through it all together as one, as if we'd always been and always would be.

Then it's gone, like the snap of a light switch being turned off.

I fall against Erik, unable to stand on my jelly legs, and he wraps both arms around me and holds me tight. He brushes a kiss across the top of my head, and I swear he says "Thank you, love," but too quietly for me to know for sure. My skin tingles with the aftermath, I assume, but there's something more that I can't put a name to. It's just there, an ember waiting to be turned into a bonfire.

"A good family patriarch—a good witch—would know all of that," Erik says, his voice tired from the obvious effort of being a conduit for that much magic. "But I know better than most that you aren't that kind of witch. Of course, it doesn't really matter now you're not a patriarch anymore."

"You've lost your damn senses," his dad says, but there's a new, unsure shake to his voice. "I *am* the Svensen patriarch. *I* control the family magic."

"Not after that power exchange ceremony," Erik says.

His dad scoffs. "You're full of shit."

"So call Cy and Sigrid. I know they're hiding from you, but you could summon them," Erik says as if he's talking about something as banal as the weather rather than a move for control so ingenious it will have all of Witchingdom talking for generations. "As the holder of the family magic, it's your power to wield and their undeniable duty to respond."

"I am the head of this family," his dad says, his voice wobbling. "I won't do party tricks for you."

"Because you can't." Erik drops another kiss to the top of my head and pulls me tight against him. "The family power isn't yours anymore."

There's silence from the phone as his dad must be calling up the Svensen magic and getting nothing but his own meager personal supply. I relax back against Erik, trying to get everything into a sensible order in my head. He's always been a solid wall of muscle, but this is different, this is—

No! Not yet!

Desperation sucks all the air out of my lungs, and I try to turn around, to see for myself what's happening, but Erik tightens his grip around me so I can't.

"And I suppose you think you're witch enough to be the family patriarch I never could be."

Erik lets out a harsh laugh. "A half-dead slug stuck on the sidewalk after a big rain would be a better patriarch than I would, but no, I don't hold the family magic—LeLe does."

His dad's voice explodes out of the phone, yelling and screaming obscenities at a volume I didn't think could be achieved by a witch, but Erik doesn't say anything to cut off the diatribe. He just reaches over and taps the end call button.

"But that's not possible, right?" I ask as I finally manage to turn around in his arms to face him. "How did you—"

The words die on my tongue as I take in the changes already happening. His hair is growing and thickening like branches reaching upward toward the sun, his skin darkening into the dark brown of an oak, and the fine lines in his face turning into deep, bark-like grooves.

He tucks a hair behind my ear, the tip of his finger hard and rough, while he looks at me as if he's memorizing my face because it's the last time he'll ever see it. "When you have access to a golden apple while in the pixie forest where the rules of witch magic don't apply, you can do just about anything."

"You could have saved yourself."

"Saving myself is what I've been doing my whole life." His lips curl in a small smile and he stiffly leans down and kisses me with an intensity that makes my heart ache. "Figured I'd try something new."

"So what's the plan for you?" Using the back of my hand, I wipe away the tears starting to fall, unable to tap into the iciness I've depended on for years. "How do we get you out of this?"

"We can't," he says, his voice deeper than before. "I gave my word, and honestly, I kind of like not breaking it." He takes me by the hips and puts space between us. The few inches feel like miles. "Maybe Svensens aren't naturally all bad."

Racking my brain, I run through every spell I've ever memorized, every magical theory I've ever heard, and every lecture on enchantments I've ever sat through looking for something—anything—that I can do to stop this and come up with exactly nothing. Stupid. I am being stupid. There has to be a way. I just need to find it. I *have* to find it.

"But you said there's always a loophole," I say, my voice breaking. "There's always a way out."

"Every rule needs an exception, and this is it." He takes a few steps back so he's in line with the other trees. As soon as he does, gnarled roots shoot from his feet, diving down into the ground and locking him in place. "Take the golden apple to the pixie queen, get The Liber Umbrarum, and get out of this forest. I just took care of my father. It's up to you to be Witchingdom's hero. I love you, Le—"

Before he can get my nickname out, the transformation comes to completion, sealing his lips closed so it looks like someone carved Erik's face into an oak tree, and I collapse in a heap on the ground in his shade.

"You better go," Addison says, not unkindly as she looks into the distance. "The wolves are at the door."

That's when I hear the motorcycle.

Chapter Thirty-Eight

LeLe . . .

*F*uck the werewolves. I'm not going anywhere without Erik.

I may not be a Svensen anymore, but they aren't the only ones who can sniff out a loophole when necessary.

But first, I have to deal with the werewolves.

Wiping my tears away with the back of my hand and willing my nose to stop running, I scramble up from the ground. Doing my best to ignore the sound of the motorcycle engine getting closer and the rush of blood in my ears as the adrenaline spikes in my veins, I pick up the golden apple from the rock and hold it tight against my chest as I call on my magic to pour into it so it can amplify it. The scent of warm donuts is weak, but it's there, fighting against the pixie prohibition against witchy magic in their forest as I summon everything

I've got. Beads of sweat slide down the back of my neck as I dig deep, focusing on the apple to unlock its power.

But nothing happens.

Letting out a deep breath, I try again. And again. And again. Each time I get the same result. Not a damn thing.

There's not a thrum or a quiver coming from the apple, nor does it give off even a single wattage of light, let alone enough to keep the world's darkness at bay. Instead it's just magical pyrite—a heavy, cold metal dud.

"It's a one-time-use object," Addison says.

"And more trouble than they're worth," Asher adds. "Especially since I'm an oak tree, not an apple tree."

"It's called the wonder of magic, Asher," Addison sighs. "Do you have to suck the joy out of everything?"

As they continue to bicker, the sound of the motorcycle goes from distant thunder to a tornado. Squaring my shoulders, I ready myself for whatever fresh shitstorm is about to rain down. Honestly, after everything that has happened since I saw Erik at that pool bar in Vegas, I'm prepared for every possibility.

Check that, because I'm definitely not prepared for seeing my older sister behind the handlebars of the alpha Aetos's motorcycle while he keeps pace beside her in his wolf form. Looking like some kind of avenging goddess with her long dark hair flying in the wind as she guns the engine, Effie swerves around trees and dodges the animals scurrying to safety as if she's been doing it her entire life. The motorcycle roars as it heads straight for me, turning at the last minute and coming to a hard stop. She's off the bike a second later and sprinting over to me, wrapping her arms around me in the kind of hug only a sister can give.

"Who *are* you?" I ask when she lets go enough for me to get a breath in.

"Your big sister, you lucky witch." She narrows her eyes as she takes a step back and holds me by the shoulders as she gives me a serious once-over. "If you offed him, I know how to hide the body."

The huge werewolf lets out a low growl and bares his teeth before sitting down next to Effie.

Completely unbothered by the massive werewolf acting as her shadow, she rolls her eyes. "Just because I watch a lot of true crime shows. Don't get your fur in a twist, Darius."

He lets out a wolfish huff and then turns his eerie golden gaze on me. He contemplates me for a second before the air shimmers around him, taking on that wavy look the road gets on a hot day that gives you an idea of what's ahead without giving you a clear picture. There's a distinct cracking sound as he starts to shift, going from wolf to man in less time than it takes me to order my morning elderberry tisane at the Alchemist's Bookshop and Tea Emporium. I try not to notice that he's buck-ass naked, but there's really no way to avoid it. Werewolves are kind of known for being clothing optional, but it's overwhelming when you're not used to it. He walks past my sister to his motorcycle, reaches inside the leather saddlebag attached to it, and pulls out a pair of jeans.

Lifting a single dark eyebrow, he grins at Effie. "Get a good look, or should I wait to put these on?"

She shrugs one shoulder as if there weren't a naked six-foot-seven man standing in front of her. "Like I care either way." Then she turns back to me and gives me another hug. "Ignore him. He's just my ride."

"Effie," I say, my voice sounding as broken as I feel. "What's going on? What are you doing here?"

"Short answer? I used a hot-wire spell on his motorcycle and came after you before he could stop me," she says. "Long answer? Considering I arrived with the scion of Witching-dom's criminal underworld, it's better you have plausible deniability on that one. Trust me."

Speaking of our dear mother . . . She pulls a burner phone out of her jacket's inside pocket and hands it to me. "She sent me with this."

The phone rings as soon as I take it. "Hello?"

"Darling, I've been worried about you. How are you?"

I am a grown woman, yes, but in this moment, hearing my mother's voice, all that age and experience fades away and I'm twelve again, pouring my heart out to my mommy. I tell her everything—almost everything—about my secret marriage, the road trip with The Liber Umbrarum, and the realization that I am in love with my no-longer husband.

"I was curious about how all of that would work out," Mom says. "He is a rather interesting match for you. Not expected, but very, very interesting."

Dumbfounded doesn't begin to explain how I feel as my legs give out and I plunk down on the flat-topped boulder. "You knew? Is that some special power the family magic gives you? Could you see the handfast mark?"

My mom snorts. "I knew the moment you came back from Vegas because I am your mother and I *know* you."

"I'm so sorry." My voice shakes as I barely get the words out. "You're disappointed. You made all those plans for me, for the family, for Witchingdom and—"

"Oh, Leona," Mom interrupts with a sigh. "It's me who is sorry. I've failed you because I never taught you the most important thing about being the family matriarch. You can't take care of anyone else if you don't take care of yourself. It's that whole in-case-of-a-magic-carpet-losing-altitude-put-your-oxygen-mask-on-first thing. You can't save the world or your family if you're suffocating."

It makes sense, but I can't shake the weight of expectation and responsibility that comes with being the heir. I've been carrying it my whole life and it's not like I can just shrug it off. The entire family is depending on me. "But our family needs me to—"

"Do the right thing?" Mom cuts in and then lets loose with a wry chuckle. "No one ever does the right thing every time. It's just not possible. And what's right may not always look that way at first. That's why it's so important that you listen to that little voice of truth inside you. It's the itch you can't reach, the feeling you can't explain, and the certainty that has no basis—

it just is. And you've always had that in you. The magic saw it the moment you were born and glommed on to you, making you the Sherwood heir because it knew it would always be safe with you." She lets out a weary sigh. "No one can ever understand what that's like, the joy and fear of being responsible for an entire family and its legacy—except another heir, of course. It's quite a gift when you can find someone who understands you at a level no one else ever could—someone named Erik Svensen, for example."

Am I crying hard enough at this point that Effie is fast-walking over to me? Yes. But even through the tears I can see something that I somehow missed before. My family—annoying, demanding, hilarious, quirky, always in my business, who I will spend the rest of my life looking out for—watch out for me just as much. Being the heir doesn't mean I'm alone.

Effie sits down beside me, wrapping me up in her big sister love as I say the one thing an heir is never supposed to admit. "I don't know how to fix this."

"Of course you do," Mom says, her voice so full of confidence that it fills me up a little too. "You save your husband."

She says it like it'll be easy. Maybe for her, the family matriarch. But for me? I'm just the witch who slips coming out of the shower and ends up with Barkley roosting on my ass.

"Now, the pixie queen should be there any second with The Liber Umbrarum. Lucille and I go way back, but that doesn't mean you should trust her, and whatever you do, don't accept another challenge from her. It was hard enough to negotiate

AVERY FLYNN

terms for the last three so they could actually be accomplished. Those pixies do love setting the odds in their favor, which is why we only play our weekly poker game on neutral ground, so I'm up six hundred dollars on her." She chuckles. "I love you, Leona."

"Love you too, Mom."

I no sooner hang up than an earsplitting crack of thunder echoes across the forest and ten pixies appear, hovering in the air while holding the queen's throne. She peers down at us and mumbles something about interlopers and double-crossing werewolves who can't be trusted.

"You owe me a golden apple," she says, pointing her delicate gold fan at me before turning it toward Darius, standing next to his slightly dinged-up motorcycle from Effie's daredevil driving. She shoots him what must be the pixie equivalent of a flirty smile that shows off her point-sharpened teeth. "And *you* were warned to never come back here again."

"It wasn't by choice," Darius says without looking up from his motorcycle as he checks it over, grumbling under his breath with every new ding or scratch he finds that my sister must have given it during her wild ride through the forest.

The color rises in the queen's cheeks. This is a woman who is most definitely not used to being ignored.

Stepping forward before things get nasty, I drop my head in deference. "I need your help."

"You need more than that, but before you get to the begging portion of the show, I want my apple." She flicks a bit of pixie dust into the air and the apple flies out of my hands over to her while The Liber Umbrarum appears out of thin air, to float in the middle of the clearing.

Now *that* gets Darius's attention. He lets out a low, growly sound that's more wolfish than human.

"Don't even think about it," the queen snaps before hard-tapping one of her attendants on the shoulder. The lady's maid winces and pulls a set of keys out of a small canvas bag and tosses them to me. "Pity about the man, but he does make a fine oak tree. Your car is at the river's edge. I strongly recommend you take The Liber Umbrarum, go to the car now, and never return."

I can't do it. I can't go without Erik. But even with the Svensen family magic merged with my own, I can't summon enough power to activate any of the spells in The Liber Umbrarum while in the forest. The book is as useless as holding nothing but a high card in your hand during the most important poker game of your life.

Poker.

I whip my head around to look at the queen and her cadre of royal attendants. The pixie at the whiteboard is already putting up the odds for when the next golden apple will appear. That's when it hits me. I've been training my whole life for this moment. All the lectures about the political factions in Witchingdom, the numerous lessons about negotiation tactics, each and every one of the gossip items and secret backstories of the various family heads and political leaders have all led to this moment. I am the Sherwood heir, and because of that I know exactly what to do next.

The queen glares at me and pauses in fanning herself. "Why are you staring at me like that?"

Play this cool, Sherwood. Play. It. Cool.

Not letting even a hint of the desperation swirling around inside me show on my face, I shrug a shoulder as if bored. "No reason."

"Of course there is a reason." She snaps her fan closed and points it at me and snarls an order to her attendants. "Take me closer to her." The pixies bearing her throne grimace, but they don't say a word as they fly her to just beyond my reach. "Tell me why you've got the same look on your face as a troll with an unsolvable riddle right this moment or I'll find a way to make you regret it."

Nope. Not yet. That would make it too easy for her, and she wants to feel like she won; that's what matters to the queen.

So I stay silent.

I let the quiet grow.

Desperation eats away at me, gnawing on the tethers keeping me from going into full freak-out mode, but I fight against it to draw the stillness out until the forest itself seems too hushed to have ever made a noise.

The queen sits back in her throne with a weary sigh that sounds as fake as a gnome's height on his driver's license. "Burn the tree."

Sheer terror rips through me like a nuclear blast of pure fear, obliterating any heir training I've ever had about keeping a cool head during negotiations.

Head Witch in Charge

"No!" I yell. "Please. Wait!"

The queen's lips curl into a tight smile of true satisfaction. "I thought so."

"I'm staring," I say, the shake in my voice one hundred percent real, "because I need a favor."

The queen lets out a long and over-the-top sigh. "I've given out too many of those recently—the latest being to make your challenges actually achievable. Your mother drives a hard bargain—but I'll get the better of her during our next poker game."

And there it is, my way to bring this deal home.

"What if I could help you with that?"

"Why would you?" the queen asks as she leans forward in her throne, fully engaged and curious.

So, right where I want her.

Holding tight to the control I learned from watching my mother even though I want to run around and scream with triumph, I keep my tone deferential and my volume low. "So you'll reverse the transformation and free Erik."

Right on cue, Asher lets out a groan that shakes the leaves hanging from his branches. "She can't do that," Asher grumbles. "It's against the rules. He agreed of his own free will. It's not her place to make changes to that."

"My place?" the queen screeches, her voice like an ice pick to the ear. "This is *my* forest."

"So you *can* do it?" I ask as if I don't already know the answer.

"Never doubt me, witch," the queen snarls, turning her ire back to focus on me. "However, do you really think *you're* in a position to make requests of me?"

My hands are trembling with nerves with Erik's life riding on what happens next, so I clasp them together in front of me and send up a quick plea to the fates that I'll be able to safely land this magic carpet.

"Yes, because there's something you want that only I can give you." When she just lifts an eyebrow in question, I continue. "My mother's poker tells."

I barely get the words out before a quill and piece of parchment appear out of thin air in front of me.

"Write them down," the queen says, "and we have an unbreakable deal."

As I do, the wind begins to whirl around us, sending up leaves, dirt, and twigs into the air like a smoke screen. I can only just see the parchment well enough to write down my mother's tendency to wrinkle her nose when she bluffs and scratch her chin when she's underselling her hand. The queen begins to chant in pixyish, her voice going from high-pitched and nasally, almost squeaky, to a low bass boom. I can't tell what she's saying, exactly, but it is the same phrase over and over and over again. A shower of pixie dust wipes out the airborne debris, and the forest looks exactly as it did before, with Erik's face still staring back at me from the bark of his oak. The forest floor starts to shake, and a deep chasm appears, the line of broken earth moving like a runaway train straight for Erik's tree.

A scream rips from my throat half a heartbeat before the ground opens up and swallows Erik's tree whole.

When the last of the pixie dust settles, the only sound in the forest is the roar of Darius's motorcycle as he races away, the top of The Liber Umbrarum that wavers in the light like a mirage sticking out of his saddlebag as the scent of fresh-brewed coffee lingers in the air.

The queen sucks her teeth and makes a tsk-tsk sound. "That was your fault for not securing The Liber Umbrarum immediately. Don't even think of blaming me for it."

Like I give two shits about the spell book right now. All I care about is my husband.

Looking around like he'll just appear like The Liber Umbrarum, it takes everything I have not to break completely as the weight of how I failed Erik pushes down on me. "Where is he?"

"Where you left him. My fates, do I have to do everything?" The queen flicks her fan open and begins waving it back and forth in front of her face. "I swear I have dust in every possible nook and cranny. Take me to the royal baths immediately."

There's another crack of thunder as she leaves, but I barely hear it over the sound of blood rushing in my ears as I sprint toward the huge hole in the ground where Erik's tree was. Heart pounding in my chest, I run right up to the edge. I don't know what I'm expecting to find, but fear has my lungs in a death grip and I'm about to pass out from the lack of oxygen when I look down into the dark depths and see Erik—my Erik—his face smudged with dirt and more than a few twigs sticking out of his hair, looking up at me.

The look of love on his face breaks the vise, and I suck in a deep breath filled with all the hope for the future I never thought I wanted. I really am the luckiest woman in Witchingdom.

"You found a loophole," he says.

"I learned from the best," I say, and scramble down to him, the dirt giving way beneath my feet as I half fall, half run and throw my arms around him. "Welcome back, husband."

He pulls me close and dips his head down, stopping when his lips are only an inch from mine. "I love the sound of that."

And then he's kissing me or I'm kissing him, it doesn't matter. He's kissing me like he's going to be the man I wake up with every morning for the rest of my life, and I've never been more excited for someone else's morning breath in my entire life.

Effie clears her throat with all the subtlety of a sentient house intent on matchmaking and hollers, "Hello down below."

Reluctant to stop but knowing I'll be able to continue later, I look up at my sister.

She looks from me to Erik and back again. "You two good here? Because I need to go chase after that duplicitous jerk Darius before he sells The Liber Umbrarum to the highest bidder."

"You need help?" Erik and I ask at the same time. Once an heir, always an heir, I guess.

"Believe me, I can take care of one little werewolf on my

own," she says with a grin that always means trouble—the kind she is more than capable of handling on her own.

"We're good," I tell her, my attention already going back to the man I love.

"Now we are," Erik says, and kisses me again.

Chapter Thirty-Nine

Erik . . .

It's been a wild fucking day.

I was an heir. Now I'm just a regular witch.

I was a tree. Now I'm not.

I was a husband. Then I wasn't. And now it seems like I might be again.

Life really does come at you fast when you fall in love with a Sherwood.

Shifting in my seat behind Bessie's steering wheel, I turn and look at LeLe. My LeLe. For real this time. Honestly, I'm having a hard time believing it's real.

"What you said before," I say. "Did you mean it?"

"When I called you 'husband'?" LeLe asks with a huge smile. "Yeah, I did."

It's more than a guy like me deserves, but I'm sure not gonna walk away from it. I'm an asshole, but I'm not *that* kind of asshole.

"So, where to next?" I turn the key in Bessie's ignition. "The Council isn't going to give up. I suppose you need to get home so you can help plan the next move."

"Yes, but there's one thing we need to do first," she says as I shift Bessie into drive and guide her onto the bridge over the river marking the pixie's territory. "Did you know there's a full moon tonight?"

I gun the engine without meaning to as I process her words. "Are you asking me to handfast marry you, Leona Sherwood?"

She scoots closer on the bench seat and kisses my cheek. "I am, Erik Svensen."

This time I stomp down on the gas with full intent. "Well, we better get moving then if we're going to drop The Liber Umbrarum at the secured facility and then make it to the Hunka Hunka Burning Love Wedding Chapel in time."

Twisting in her seat, she looks up at me and raises an eyebrow in question. "But the werewolves have it."

"Do they?" I summon a quick spell that undoes the locks on Bessie's glove box and the door pops open, revealing The Liber Umbrarum safely tucked inside.

LeLe gasps, her gorgeous eyes round with surprise. "But you were a tree, how could you?"

"There's always a loophole, soon-to-be-again wife," I say, grinning down at her as I curl my arm around her and pull her closer against me. "I wasn't just a tree, I was a witch transformed into a tree, meaning that I still had magic. And as a tree, I was an official part of the pixie's forest; the ban on outsider magic didn't apply to me."

She snort-giggles and shakes her head. "You swapped out the spell book."

"And there's more." My gut tightens because this one just might really piss her off, but coming clean to her seems right.

I don't have to hide the truth from her because she'll use it against me. I don't have to pretend not to care because she'll find a way to leverage that knowledge. I don't have to always be on guard. I can just be Erik Svensen, patriarch to a family that maybe isn't born to be bad. Who'd have ever thought that could even be a possibility? Not me before LeLe.

"I haven't told you the complete truth about getting to the facility," I go on. "*We* can make better time."

I rest my fingers on her waist and the magic starts building between us before I can even ask if she'll help. Like a couple that's been together for decades—or two heirs who've found their matches—our magic is already intertwined enough to work together without a conscious spell.

"Hold on," I say as I move the gearshift from drive to drive two, "it's gonna be a bumpy ride."

In half a heartbeat we go from cruising speed to what feels like light speed when you're in a classic convertible with the top down speeding down the road. Houses and fields go by in a blur as Bessie automatically swerves around slower vehicles and the occasional bridge troll standing in the middle of the highway.

"Bessie had super speed this whole time?" LeLe asks, her hair flying every which way as we race so fast if anyone watching blinked they'd miss us. "We could have driven this fast the whole time?"

"There's always a loophole"—I dip my head down so our mouths are so close we're nearly kissing, teasing her because I know she loves it—"wife."

Her lips curl upward even as her gaze goes hazy with want. "What am I going to do with you, Erik Svensen?"

There's a million answers to that question, but one rises above all the others. "Marry me."

LeLe lets out a sigh of a yes as she reaches up and curls her fingers in my hair before pulling me down to deliver on that kiss.

Yeah, I'm still not the good guy—well, not completely—but I'm *her* guy, and there's no happier ending than that.

Epilogue

Leona . . . LeLe . . . Mrs. Sherwood-Svensen . . . Wife . . .

Three years later . . .

You ever have one of those family picnics when your brother-in-law keeps sprinkling manufactured fairy dust on Witchingdom's biggest (in literal size and audience numbers) troll influencer?

Then you turn around and your personal nemesis (aka your sister's rooster familiar Barkley) is gobbling down a plate full of speak-your-mind cooked rice fritters made by your oldest sister as a gag and so now he's telling everyone exactly what he thinks in plain English instead of cock-a-doodle-doos?

And all of that is followed by the sound of your great-aunt Luna getting a howling lesson from her favorite werewolf-in-law, who may or may not be wanted in three states for a string of bank robberies that were almost immediately followed by customers' loans being paid off in full by an anonymous donor?

Did I mention all of this is taking place on a meadow next to a lake where hippocamps are frolicking in the water under the watchful gaze of a farmer who is completely in the thrall of a pack of pixies?

No? You haven't experienced that?

Well, then, I'm sorry, because it is exactly the kind of who-knows-what's-going-to-happen-next chaos that doesn't follow the rules that makes life as the Sherwood matriarch fun. Trust me, it's way better than the political elbow-rubbing that comes with the job, which is mercifully a lot less since the Council was exposed and gloriously decimated to the point that there isn't even a metaphorical corpse of the organization to be buried in salted earth. Bloodthirsty? Yeah, maybe I do have a little of that Effie vengeance gene in me when it comes to small-minded bullies with delusions of grandeur.

Exactly how did that happen? Well, it started with the werewolves, then the vampires got involved, and by the time Juniper got herself banished to The Beyond, where she hooked up with an outlaw band of witches, it was only a matter of time until the Council was done in. My sisters will have to tell you their parts in it, but let's just say, there's no way for those authoritarian assholes to claw their way out of the ground again anytime soon.

A wolfhound's happy yelps fill the air, and I look up to see an almost two-hundred-pound shaggy dog float by just out of reach of the ten-foot-tall troll hollering that everything will be okay while another troll livestreams the whole thing.

"If your brother makes Cupcake float up one more time," I say as I stow away my phone after my weekly catchup chat with Witchingdom's president, "Walter is going to start eating witches again."

"Cy's testing out the manufactured pixie dust he made up in the lab," Erik says as he pulls me back down next to him onto the red-and-white-checked picnic blanket. "Don't worry, I snuck some out of his lab so we could try it out in private later."

I roll my eyes. "We're witches, we can float on our own power."

"But can we do that?" he asks, looking up at the wolfhound.

The air around Cupcake starts to vibrate and the dog starts kicking one leg as the air massage hits that one perfect spot.

It's like a personal air vibrator that just knows exactly where to go and how hard to buzz.

"Not as of yet." Suddenly hot and beginning to have all sorts of ideas, I fan myself with the stack of napkins embossed with an S intertwined with another S. "But I think I'm going to start researching the family spell cookbooks for just that option."

Erik dips his head and whispers into my ear, "Or we can just go somewhere and try it ourselves."

I look around. In addition to my family, there are some of Witchingdom's most powerful people at the picnic, including the witches who are allied with the Sherwoods. They formed an impenetrable bloc against the Council and saved Witchingdom together.

I let out a sigh. The fact that I want to go with Erik so both of us can get just that happy is a given. However, I really should stay. Witchingdom still expects certain things from the Sherwood family matriarch.

It comes with the job.

But I am not *only* the job.

And as I learned, the only expectations that really matter are the ones I have for myself. The rest of Witchingdom can go take a ride on a hippocamp.

Already prioritizing what we should do first with that manufactured pixie dust, I turn back to Erik. "Let's go."

Looking every bit like the rogue he is, he snaps his fingers, and a blast of coffee scent fills the air half a second before we disappear. Before I can blink, I'm standing face-to-face with a marble statue of a faun in a room decorated in jewel-toned velvets where the wallpaper offers up so many ideas.

"So tell me, wife," Erik says, coming up behind me so close I can feel every inch of him even though we aren't touching, "what do you want?"

I don't even have to think about it. "You, husband."

And, as always, that is *exactly* what he gives me.

Acknowledgments

This book would definitely not exist if it weren't for a lot of very patient people who didn't give in to their justifiable urge to knock me upside the head while I was writing it. Thank you so much for everything.

I'd especially like to thank my agent, Elaine Spencer, and editor, Kristine Swartz. I will always share my Oreos with both of you. Thank you for not giving up on this book. I'd also like to thank the many people at Berkley who worked on this book. My apologies to the copy editors and proofreaders who have to deal with all of my grammar errors. There is a special place in Witchingdom just for y'all. A million thanks to artist Leni Kauffman for another gorgeous cover. It really is the most beautiful!!!

As always, I couldn't do this without the help of my own little coven. Kim, Robin, and Kristen, y'all are amazing.

My family's tolerance for me muttering to myself and spending way too many hours in my PJs has increased with each book I've written, but their support has always been at one hundred percent. Thank you, I love you guys.

Of course, this story wouldn't exist without the fabulous readers who give up their limited free time to read one of my books. Y'all really are the absolute best. THANK YOU!!!

xoxo,

Avery

Keep reading for an excerpt from
Avery Flynn's next novel . . .

Hexy Beast

Chapter One

Effie . . .

*F*ated mates is bullshit, right?

Right?

Tell me I'm right because otherwise that means the fact that I can't get more than a room away from the most one-grunt-for-yes-two-grunts-for-no grumpy-ass werewolf shifter in all of Witchingdom is more than a curse. It's a life sentence— and I'm not the kind of witch who can do that kind of time.

But I'm getting ahead of myself, which is not a surprise to anyone who knows me or follows me on Witchygram, where I post all of my escapades (much to my family's dismay about my wild behavior).

I'm Effie Sherwood, the oldest daughter of the magically badass Sherwood family, one of—if not—the most powerful families in all of Witchingdom. As the eldest, everyone expected me to inherit our family magic and become the head witch in charge of the family because that's how the world works.

Every witchy family has their own stream of magic that flows through the head of the family and to all of the other members. Magic binds and empowers them. Then, when the firstborn of the next generation hits their 30s, they move from being the heir to the family's magic to the head of the family.

That's the way everyone's family magic worked in Witchingdom going from firstborn to firstborn like clockwork—boring, never varying, watching-paint-dry clockwork.

Until I came along.

The story of my birth hit legendary status before I was even old enough to understand the whispers. It was a dark and stormy night. Kidding! It was a bland and sunny Tuesday morning when I came into the world.

Sherwood magic filled the room in anticipation of my birth. My mom went through labor without a hair out of place while my dad had fully shifted into literal bear mode because of the stress. I came out bald as a troll and screaming my lungs out—I never have liked being woken up before noon.

The family magic flew around the world going from invisible force to a sparkling purple stream of pure power. It swirled around the room, a circle that tightened and tightened until it resembled a wreath small enough to sit on a newborn's head and thus bestow status as the family's heir.

The thing is, with me, it didn't.

Oh it got close. If I would have had any of the frizzy bright orange and red hair I have now, the magic would have touched it. But instead of coming to a rest on my slightly pointy head, it poofed out of there leaving behind a thick dusting of honeysuckle-scented sparkles that landed on my cheeks in the exact spots where today I have a bazillion freckles.

That outcome was very not expected—unless you're me because I don't do what's expected.

Not as a newborn.

Not as a grown-ass witch.

I'm a free spirit. The wild one of the family. The Sherwood voted most outrageous on Witchygram five years running. And there's a reason why I'm not the heir to our family's magic and destined to be the family matriarch.

I wish I knew what it is.

The best reason I can come up with is that I'm just not that witch. My sister Leona is, and she's fantastic at it, and that's why when she was born, the wreath landed on her infant head without a second of hesitation.

Yeah, it's a little weird and can be kinda (read: so fucking very) awkward when people start giving me pitying looks and wondering aloud just what's wrong with me that would result in what ninety-nine percent of Witchingdom sees as a demotion. But it is what it is.

It hardly ever bothers me.

And when it does?

Well, that's when I double down on bringing the shenanigans to Witchingdom, like when I hosted a unicorn shifter

Lucky Charms eating contest with the winner getting their body weight in cereal marshmallows. The catch? Participants had to do it while dressed in rainbow tutus and balancing on floating surfboards. That one totally got me trending on Witchygram.

It's not the life anyone expected of me, but it's mine, and I love it just how it is.

I'm the family bon vivant, showing my four younger sisters how to live their best lives (and kicking the ass of anyone who tries to stop them). I've got a big mouth, a big attitude, and big thighs—all of which, for the record, I love about myself. The first two definitely get me into big trouble of the societal snubs kind, while the third gets me all the good kind of trouble I can handle—and believe you me, I can handle a lot.

Does that mean things just seem to spin out of control when I get involved?

Fine.

Yes.

That's why I wasn't surprised to find myself on a Tuesday (why is it always Tuesdays?) being accidentally kidnapped by Darius, the alpha of the Aetos werewolves and the man with the best ass in Witchingdom.

Don't get distracted by that last one. Trust me. Just look, appreciate, and go on with your day because his butt may be glorious but it's not enough to distract from the rest of him. All six-foot-seven inches of muscular, tatted-up him. The man has a personality disorder called head-up-the-ass-itis. He's a tightly wound accountant inside the body of an MMA fighter.

Shit.

I'm getting all ahead of myself again. Next thing, I'll be explaining to you how right now at this very moment I'm naked, horny, and howling at the moon with the alpha wolf who is most definitely not my fated mate—the first two kinda happen to me a lot, but the last one is a new one for me.

So this whole mess started a week ago when I magicked myself onto Darius's motorcycle while he was riding hell-bent for leather with The Liber Umbrarum he'd stolen from my sister Leona and her secret husband.

Really, I didn't have a choice but to make a dramatic appearance and retreive the spell book. It's only the most powerful collection of ancient charms and hexes in Witchingdom. If that fell into the wrong hands, it would be devestating. Yes, a pack of lawless werewolves who'd probably sell it to the highest bidder qualifies as wrong hands but so does the Council—even more so.

Who's the Council? Just an evil coven determined to drag Witchingdom back to the Middle Ages, lock everyone into rigid roles, and snuff out any flicker of fun, originality, or not being an awful, horrible, judgmental witch with a hard-on for fascism. They are the last people in the world who should possess The Liber Umbrarum, and they'd definitely be willing to pony up the most cash for a black-market deal for the spell book.

So when Darius—the uptight alpha—rode off on his motorcycle with the stolen Liber Umbrarum tucked in his saddlebag, I didn't even think before I acted.

Why would I? I knew what needed to be done—the totally unexpectedly expected.

One second Darius was getting away with it and then—abracadabra—I'm on his lap ready, willing, and able to steal The Liber Umbrarum right back.

Chapter Two

Darius . . .

A week earlier . . .

With Witchingdom going to shit in a half-shredded, rat-eaten handbasket, you've gotta love when a plan comes to-gether, and you get to send a pack-collective fuck-you to the rest of Witchingdom—especially the witches.

Fucking witches.

They think they know everything, control everything, win everything.

Well, not this time.

Not with the prize I've got in my saddlebag. That spell book with some stupid Latin name (like anyone speaks that shit anymore) has been all anyone can talk about on the Croesus Network for the past six months. The thieves, crooks, and everyday villains who posted on the LinkedIn of Witching-dom's law adverse called stealing the spell book the job of all jobs.

How was I supposed to walk away from a challenge like that? I'm Darius Aetos, the first of my family to be the alpha of our namesake pack in three generations. There was no way. So I didn't. Now it's mine.

How did I make that happen? The same way I do every-thing else, by putting together a plan all the way down to the minute details and then working that plan. No changes or sub-stitutions allowed.

I don't yammer about it or bounce ideas off of other people. I don't need to.

I learn.

I observe.

I act.

Period.

It's my system, and it works. I don't need to mess it up by talking through ideas or being anything other than completely analytical about it all. Feelings only fuck things up—all you have to do is take a look at the mess the past two alphas have made of the pack to understand that.

I'm in the process of cleaning it all up, which is why I de-cided to take The Liber Umbrarum.

The thing about stealing the spell book, though, is that the people on the Croesus Network weren't wrong. Swiping it was a giant pain in my ass.

Not only did I have to track it down, which was its own headache, I had to deal with Effie Sherwood—the Sherwood family's resident troublemaker. She's the daughter most likely to throw a party in the woods, put a spell on your phone so every text includes an eggplant emoji, and go skydiving without a magic carpet.

The witch is a menace.

And she stole my motorcycle.

No one takes the alpha's bike—especially not a wild witch with an attitude problem. But she did. So, of course, I had no choice but to chase her down, which served my purposes just fine because she led me to the spell book and the solution to all of my pack's problems. Taking it was comically easy, and the payday for this thing is going to be huge.

It has to be.

"Darry," Nikos's voice fills the inside of my helmet as I speed away from the scene of my latest crime. "You got it?"

Which answer he'd prefer is a toss-up.

Yes, it means we've made the score of scores, and everyone in the pack will live like kings through the winter instead of scrounging for scraps.

A no means that I, as the alpha, failed the pack, and Nikos will finally have his opportunity to challenge me out in the open rather than by shit-talking me behind my back.

I'd kick his ass in a fair fight, but Nikos isn't known for playing fair. The last alpha had been bad, but Nikos would be so much worse. He'd fuck the pack over in a heartbeat if it meant he'd benefit.

"Affirmative," I say into the mic in answer to his question.

"Great," he says, sounding like I'd just poured a Coke in his gas tank and ruined his ride's engine. "We'll meet at the guard checkpoint outside of Arcadia."

I grunt an acknowledgment before clicking off my comms.

There's really no point in keeping them on. Until I get close to our home hidden in the hills, I don't need to hear my number two's thoughts. Fuck. I'd rather never hear them at all, but that's the downside of being the alpha and what Nikos has never gotten about the job—you have to listen because it's not just about what you want. It's about the pack and keeping everything in order and on schedule to keep the chaos of whatever was happening from happening again.

I climb the Oros Hills heading toward Arcadia. It's just me and the peace and quiet of the open road.

That lasts for about a quarter of a mile before the air shifts around me and the unmistakable warm rich scent of honeysuckle that fills the woods around Arcadia hits me like a knockout punch. But what lands against me isn't a fist. It's a witch. And not just any witch but the madam of mayhem herself, Effie Sherwood. One second I'm alone on my bike and the next she's wrapped around my front like she's about to give me the best lap dance of my life.

Unfortunately, she's not about to grind against me in the champagne room. Too bad because with a thick, curvy body like hers, I have no doubt she'd rock my world if she decided to give it a try.

My grip tightens on the steering wheel but otherwise I manage to keep an unbothered outward appearance even as she settles against me as if magicking herself onto someone's lap is a normal, everyday occurance for her. Going by what she posts on Witchygram, it probably is. But we both know better about why she's here. She's not here for fun. She's here to get the spell book back.

"Miss me, honey?" she asks, curling her full pale peach lips into a teasing smile.

"No," I grumble, already planning what my next move should be.

"Ow," she says, seemingly not the least bit disturbed by the fact that we're doing one-ten through the twists and turns of the Oros Hills. "If I had feelings you could hurt, my mascara would be ruined by all the tears I'd be crying."

The urge to wrap my arm around her to cradle her close— the witch doesn't even have a helmet on—is getting hard to resist, so I buy time to get my shit together by asking, "No feelings, huh?"

"Not ones you can fuck with," she says with a piss-off-asshole grin. "Now, be a good little pup and hand over The Liber Umbrarum."

"The what?" I'm not dumb, but I've found most witches assume every shifter is, so I might as well use it to my advantage.

"Don't make me tap that been-broken-a-time-or-twelve nose of yours with a rolled up newspaper for being naughty," she says with a teasing lilt before her tone goes harder than a lead-lined vault. "The spell book. Now."

I flick my gaze from the road to her. It's a mistake. The wind is tossing her sunset-colored hair all over the place, and some of it is sticking to her lips, drawing my attention to her mouth where it most definitely should not be.

"Not happening," I say to myself as much as to her.

She purses her lips together and stares at me for a second. I swear I can see the gears turning as she works me out like I'm a puzzle. Then, a turn in the road shifts her, and she goes from close to plastered against me. The metal of my handlebars bends in my grip before I loosen it.

"Such a tough guy," Effie says, using my biceps to brace herself as she puts a sliver of space between us. "Seriously, do you guys have like MMA fights under the full moon?" She glances down at my chest and lower. "Are you naked when you do it like it's ancient times again?" She lets out a little mmh-mmh-mmh sound as if she's picturing it. "Do you sell tickets?" She leans forward, pressing her full breasts against my chest before she asks, "Can I sell tickets?"

This was what it had been like when she'd approached me outside of the Pixie Forest prior to stealing my bike. She'd gone into a motormouth shock and awe campaign to distract and disorient me before taking my motorcycle and speeding into the forest.

It had worked once. It isn't going to work again.

She might have spells that make her appear out of thin air, but I've got shifter reflexes. I reach back and grab her wrist before she gets her hand inside my saddlebag, no doubt to snatch the spell book and pull a disappearing act with it.

"Bag's shielded," I say before she gets other ideas to magic it out of my possession.

Her huff of annoyance is almost cute. "You're no fun."

She's not the first with that opinion. She won't be the last.

I keep my eyes on the road and not the deep V of Effie's black sweater when her tits sway as we round the bend in the road—well, mostly. And thank the fates because as soon as we clear it, I spot the five motorcycles parked in the middle of the highway. Nikos is standing cross-armed in front of the bike at the front, wearing aviators and a smug expression like he's about to bust me for running moonshine.

I'm going through scenarios in my mind before I even start to slow down. The plan is to get off as soon as I stop in front of Nikos's bike, but Little Miss Fuck with You doesn't move off my lap when we come to a halt. Her honey-eyed gaze stays locked on mine.

A challenge? A promise? Who the fuck knows or cares.

Not me.

Not even a little.

Fine, maybe a little, but I have other shit to deal with right now.

I hook my arm around her waist, noting against my will the easy, soft give of her and the way her eyes darken with at-traction when I do. Her mouth rounds with a little gasp when I get up, holding her tight against me, and get off the bike. She's at least half a foot off the ground with all of those bountiful curves of hers tucked against me. Suddenly, putting her down is the last thing on my mind.

The full moon isn't for a few days but the wolf inside wants to snarl at anyone who dares to look at her. He's desperate with the need to make her want him, to claim her, to be the last man to ever touch her. The feeling rushes through my veins like fire and ice at the same time. In a heartbeat I can hear every bird in the forest, every tree leaf in the wind, and every beat of her heart in sync with my own.

Something dark and hungry swirls in her eyes as she watches me, neither pushing away nor pulling closer. I smell it again, the honeysuckle that makes me think of dusk in the hills when the flowers let everyone know the night's coming. But it's nowhere close to twilight, and whatever is about to happen is more permanent than the moon coming out for its turn in the sky.

But that's something I'll have to deal with later because Nikos isn't about to wait.

Tearing my gaze away from Effie, I set her down and step in front of her as I focus my attention on the man who'd love to take my place.

"Nikos," I say since "what the fuck are you doing here instead of waiting at the rendezvous point like you're supposed to be" is too many words.

"What the fuck is she doing here?" he snarls.

"Oh, Rover," Effie says as she steps up next to me, not a hint of worry coming off of her. "If I didn't know better, I'd think you weren't happy to see me."

He takes a step toward her, and my growl comes out before he even finishes the step.

He doesn't come any closer but sneers at her, "The name's Nikos."

She makes a dismissive tsk-tsk. "Really? You look more like a Rover—maybe a Spot."

"Darry," my second-in-command growls—literally. "Why was there a witch—especially that fuckin' witch—on your bike?"

And my day was going so well. Every line item on my agenda had been checked off. The mental files for this job were alphabetized and color-coded before I'd slid them into the filing cabinet marked "Shit Done Right." I'd already tallied the sums for what the pack's take would be when we fenced the spell book. It would be more than enough to right our accounts after the last alpha had screwed the pack over by running it like his own little medieval fiefdom.

Now the wolf gunning for my job—and my throat—is about to lose his shit because of the witch who appeared out of nowhere onto my lap. What is she doing here? Besides busting my balls and making my cock rock hard? I have no fucking clue, and I'm sure as shit not about to admit that or the status of my dick to Nikos.

"Kidnapped her," I say, the words coming out in total surprise to myself.

Fuck.

Fuck.

Fuck.

This is why I plan out every syllable of anything I say. Spontaneity is everyone's privilege except the alpha.

Effie turns her head to me and lifts one pierced eyebrow but doesn't call me out on my lie in front of the pack.

"We can ransom her." In for a penny, in for a pain-in-my-ass witch.

That shuts Nikos up, but it does not have the same effect on the sexy witch pressed up against my side.

Effie raises herself up on her tiptoes and whispers against my throat (as high as she can get, which somehow makes the effort even hotter), "Role playing as the Big Bad Wolf, Darius?" she asks. "Does that make me Red Riding Hood? Are you going to nip at me with those teeth of yours? Be careful, I might like that."

The mental image of Effie Sherwood in a dark red velvet cape and nothing else running through the woods jolts me enough that I stop breathing. The idea of biting that sensitive spot where her shoulder mets her neck as I sink deep inside her nearly makes my brain go into buffer mode. I'm stock-still and every muscle is tensed to make sure I don't give anything away but that doesn't slow my heart, which is going faster than my odometer.

But Effie? She looks like she's about to throw up her arms as if she's cresting the highest peak on a roller coaster and having the time of her life.

Of course, I would end up accidentally kidnapping a thrill seeker—just the type of person I avoid even more than witches. Nothing good is going to come from this woman appearing out of thin air onto my lap. I already have too much pack shit to deal with—including keeping my place in it—to take on ransoming a troublesome witch no matter what my Aunt Artemis predicts about my future.

The witch standing next to me is not the witch Aunt Artemis talks about.

Fuck. No.

The frustrated growl rumbles out of my chest before I can stop it. I know what the wolf inside me wants, but this isn't her.

Effie lets out a thin, half-assed witch growl of her own before lapsing into giggles.

"Is this when I'm supposed to be scared of the oh-so-dangerous werewolf alpha?" she asks when she finally can.

If it is, she's failing miserably at it. She doesn't sound like she is even the least bit spooked. In fact, Effie sounds like she's planning to be the one to eat me up—and fuck me, I like the way this curvy little witch thinks.

Photo by Passion Pages / Annie Ray

USA Today and *Wall Street Journal* bestselling romance author Avery Flynn has three slightly wild children, loves a hockey-addicted husband, and is desperately hoping someone invents the coffee-IV drip. She lives outside of Washington, D.C., with her family, Dwight the cat, and a pack of five dogs all named after food. If she is not reading romance or binging reality TV, she is most definitely plotting to take over the world so she can banish Crocs from existence.

Ready to find
your next great read?

Let us help.

Visit prh.com/nextread

Penguin
Random
House